Ithanalin's
RESTORATION

Ithanalin's
RESTORATION

Lawrence Watt-Evans

TOR®

A Tom Doherty Associates Book

NEW YORK

ITHANALIN'S RESTORATION

Copyright © 2002 by Lawrence Watt-Evans

A Tor Book
Published by Tom Doherty Associates, LLC
175 Fifth Avenue
New York, NY 10010

Tor® is a registered trademark of Tom Doherty Associates, LLC.

ISBN 0-765-30012-5

Printed in the United States of America

In memory of
Jenna Felice

Ithanalin's
RESTORATION

Chapter One

The room was quietly comfortable, and not at all like the popular image of a wizard's workshop. There were no cluttered shelves, no steaming cauldrons, no mysterious books, just a few pieces of fairly ordinary furniture, most of it in need of a little dusting. It did not smell of strange herbs or exotic incense, but only of wood and cloth and sunlight.

But then, Lady Nuvielle told herself, this probably *wasn't* a workshop. This was the parlor where the wizard dealt with his customers; undoubtedly he had a workshop elsewhere in the house, and it might well be jammed with dusty books and mummified animals. The parlor furnishings were more mundane.

Still, some of the pieces appeared as if they might be rather valuable, she thought as she looked around with interest. The mirror above the mantel, for example, had no visible flaws at all, in either the glass or the silvering. Glass that fine must have come from Ethshar of the Sands, more than fifty leagues away, or perhaps from somewhere even more distant—possibly even Shan on the Desert, halfway across the World.

Or perhaps it had been created by magic; after all, Ithanalin was a wizard.

Wherever it came from, Nuvielle was sure it must have cost a goodly sum.

And beneath the mirror there was the smallish velvet-upholstered couch, with its ornately carved wooden arms curling elegantly at either end. This was *not* ordinary furniture, but a unique item—Nuvielle had never seen anything quite like it. The velvet was an unusual and striking color, a vivid crimson, and was perfectly smooth, perfectly fitted. Whoever had decorated the arms and legs had been exceptionally talented with a woodworker's knife, and perhaps slightly insane. The very dark wood made it hard to see details, but she could make out some rather disturbing designs. If anything here had been made by magic, the couch was a likely candidate.

The little table beside the couch was of the same wood, and had apparently been meant to match, but the craftsman who made it had not had the same eccentric flair as the artist—or magic—that had carved the couch frame.

The mirror was very nice, in any case.

Lady Nuvielle knew that many people wouldn't dare leave the front door unlocked if they had such things on display, but wizards did not need to worry about ordinary thieves; only the worst sort of fool would steal from a wizard.

Other items, like the oval braided-rag rug just inside the front door, were nothing special at all—at least, not to her relatively untrained eye. She smoothed out a large hump in the rug with the toe of her velvet slipper and wondered idly if any of the furnishings might have unseen magical attributes.

It didn't seem very likely—though she wouldn't rule out the possibility in the case of the couch or mirror. The wizard's front room was a pleasant little parlor that could have belonged to anyone.

When she had spoken with Ithanalin before, she had summoned him to the Fortress rather than trouble herself to venture a mile across the city, but today she had been bored, and had come out to the shop on Wizard Street in person in hopes of seeing some entertaining magic while she was here. So far she had been disappointed. She hadn't seen much of anything, in fact. She hadn't yet seen the wizard, or the apprentice her messenger had reported lived here. All she had seen was this uninhabited room. She had knocked, found the door open, and walked in—and now she had resorted to studying the furniture, for lack of anything better to do. The room was small, with a single door and a single broad window opening on the street, and a single door at the rear; there were no books, no paintings, no statues to keep her attention.

She waited for a few moments, expecting some response to her entry—surely, the wizard must have known she was here! Didn't magicians all have mysterious sources of knowledge to keep them informed of such things?

Eventually she got sufficiently bored to call out, "*Hai!* Is anyone here?"

Almost immediately, a young woman's head popped through the doorway at the back. Her face was unfamiliar, but Nuvielle assumed this was the wizard's apprentice—though she was not wearing the formal gray apprentice robes.

"You must be Lady Nuvielle!" the supposed apprentice said. "Please forgive us; we hadn't expected you quite so soon. I'll be right out."

"That's quite all right," she said in reply, but the girl had vanished before the visitor had completed her sentence.

She smiled wryly, then settled cautiously onto one end of the well-made couch, only to discover that its upholstery of fine, oddly hued crimson clashed horribly with her own forest green velvet gloves, skirt, and slippers. Always aware of her appearance, Lady Nuvielle spread her black cloak over the cushions to provide a neutral buffer between the two colors.

This was a major reason she wore the cloak despite the late-summer weather—a vast expanse of black cloth could be very handy for adjusting appearances, even in the lingering heat of Harvest.

She was still straightening her skirt when the young woman reappeared. This time she entered gracefully, stopped a few feet away at the far end of the couch, and curtsied politely.

"Hello, my lady," she said. "I am Kilisha of Eastgate, apprentice to the master wizard, Ithanalin the Wise."

Lady Nuvielle smiled with a polite pretense of warmth. "And I am Nuvielle, Lady Treasurer of Ethshar of the Rocks." She nodded an acknowledgment of the formalities. "Where's your master?"

"In his workshop, my lady, finishing up the spell you ordered. He should be out in a moment."

Then there was indeed a workshop, as she had suspected. "And the spell succeeded?" she asked.

Kilisha hesitated. "Well, to be honest," she said, "I'm not really sure. My master has not informed me of the details. You wanted an animation of some sort?"

"A pet," Nuvielle agreed. "Just a pet, to ride on my shoulder and keep me company. Something out of the ordinary, to amuse me."

Kilisha smiled with relief. "Then I think it's succeeded," she said, "and I think you'll be pleased."

"Good!" For a moment the two women stared silently at each other; before the silence could grow awkward, Nuvielle asked, "How is it I didn't meet you before, when I summoned Ithanalin to the Fortress to take my order? Shouldn't you have accompanied your master?"

"That was a sixnight ago? Oh, I was running some errands for Ithanalin—for my master," Kilisha explained, with assumed and unconvincing nonchalance. She glanced about nervously, and tried to unobtrusively use her skirt to wipe the worst of the dust from the square table that stood beside the little sofa.

The truth was that Kilisha had been left to baby-sit her master's three children that night, as their mother Yara had been visiting a friend in the countryside somewhere. Kilisha suspected the timing of that visit had been deliberate, to keep her at home where she would not risk embarrassing her master in front of the city's elite.

Sometimes she thought her master didn't need *her* to embarrass him. Kilisha hoped that Lady Nuvielle hadn't noticed the dust on the furniture—and in particular, that she hadn't noticed the footprints visible in it. Kilisha recognized them as spriggan tracks, and some people thought spriggans were disgusting, unclean creatures.

Kilisha thought those people were probably right—but spriggans were attracted by wizardry, and keeping them out of the shop was almost impossible. They seemed to be able to get inside no matter how carefully doors and windows were closed and locked— Ithanalin's children thought they came down the chimney, and Kilisha was not ready to rule that possibility out.

Warning spells could announce their arrival, but none of the wards and barriers Ithanalin knew—which was admittedly not many, as that sort of magic was not his area of expertise—could keep them out, any more than locked doors could. Spriggans ran hither and yon almost unhindered, and one of them had clearly run across the end table.

If there were only some way to make the little pests *useful,* Kilisha thought—but then she pushed the thought aside and tried to concentrate on Lady Nuvielle. Ithanalin always told her to focus on the customer—magicians were paid for pleasing their patrons, not just for working magic.

And pleasing the Lady Treasurer, who happened to be not merely a top city official but the next-to-youngest of the overlord's several aunts, was especially important. Kilisha could not help being aware that she was in the presence of high-ranking nobility.

Lady Nuvielle noticed the girl's nervousness and smiled again, debating whether to try to put the girl at ease, or whether to tease her and enjoy her discomfort. Still undecided, she asked a neutral question.

"Ithanalin is an unusual name. Is it Tintallionese?"

"I don't know, my lady," Kilisha replied. "I'm not sure it's any known language. Wizards often take new names, for one reason or another." She shifted nervously. She was shading the truth; she knew her master had taken his name from an old book he had read as a boy, and the book was not Tintallionese in origin.

"I take it you have not dealt with many of your master's clients?" Nuvielle asked.

"Well," Kilisha said, shifting her feet, "I have assisted Ithanalin with his customers for a few years now, but none of the other customers were as . . . as distinguished as yourself, my lady."

Nuvielle knew exactly what Kilisha referred to, and that it wasn't just her office of treasurer for the city of Ethshar of the Rocks. She grew suddenly bored and annoyed with the apprentice's unease—she was tired of being feared because of who her brother had been, and who her nephew was. "Oh, calm down, girl," she said. "Sit down and relax. I'm not going to eat you."

"Yes, my lady," the apprentice said, settling cautiously onto a straight-backed wooden chair set at an angle to the couch. She tucked her brown wool skirt neatly under her as she sat.

Nuvielle looked Kilisha over. She was a little on the short side, and plumper than was entirely fashionable just at the moment. Her hair was a nondescript brown, pleasant enough, but utterly dull, worn long and straight and tied back in a ponytail. Her eyes were hazel—not brown flecked with green, or green flecked with brown, either of which might sometimes be called hazel—but the real thing, a solid color somewhere between brown and green, neither one nor the other. Instead of apprentice robes she wore a plain wool skirt a shade darker than her hair, a pale yellow tunic that came to mid-thigh, and a stiff leather pouch and a drawstring purse on her belt. A leather-and-feather hair ornament was the only touch of bright color or interest anywhere about her, and even that was something worn by any number of girls in Ethshar of the Rocks. Her appearance was absolutely, completely, totally ordinary. The city held thousands just like her, Nuvielle thought.

Though most, of course, weren't apprenticed to wizards. What sort of a future could anyone so boring have, in so flamboyant a profession as wizardry? This girl looked utterly dull.

The noblewoman watched Kilisha for a moment, then turned away, determined to ignore the poor little thing until the wizard arrived.

For her part, Kilisha was admiring this gorgeous customer—or rather, client, as the lady would have it. The long black cloak, the rich green velvet, the white satin tunic embroidered in gold and scarlet, the long gloves, the black hair bound up in an elaborate network of braids and ribbons, all seemed to Kilisha to be the absolute epitome of elegance. When Nuvielle turned her head, Kilisha marveled at the graceful profile and the smooth white skin.

Kilisha had always thought that Yara, Ithanalin's wife, was just about perfect, but she had to admit that that common soul's appearance couldn't begin to compare with Lady Nuvielle's.

And Kilisha's own looks, she thought, weren't even up to Yara's.

Then, at last, before she could pursue this depressing line of thought any further, Ithanalin finally emerged from the workshop, his hands behind his back.

"My apologies for the delay, Lady Nuvielle," he said, with a sketchy sort of bow. "I wanted to be sure everything about your purchase was perfect."

Kilisha grimaced slightly, unnoticed by the others. The real cause for delay had been the need to change clothes, from the grubby, stained old tunic that Ithanalin wore when actually working to the red-and-gold robes he wore for meeting the public. It wouldn't do for customers to see the wizard as dirty and unkempt as a ditchdigger.

"It's ready, then?" Nuvielle asked.

"Oh, yes," Ithanalin said, bringing one hand out from behind his back.

There, standing on his palm, was a perfect miniature dragon, gleaming black from its pointed snout to the tip of its curling tail, with eyes, mouth, and claws of blazing red. It unfurled wings that seemed bigger than all the rest of it put together; they were black on top, red beneath. It folded back sleek black ears, hiding their red interiors, and hissed, making a sound Kilisha thought was very much like little Pirra's unsuccessful attempts to whistle.

Nuvielle leaned forward on the couch and studied it critically.

"Does it breathe fire?" she asked.

"No," Ithanalin replied. "You hadn't said it should, and I judged that fiery breath might be unsafe—a spark might go astray and set a drapery aflame."

Nuvielle nodded.

"Does it fly?"

For answer, Ithanalin tossed the little beast upward; it flapped its wings, then soared away, circling the room once before coming to land on the arched arm of the couch by Nuvielle's elbow. It wrapped its tail under the arm, securing itself to its perch, and then stared intently up at its purchaser.

She stared back.

"What's it made of?" she asked.

"Glass, wood, and lacquer, mostly," Ithanalin said, stepping back. "I'm not certain of everything, as I subcontracted part of its construction. My talents lie in magic, not in sculpture." Noticing something, he turned and surreptitiously kicked his heel back, straightening the rag rug, which had humped up again.

"It will never grow?" Lady Nuvielle asked.

"No. That's as big as it will ever be."

"Is it male or female?"

"Neither; it's an animated statue, not a true living creature."

Nuvielle nodded slowly. For a moment she was silent. The dragon lost interest in her and began studying the crimson fabric of the sofa, the black of her cloak, and the carved wood beneath its talons.

"Can it speak?" Nuvielle asked at last.

"Only a few words, as yet," Ithanalin said, apologetically. "I thought you might prefer to teach it yourself. I also didn't name it, but it responds to 'Dragon.' "

At the word, the little creature looked up, then craned its long neck around to peer at its creator.

"Dragon," Nuvielle whispered.

The head swung back. She held out a hand.

"Say 'here,' " Ithanalin advised.

"Here," she said quietly.

The dragon unwound its tail and leapt from the arm of the couch to the back of her hand. It stared up at its new owner, and she stared back. Then she looked up. "Excellent, wizard," she said. "Excellent. I'm very pleased." She rose, and Kilisha hurried to help

her on with her cloak—with the imitation dragon perched on one
hand, Lady Nuvielle was limited in what she could manage by
herself.

Her free hand brushed against a small purse on her belt; the
thong came loose and let it drop to the upholstery. Kilisha started
to say something, and then realized that this had been deliberate,
a way of paying for the purchase without the indignity of haggling.

Nuvielle headed for the door, then stopped and turned back
to the wizard. "Does it bite?" she asked.

"No," Ithanalin assured her. "It has no teeth. And its claws
are as dull as I could make them without spoiling its appearance.
It needs only a few drops of water each day to keep the wood
from cracking, and no food at all. You needn't worry about feeding
it."

"Excellent," Nuvielle said again. She swirled her cloak about
her and swept out onto Wizard Street, her pet held high before
her.

✦

Chapter Two

Kilisha watched Lady Nuvielle go, but Ithanalin didn't bother; he picked up the purse and opened it. He smiled at the sight of its contents, then turned to the workshop door.

"You can come out now," he called.

"I know," Yara answered from the doorway, "but Pirra and Lirrin were fighting again." She emerged, with her two daughters on either side. Lirrin was eight; Pirra only three. Yara released them, and they immediately dashed to the front window.

"She's pretty, Daddy," Lirrin remarked.

"I do enjoy working for the nobility," Ithanalin said, as he poured a stream of golden bits into Yara's outstretched hands.

"You did that with the Familiar Animation?" Kilisha asked, still staring after the departed customer.

"That's right," Ithanalin agreed, his head bent over his wife's hands, counting the coins. "A variant, actually."

"When are you going to teach me that spell?" Kilisha asked.

"Soon," Ithanalin replied, still counting.

"And when are you going to dust in here?" Yara asked. "Or let me dust it?"

"Soon," he repeated. Then he paused and looked up. "We'll

have to close the drapes, of course. We can't let anyone see you doing it." He kicked at the rag rug, which was humped again. "You know, I think I've accidentally animated this stupid thing, at least slightly. This wrinkling can't be natural."

Yara sighed. She suspected Ithanalin was right about the rug, which was certainly a nuisance; she was convinced he was wrong about the drapes, though. She would have been glad to dust the place in broad daylight, with an audience, but Ithanalin wouldn't allow it. He insisted it would look bad if anyone saw an ordinary human being dusting his furniture, rather than a sylph or homunculus.

Yara had argued often enough that not having *anyone* dust it looked even worse, but Ithanalin was adamant. He would only allow housework to be done in the front parlor, the only public part of the shop, when no customers were expected, and only behind tightly drawn drapes—and since he kept the shop open long hours, and Yara did like to eat and sleep on occasion, that meant the dusting wasn't done very often.

Yara thought it was a foolish minor annoyance.

Kilisha thought it was bad advertising, to let the place get so dusty, but she knew better than to argue with her master. She was just an apprentice; it wasn't her place to say anything, let alone to side against her master, even if it was only with her master's wife. She had acquired a bit of a reputation for rushing into things without thinking, but even she wasn't going to argue with the man who controlled almost every detail of her life.

It had long since occurred to her that as the apprentice in the household she probably ought to do the dusting herself, but as yet Ithanalin hadn't told her to, and she had enough other obligations that she didn't care to volunteer.

Ithanalin himself clearly thought that it was in keeping with a wizard's image to let the place get a little dusty. Wizards were supposed to be somewhat unworldly, after all.

Even so, for the sake of peace, he kept promising to animate something that would do the job, but as yet he hadn't gotten around to it.

Yara maintained that he never *would* get around to it, and every so often she would sneak into the room when Ithanalin was out and run a surreptitious rag over the most offensive surfaces, without worrying about whether the drapes were drawn.

Kilisha did wonder why the wizard hadn't just animated something long ago and gotten it over with. She knew Ithanalin was capable of it; the little creature that Lady Nuvielle had just bought was not the only such she'd seen pass through the shop, so she knew that Ithanalin could make a very nice little homunculus indeed, if he chose to. Animations were his specialty. He claimed to know more animating spells than any other wizard in the city, and Kilisha believed him—though as yet he had not taught her any of them; she had been working her way up through more mundane magic.

He knew all the spells, yet there wasn't a sylph or homunculus or even as much as an animated serving dish in the entire house. He had just created a familiar for a noblewoman, but had none himself. Everything he had ever animated had been given away or sold. He claimed that he didn't want the place cluttered up with creatures that might interfere with his work, but Kilisha thought he just couldn't be bothered.

Maybe someday, Kilisha thought as she turned away from the door, she could make a homunculus for Yara on her own, if Ithanalin never did get around to it; it would be an expression of gratitude for the treatment she'd had.

Ithanalin was a fine master—polite, informative, an excellent teacher, never beating her or working her too hard, rarely even yelling at her when she messed something up. A girl could hardly ask for better, really.

But Ithanalin could be absentminded and careless, and often left Kilisha to fend for herself in the workshop for extended periods of time, or let her improvise complicated jury-rigged solutions to magical problems that Ithanalin himself could have solved with a single simple little incantation. He kept telling her to plan, to think things out for herself—but when she tried, it never seemed to work out, and often because there was some little detail that Ithanalin had failed to provide.

Yara, though—Yara was always considerate. It was Yara who made sure that Kilisha had clean bedding, good food, safe water, and all the other basic necessities of life.

Of course, she did the same for her husband, and the three children, and herself. It was she who kept the entire household running smoothly at all times. She was more than just a house-keeper, though—she loved her husband and her children and showed it, she provided the household with firm common sense when it was called for, and she was even sometimes a friend when Kilisha needed one. Ithanalin was fine, but he was her master, and sometimes she needed someone to talk to who *wasn't* her master. The three children—Telleth, Lirrin, and Pirra—were sweet enough, but too young to understand the concerns of a girl of seventeen. Telleth, the oldest, was only ten. Kilisha couldn't often talk to her parents or her brother Opir—they still lived in Eastgate, a mile away, and she was rarely free to visit there.

Much of the time there was only Yara—but she was usually enough.

Kilisha knew she would have to animate a few things herself in order to learn the relevant spells; perhaps, as part of her training, if Ithanalin didn't insist her creations be sold, she could provide Yara with the magical servants Ithanalin had never bothered to create.

But she had less than a year of her apprenticeship remaining, and had not yet been taught a single one of the spells that were Ithanalin's specialty and primary source of income—a fact that distressed her.

"Master," Kilisha said, "please—could I *please* learn an animation spell next?"

Ithanalin looked up at her, startled by the intensity in her voice.

"All right," he said. "We'll start on the seventeenth, the day after tomorrow—I have another important customer coming tomorrow, and it will take me most of the day to get his spell ready, so we can't do it then. But Kilisha, it may still be more than you can handle, even yet—animation spells are tricky." He thought for a moment, then added, "We'll start with the simplest I know. It's called the Spell of the Obedient Object—you've seen me use it. It's not the simplest there *is,* by any means, just the simplest I *know.* We'll need the blood of a gray cat, and one of these gold coins—I'll have to look the rest up. Day after tomorrow, right after breakfast, then. You'll have to find a gray cat tomorrow—I don't have any more cat's blood in stock. Besides, it'll keep you out of the way while I'm working."

Kilisha grinned. "*Thank* you, Master!" she said. She almost bounced with joy.

"That's tomorrow," Yara said, bringing her back to earth. "Right now, I'd like you to watch Pirra while I get our dinner."

Kilisha sighed, and smoothed out a hump in the rag rug by the door. "Yes, Mistress," she said.

Chapter Three

Kilisha eyed the gray cat warily; the cat stared inscrutably back.

Maybe, Kilisha thought, she was going about this wrong.

It had seemed perfectly reasonable to chase this stray; after all, she needed a gray cat, and this one had walked right in front of her as she strolled down Wizard Street. If she had thought about it at all she would have taken it as a sign from the gods—but she should have remembered how fond the gods were of jokes.

Now she stood precariously balanced on a broken crate, trying to reach the cat while it sat calmly watching her from a second-floor windowsill that was just a few inches beyond Kilisha's outstretched fingers.

"Here, puss," Kilisha crooned. "Come on. I'm not going to kill you, I just need a *little* blood."

The cat didn't move.

Kilisha stretched a little farther, on the very edge of overbalancing.

The cat flicked its tail against the windowpane with an audible thump, then stood up and stretched. Kilisha waited, hoping it would jump down, back within reach.

Something rattled, and the window casement swung inward.

"Come on in, Smoky," a child's voice said.

The cat gave Kilisha one last look, one the apprentice would have sworn was a supercilious sneer, and then climbed in through the open window, out of sight.

"No, wait!" Kilisha called. "Wait!" She reached too far; the window closed with a thump, wood cracked under her foot, and she tumbled down into the alley.

A moment later she had untangled herself from the wreckage and gotten upright once more; as she brushed dirt and splinters from her tunic she concluded that yes, she *was* going about this wrong. Trying to find a stray gray cat in the streets of Ethshar was simply too haphazard an enterprise; for one thing, as this latest incident demonstrated, there was no way to tell a true stray from someone's pet. Not everyone put bows, bells, and collars on their cats.

She had set out with no definite plan of action, and Smoky's appearance had convinced her she didn't need one.

She should have known better. Ithanalin was always telling her to plan ahead, and she kept forgetting and charging ahead without thinking.

She looked around thoughtfully. She couldn't ask Ithanalin for advice; by now he would be deep in his spell-casting, and an interruption might be disastrous. Yara and the children were out for the day—Yara at the market, the children playing with neighbors across the back courtyard—so as not to disturb Ithanalin. It was up to her.

Finding a cat shouldn't be a problem, though. It wasn't as if she'd been sent after dragon's blood or the hair of an unborn babe. Ethshar of the Rocks might be short of dragons, and its unborn children might be inaccessible, but there were plenty of cats.

Many of the aristocrats of Highside and Center City, westward toward the sea, kept cats—as well as any number of more exotic pets, such as Lady Nuvielle's miniature imitation dragon. Kilisha doubted that she'd find any aristocrats who cared to let a scruffy apprentice draw blood from their pampered darlings, though. At least, not without demanding more money than she could afford.

To the east was the Lakeshore district, and to the north was Norcross—both solidly middle class, home to assorted tradesmen and bureaucrats. Kilisha had the impression that their taste in pets ran more to watchdogs than cats.

The Arena district was a few blocks to the south, though, and that seemed promising.

Or if she just strolled along Wizard Street . . .

She knew several cats, belonging to magicians of every sort. Unfortunately, none of them were really *gray*—most magicians seemed to prefer black, and while there were a few tigers and tabbies mixed in, she didn't remember a single gray.

Maybe someone else would, though.

And if all else failed, she could go to a professional wizards' supply house—there was Kara's Arcana, on Arena Street just around the corner from Wizard Street. That would be expensive, even for something as simple as cat's blood, she was sure.

She sighed again and began walking.

Five hours later, around the middle of the afternoon, she finally headed homeward, a tightly stoppered vial of dark blood tucked in the purse on her belt. She owed the priestess Illuré a favor for this, and she hoped it wouldn't be too difficult to repay.

At least a priestess wouldn't want anyone turned into a newt or otherwise seriously harmed; the gods didn't approve of that sort of thing.

It seemed silly, spending all this time, half the day, just getting a little cat's blood. She knew Ithanalin had always said that the hardest part of any spell was getting the ingredients, but if it took this long for something simple like cat's blood . . .

Well, that was how wizards' suppliers like Kara or the infamous Gresh stayed in business, and why they could charge so much.

At least this way Ithanalin had probably had plenty of time for his spell and his mysterious customer, whoever it was—not many spells took more than a few hours. Yara and the little ones wouldn't be back yet, and the wizard had had the whole morning without an apprentice underfoot.

She came within sight of the shop and noticed that the drapes were still drawn. She sighed. Yara would never have allowed that, had she been home. Usually Ithanalin agreed that the drapes should be open during business hours, but sometimes, when he was busy, he forgot.

The door was open, though, so people would know that the wizard was home.

And he must be done with his spell, if he had left the door wide open. Kilisha hurried the last few paces.

"Hello, Master," she said, as she stepped into the dim room. "I'm sorry I—"

She stopped dead in her tracks. Something was wrong here.

Something was *very* wrong.

Ithanalin was crouching on the floor just a few feet inside the door, as if in the process of rising from a sitting position, but he was not moving. He wore his grubby working tunic and a worn leather apron, and he was utterly, perfectly still, his face frozen in a beard-bristling expression of severe annoyance.

Kilisha stared at him for a moment, then looked straight down at her own feet, not realizing why she did it until she saw that she was standing on bare planking.

The rag rug was gone.

She stared, then quickly looked around to see whether it might have slid off to one side.

It hadn't. It was gone.

And the red velvet couch was gone.

And the square black end table was gone.

And the humpback bench was gone.

And the coatrack was gone.

And the straight chair was gone.

Everything was gone—the room was totally empty except for herself, Ithanalin, and the mirror above the mantel.

"Master?" Kilisha said.

Ithanalin didn't respond.

She stepped closer, and, very carefully, reached out and touched the immobile wizard.

He was still warm—that was something, anyway—but he didn't react, didn't move; his skin felt lifeless and inert, like sun-warmed leather rather than living flesh.

"Master, what *happened*?" she wailed. She stared wildly around the empty room. She wanted to cry, but she wouldn't let herself cry; she wasn't a baby, she was seventeen years old, almost a journeyman.

This was magic, obviously. Ithanalin was clearly alive, but somehow frozen, and surely nothing but magic could freeze a person like that.

But was it hostile magic, or had something gone wrong?

She couldn't imagine who would have done this to her master deliberately. Ithanalin might not be the best-loved man in Ethshar, or even close to it, but he wasn't bad. She knew people who didn't like him, but she couldn't name anyone she would really call an *enemy*.

And if anyone attacked him—well, it would have to be another wizard, because if anyone else were to use magic on him that person would be risking the wrath of the Wizards' Guild. Nobody who was stupid enough to do that could be powerful enough to do something like this.

And why would a fellow wizard do it?

She wished she knew some decent divinations, but Ithanalin had never been much interested in such things. She had to rely on common sense to figure out what had happened here.

It might have been a wizard with some old grudge she didn't know about—but it might also be that something had gone wrong. After all, why would a wizard have stolen all the furniture?

She blinked, and looked around.

Why would *anyone* take the furniture? Most of it wasn't anything very special; the couch was unique, but so far as she knew it wasn't especially valuable. Probably the most valuable piece was the mirror, with its Shan glass and perfect silvering, and that was the only thing still here!

She reached back and closed the door; then she tiptoed carefully past the frozen wizard and peered through the doorway at the back of the parlor.

The workshop appeared to be undisturbed; the shelves and benches and stools were all still there, still cluttered with the detritus of wizardry. The chests of drawers where Ithanalin kept his ingredients were all in place, their drawers tidily closed. An oil lamp was burning in one corner of the workbench, warming a small brass bowl on a tripod—Kilisha had no idea what that might be for. Several spells required heating things, but none of the ones she knew seemed likely to have been in progress.

Cautiously, she ventured through the workroom to the kitchen at the rear of the shop, and then on up the stairs, checking for intruders, damage, or simply some sign of what had happened.

The ground-floor kitchen was untouched, just as she had left it that morning. The day nursery and drawing room on the next level were intact. A quick look in the bedrooms farther upstairs found nothing out of place.

Only the front parlor was affected.

She hurried back.

Ithanalin was still there, still motionless, still warm to the touch; everything else was still gone, save the mantel, hearth, and mirror.

What was so special about the mirror, then? Why was it still here? It wasn't bolted to the wall, or impossibly heavy; she had seen Yara take it down for cleaning once, a couple of years ago, and she hadn't had to strain to move it. If all the other furniture had been stolen, then why had the thieves left the most precious piece? Kilisha crossed the room and peered up into the smooth glass.

She saw her own image, and Ithanalin's, and the empty room. As she watched, though, shadows appeared; she spun around, expecting to see whatever made them.

Nothing was there. The room was empty and still.

She blinked, then slowly turned back to the mirror.

She knew the glass came from Shan on the Desert, far to the east, and there were rumors that Shan had been full of strange magic during the Great War, centuries ago—could there be some lingering spell that had been triggered by today's events, whatever they were? She stared intently at the reflected scene.

The shadows were still there; in fact, they were darker and sharper than before, and she realized that they couldn't be a reflection—they didn't move when she shifted angle. They were there in the mirror itself, somehow—not on the surface of the glass, but in the famously perfect silvering. That dark line wasn't across Ithanalin's face, and that one wasn't on the far wall. . . .

They grew and darkened as she watched, but it took another few seconds before she could adjust her vision and look at the thick black strokes properly. Finally, though, the runes fell into place.

HELLO, KILISHA, they said.

She blinked. "Hello," she said warily.

The shadow runes broke apart and vanished. The image of the empty room, her motionless master, and her own worried face was clear once again.

"Who are you?" she asked, after a moment of entirely ordinary reflections.

Curls of darkness swirled for a moment; then new runes appeared reading PART OF ITHANALIN THE WISE.

Her eyes widened as she realized that in fact the runes were in the familiar, slightly crooked handwriting she had seen so often—she had no doubt that the words were true. "Master!" she said. "You're trapped in there? Your spirit?"

NOT EXACTLY, the mirror replied.

Before Kilisha could react, the runes shifted again.

I AM *PART* OF ITHANALIN, they said. The three runes of the word "part" were larger and more ornately curved than the rest.

"Well, of course," Kilisha said. "Your body is right over there." She pointed.

I AM ONLY PART OF ITHANALIN'S SPIRIT, OR GHOST. NOT

ALL OF IT. The runes had to be somewhat smaller to convey this longer message, and squeezed together awkwardly.

"Oh," Kilisha said, crestfallen. She had been thinking this would be simple—if she had Ithanalin's body, and his soul was trapped in the mirror, surely there would be some way to put them back together. "What part? How many . . . I mean . . ."

I AM MOST OF THE WIZARD'S MEMORY, the mirror said.

"Oh. Then . . . then do you remember what happened?"

YES.

The single word hung there for a moment. "Then what *was* it?" Kilisha asked, almost wailing, when no further explanation materialized. "Why is your memory in the mirror, and your body petrified—or paralyzed, or whatever it is?"

Then the mirror explained the whole thing, in line after line of shadowy runes, and Kilisha stared until her eyes hurt, reading silently.

Ithanalin had been working on the animation spell for his important new customer—the man wanted a bed brought to life, for reasons that Ithanalin had not inquired very closely into, once the wizard had assurances that the customer's wife knew and approved, and that nothing murderous was planned.

Kilisha wondered about that—a living bed? She was a normal adolescent girl, with a normal interest in sex, no experience at all, and an overheated imagination; what would a living bed be for? Wouldn't that be, well, *strange*?

But people often were strange, especially those rich and eccentric enough to buy Ithanalin's spells. She tried not to think about the bed as the mirror continued.

The spell had finally been going well, after a couple of false starts, and was nearing completion; a spriggan had gotten into the workshop somehow, despite the locked front door, but Ithanalin had managed to shoo it out of the workshop and into the front parlor while he continued the mixing. He was at a point in the six-hour ritual where he had to stir a large bowl of goo for an hour without stopping—those people who made jokes about how wizards didn't need to keep their bodies fit obviously didn't know what went into some of these spells, Kilisha thought.

Then someone had knocked at the door.

At first Ithanalin had ignored it—Kilisha or Yara or the children would have the sense to realize he was busy, and could wait—they weren't due back yet, in any case—and he was not interested in talking to any customers or neighbors when he was in the middle of a spell. The door was closed and the curtains drawn, so it should have been plain that the wizard was not open for business; all the same, someone had rapped loudly.

Ithanalin had assumed that the caller, upon being ignored, would conclude no one was home and go away.

Whoever it was didn't take the hint, though—he pounded harder and started shouting, and Ithanalin had picked up the bowl, still stirring, and had marched out into the front room with the bowl tucked in his left arm, stirring spoon in his right hand. He had intended to order whoever it was to go away, and threaten to lay a few choice curses, but then he had made out some of the words being shouted—it wasn't a determined or angry customer at all. It was the overlord's tax collector on his more-or-less-annual rounds, and wizards had to pay just like anyone else.

Ithanalin couldn't stop stirring without ruining the spell, but he thought he could call through the door and explain that he was busy, and ask the tax collector to come back later—the guardsmen assigned to the treasurer's office were reputed to be stubborn but reasonable, and after all, Ithanalin had sold a miniature dragon to the treasurer herself just the day before, so surely the collector had not been instructed to be unusually difficult.

The rug by the front door had been humped up again, as usual, and as he walked and stirred Ithanalin had kicked at it, to straighten it out—but this time, instead of flattening, the rug had jumped up at him. The spriggan Ithanalin had chased out of the workshop had been hiding under the hump, and sprang out when the wizard kicked at it.

Ithanalin had been so startled that he had started to fall backward, and he had flung up his hands instinctively. The dish of magical glop intended for the customer's bed had gone flying, the spoon had gone flying, and the goo had sprayed all over the parlor in a glowing purple spatter, smearing on the ceiling, dripping down on the furniture, drifting in a thick fog every which way—not like a natural spill at all, but then, the stuff wasn't natural, it was magic. An animation magic, at that, already more than half alive.

Ithanalin had landed heavily on his backside, sitting spraddled on the floor, and had lost his temper enough to shout, "*Kux aqa!*"

"What does that mean?" Kilisha asked.

IT IS AN OBSCENITY IN AN ANCIENT, FORGOTTEN TONGUE, the mirror told her, the shadowy letters sliding across her reflected face.

"Yes, but what does it *mean*?" Kilisha insisted.

I DO NOT THINK THAT ITHANALIN, WERE HE COMPLETE, WOULD WISH TO TELL YOU.

"But he *isn't* complete, and it might be important!"

VERY WELL.

"So what does it mean?"

YOU ARE AWARE THAT PROFANITY OFTEN DOES NOT MAKE SENSE WHEN TRANSLATED LITERALLY?

"Of course!" Kilisha said, though she hadn't known any such thing.

THE PHRASE "*KUX AQA*" TRANSLATES ROUGHLY AS "A PER-SON WHO EATS POULTRY IN A DISTASTEFUL MANNER," the mirror informed her.

Kilisha blinked.

"Oh," she said.

SHALL I CONTINUE?

"Yes, please!"

The mirror continued, explaining that the phrase had served as a trigger for the incomplete spell, but as almost always happened when a spell was improperly performed, the results were not those intended. Usually, as Kilisha knew from her own failed attempts at any number of spells, an error simply drained the magic away and made the whole thing a lot of meaningless gestures; sometimes, though, it produced an entirely new spell—sometimes trivial, sometimes not. It was rumored that just such an accidental spell had created spriggans in the first place, a few years before.

In this case, the botched spell had had a very definite effect—it had absorbed Ithanalin's own life force and distributed it throughout the room, settling it into the furnishings.

That had left the wizard himself inanimate, of course—his energies and the various aspects of his personality had been drained away and scattered about, leaving an empty shell.

"Oh, gods!" Kilisha said, hand to her mouth. She looked about at the empty room.

I SEE YOU UNDERSTAND, the mirror said.

It went on to explain that all the furniture had been animated, receiving different parts of Ithanalin's life force. Because almost the entirety of Ithanalin's memory had been deposited in the mirror, however, the other pieces seemed unaware of who or what they were.

The latch of the front door had been animated, as well, and had opened itself, allowing the tax collector to enter. He had then found himself confronted by animated furniture and an inanimate wizard, and had let out a yell, whereupon there had been a general panic, and the various furnishings, after bumping around the room a little, had fled—as had the tax collector, apparently; the mirror had not had a clear view, but at any rate the soldier had not stayed.

The couch and end table, the bench, the coatrack, and the old chair had all had legs, legs they could now move; they had been able to walk, run, or scamper out the door. The rag rug had humped itself along like an inchworm and vanished into the street. And although the mirror hadn't seen just how they propelled themselves, it was fairly sure that the implements Ithanalin had carried had come to life, as well.

The dish had run away with the spoon.

Chapter Four

Since he had been interrupted in the middle of a spell, Ithanalin's book of magic was lying open on the workbench when Kilisha found it; that voided most of the protective spells that would ordinarily prevent anyone other than Ithanalin himself from using it. Of the other wards Kilisha was exempted from some, and the mirror was able to tell her how to counteract the last few.

With a glance at the mysterious oil lamp and tripod, Kilisha picked up the book and carried it into the front room. There she paged through it, reading anything that looked even vaguely relevant and holding it up for the mirror to read when she had any questions.

She had already gone through her own book of spells, which contained the instructions for the fifty-three assorted spells she had learned to date, before touching Ithanalin's. None of those fifty-three were of any obvious use in restoring her master to normal, so she had resorted to Ithanalin's own book, which held, by her hasty count, one hundred and twelve.

Even distraught as she was over the accident, Kilisha was somewhat annoyed by the discovery of just how many of her master's spells she had not yet learned; she had hoped and expected to complete her apprenticeship within the coming year and become a journeyman at the age of eighteen, but she doubted she could learn another fifty-nine spells properly in that time when it had taken her five years to get this far. She had known there were all the various animation spells, but glancing through it was plain that there were a good many others, as well.

She was sure she could have learned faster if Ithanalin had taken the trouble to teach her. She wondered whether his one previous apprentice, Istram—now a journeyman and well on the way to becoming a master himself—had learned all these, or whether he had gone out into the World only partially educated. Perhaps some of these spells were deemed unfit for mere apprentices or journeymen, and Kilisha would have to wait years to learn them.

Right now, though, Kilisha needed to find a spell to undo the botched animation, and once she found it she would probably need to teach it to herself from the book, so she certainly *hoped* she would be able to handle it, even if she *was* just an apprentice.

She hoped she would be able to read the instructions properly, that Ithanalin hadn't used any secret codes in writing up his book. She had never before been permitted to work directly from Ithanalin's written instruction; spells were taught orally, and by demonstration, never in writing, so that the master could watch the apprentice every step of the way. And the apprentice was required to write down the spell in her own words, rather than copying the master's, to make sure that she would always be able to understand it.

The spell that had gone wrong, the mirror told her, was the Servile Animation, a sixth-order spell requiring, among other things, dragon's blood, seeds of an opium poppy, virgin's tears— Kilisha had provided those tears herself, she realized, unsure whether to be offended that Ithanalin had correctly assumed she was qualified for the purpose, and had not bothered to ask her whether she was still a suitable donor—and red hair from a woman married more than a year.

Yara's hair was dark brown; Kilisha wondered where Ithanalin had found a red-haired woman.

It didn't really look all that difficult when she read the instructions, but the mirror assured her that it was far harder than it appeared.

The spell had no specified counter, and was not inherently reversible. Kilisha sighed. She went paging onward through the book.

"Here," she said at last, holding the volume up to the mirror. "Will this work?"

She had found a spell called Javan's Restorative; according to the description Ithanalin had written, this spell would restore a person or thing to a "natural healthy State, regardless of previous Enchauntments, Breakage, or Damage." It wasn't one she had ever attempted, or one she would have had any business attempting unaided for some time yet under ordinary circumstances, but she was fairly sure she had seen Ithanalin use it once, and she was willing to give it a try.

If she couldn't make it work, perhaps she could find a more experienced wizard who could handle it—if it was the right spell.

"Will it work?" she repeated.

IT SHOULD, read the reply.

"Good," Kilisha said. She lowered the book and looked at the ingredients the spell called for.

Two peacock plumes, one of them pure white—that was easy; Ithanalin kept a vase of them in the corner of his workshop, a vase Yara occasionally put out on display in the parlor, but which Ithanalin always took back as soon as he noticed its absence.

Boiling water was easy, too.

Jewelweed . . . Kilisha had never heard of jewelweed, but she assumed she could get it from any good herbalist. She would check on that.

A quarter-pound block of a special incense, prepared in fog or sea mist—Kilisha hurried to the drawers in the workshop.

Fortunately, though Ithanalin might be a careless housekeeper elsewhere, he kept *some* things tidy and neatly labeled; each block of incense was wrapped in tissue and tied with string, with a tag on the string that said, in Ithanalin's crooked runes, exactly when and how the incense had been made, and what ingredients had been used.

The right block was in the first drawer Kilisha checked, about halfway back and one layer down. She lifted it out and set it carefully on the workbench.

And that, once she had bought the jewelweed and fetched the feathers and boiled the water, was everything—except, of course, for a wizard's athame and the parts of whatever was broken.

She blinked.

Well, she had her own athame. She'd had it for years, she'd made it when she was not quite thirteen. And of course she had to have the pieces of whatever was broken; that was obvious. Something about it bothered her, though. She read through the instructions carefully, to see if she had missed anything.

No, it all seemed fairly straightforward. It was a higher-order spell than anything she'd ever done, but she could at least attempt it. She just needed to either work the spell in the front room, or bring Ithanalin and the mirror into the workshop. . . .

She blinked again.

And, she realized, all the furniture.

She needed to have *all* the pieces. The instructions were quite clear that if any significant portion was absent, the spell would not work.

And a part of Ithanalin—presumably each one significant—had animated each object now missing from the parlor.

In addition to the mirror and her master's body, she needed the rag rug, and the couch, and the end table, and the bench, and the chair, and the coatrack, and the dish, and the spoon.

She looked through the open doorway into the bare room. She would need the front door latch, too, but that was still where it belonged.

Almost nothing else was.

"Oh," she said, staring.

She would have to collect all the furniture. It had all run out the front door and vanished, and she would have to find it all and bring it back here. Her lips tightened into a frown.

Then she relaxed a little. Really, how hard could that be? After all, animated furniture wasn't exactly a common sight in the streets of Ethshar. It should be easy enough to find. The rag rug, the couch, the end table, the bench, the coatrack, the chair, the bowl, and the spoon—eight items.

She hoped she wasn't forgetting anything. She would want to consult the mirror carefully before actually attempting Javan's spell.

She sighed, and put the block of incense back in the drawer. She didn't dare close the book of spells, in case Ithanalin's magic might keep her from opening it again, but she placed it carefully on a shelf and covered it with a soft cloth.

She looked at the oil lamp, and the brass bowl. Something was bubbling darkly in there—presumably some minor spell her master had had brewing on the side while he performed the Servile Animation. She hoped it wasn't dangerous.

Well, it shouldn't be hard to find out. She went back out to the parlor and asked the mirror, "What's in that brass bowl Ithanalin was heating?"

The mirror clouded, but no runes appeared at first. Kilisha frowned.

"Hello?"

WHAT BOWL?

"The brass bowl over the oil lamp," Kilisha said.

The mirror clouded again for a long moment, but finally admitted, I DON'T REMEMBER. PERHAPS SOMETHING ELSE RECEIVED THAT PARTICULAR MEMORY.

"Oh, that's just wonderful," Kilisha muttered. She returned to the workshop and looked at the bowl again.

The stuff looked thick and oily, a brown so dark it was almost black. It smelled spicy and very slightly bitter, but not at all unpleasant. She didn't recognize it.

The obvious assumption was that something brewing in a wizard's workshop was a spell of some sort, but this smelled more like food. Ithanalin didn't cook—Yara didn't allow it, due to an unfortunate incident a few years before Kilisha's arrival—but perhaps this might still be something other than a spell. Kilisha drew her athame and held it out cautiously toward the bowl to check.

The point of the knife glowed faintly blue, and she could feel magic in the air. Whatever was in that bowl was definitely magical.

So it *was* a spell, and one she didn't recognize.

"Oh, blast," she said.

She sheathed her dagger and stared at the bowl for a moment, then glanced at the book of spells on the shelf above the workbench. She had no idea which of them might have produced this stuff, and simply going through and looking at the ingredients would not tell her—magic didn't work that way; the dark goo might bear no resemblance at all to its ingredients.

It didn't look dangerous, at least not yet, but she really needed to restore Ithanalin to health *quickly,* before that concoction set off some other weird spell, or blew up, or went bad.

It would probably be strongly advisable to restore him before that lamp ran out of oil, too. She peered into the reservoir; it looked fairly full.

She needed to find the missing furniture and get it back here as soon as she could. She took a final glance around, then hurried back out to the street, calling a quick farewell to the mirror.

She'd already spent the whole morning and half the afternoon tracking down cat's blood, an hour or more consulting the mirror and the books of spells, and she was not looking forward to spending the rest of the day hunting furniture. . . .

She had reached the middle of the street when she realized that the cat's blood was still on her belt. She did not want to risk spilling it, after all the trouble she had gone to to obtain it. She sighed again, and trudged back into Ithanalin's workshop, where she placed the vial of blood in a rack, then looked around again.

Was there anything else she was forgetting?

Of course there was. Yara and the children. What would *they* think, when they came home and found Ithanalin petrified and the furniture gone?

She found a piece of paper and wrote a note—Yara and Telleth could read, and Lirrin was learning.

"Master's spell went wrong," she wrote. "Am seeking ingredients for antidote. Mirror is enchanted, can answer questions. Back as soon as I can be." She signed it, "Kilisha, app."

Just as she finished something chimed—the brass bowl on the tripod had rung like a bell. She looked at it, startled.

It looked exactly the same—the lamp was burning, the brown goo was bubbling, and the spicy smell was stronger than ever.

Presumably the chime was some part of the enchantment; probably it was a signal that something was ready, or something needed to be done to continue the spell. Unfortunately, Kilisha had no idea what it meant or what should be done. She stood there for a moment, her note in one hand, staring at the bowl and trying to decide what to do.

Eventually she decided that the best thing she could do, in her present state of ignorance, was to leave the thing completely alone and hope for the best while she did everything she could to restore her master. If the brass bowl exploded or started spewing dragons she would deal with it then. For now, she wanted to leave her note and get on with the furniture hunting.

She considered adding a line or two advising Yara to leave the lamp, tripod, and bowl alone, but surely a wizard's wife would have the sense to do that without being told by a mere apprentice. The note would be fine as it was.

She thought about where to post it, and for a moment she considered leaving it on Ithanalin's lap, but she decided that would be disrespectful. Instead, she laid it carefully on the floor just inside the front door.

Then she stepped out into the street, closed the door cautiously behind her, and looked around. She wanted to recover the furniture—but where should she start?

She was on Wizard Street, in one of those ill-defined parts of the city that weren't really part of any recognized district—the magistrates said this was part of Lakeshore, but no one else thought so. Ithanalin's shop was on the north side of the street, in the middle of a long block. Two blocks to the north—a little over a hundred yards—was the East Road, which ran through the center of the city from just below the Fortress to the market at Eastgate; a couple of blocks beyond that was Wizard Street again, as it looped back on itself half a mile to the east, making a U around Eastgate Circle.

To the west Wizard Street ran through the valley between Center City and Highside and down to the shipyards, then wound its way southeast to Wargate.

A hundred feet to the east and across the street was the entrance to Not Quite Street—so named because it stopped two blocks short of the East Road at this end, and one block short of Cross Avenue at the other.

Kilisha could see a good two hundred yards in either direction—the street was surprisingly uncrowded for this time of day—and saw nothing out of the ordinary. No end tables or couches were anywhere to be seen, nor any crowds of curious bystanders that animated furniture might have attracted.

She trotted quickly over and peered down Not Quite Street, and saw nothing down that way.

She had come home, she remembered, along Wizard Street—Illuré's little temple was up to the east, toward Eastgate. She hadn't seen any furniture along that route.

Walking furniture would attract attention, she thought; why weren't there crowds around the missing pieces?

Frowning, she went back toward Ithanalin's shop, but stopped at the shop next door and rang the bell.

Nissitha the Seer was not Kilisha's idea of the perfect neighbor, but she could certainly be worse; she was a fortune-teller, and Ithanalin suspected her of being a fraud. She spent a good bit of her time, when no customers were expected, gossiping in the courtyard out back, but never offered to help out with anyone's chores. She had refused to mind Pirra a few weeks back, when Yara had been out somewhere with Telleth and Lirrin, and Ithanalin had wanted Kilisha to help with a spell. She kept no chickens or other livestock—just a pampered long-haired black cat. And she made stupid jokes about the supposed similarities between her own talents and Ithanalin's.

But she didn't intrude, didn't make noise other than her court-yard chatter, and kept her place clean.

The door opened, and Nissitha looked down her long nose at Kilisha. The Seer's long black hair hung loose in curls and ringlets.

"Oh, hello, Kilisha," she said. "Did you have a question? I'm afraid I don't work for free for anyone, but I could give you a discount. Is it a boy?"

"No, it's nothing like that," Kilisha said. "I was wondering if you'd seen our furniture."

Nissitha blinked at her. "Your furniture?"

"Yes." Kilisha hesitated, then explained. "There's been an accident, and some of our furniture was inadvertently brought to life, and it got loose. I was wondering whether you saw which way it went."

"I'm afraid not," Nissitha said, staring at the apprentice. "When did this happen?"

"I'm not sure exactly," Kilisha said. "Sometime today. A tax collector interrupted a spell."

"Oh!" Sudden comprehension dawned on Nissitha's face. "Oh, I'm afraid I was hiding upstairs. I saw the tax collector coming, you see, and I just really didn't want to be bothered."

"You didn't want to pay," Kilisha said.

"I didn't want to pay," Nissitha admitted with a smile.

"He'll come back until he catches you, you know," Kilisha said.

Nissitha sighed. "I suppose so," she said, "but I'm in no hurry to be caught."

Kilisha nodded—then stopped.

What if the furniture was in no hurry to be caught? She'd been assuming it had wandered off more or less at random, but what if it was deliberately *hiding* from her?

That might make the task of restoring Ithanalin to life considerably more difficult than she had anticipated.

"Listen," she said, "if you see any animated furniture, let me know, please? It's very important. I'll owe you a favor if you help me—I know I'm only an apprentice, but I do know a few spells."

Nissitha cocked her head to one side. "Oh?"

"Yes. It's not worth anything to anyone else, really—I mean, no more than any animated furniture—but really, it's very important to me."

"I'll keep that in mind."

"Thank you." Kilisha bobbed in a polite half-bow, then turned away and looked up and down the street.

The furniture had been *scared*, the mirror said—or at least startled. And it didn't remember it had been Ithanalin. Any given piece might not remember anything. It might not realize that Ithanalin's shop was its home.

So where would it go?

A rag rug, a couch, an end table. . . .

Behind her, Nissitha shrugged and closed her door.

Furniture, Kilisha said to herself. Where would *furniture* go to hide?

The rag rug surely couldn't hump along very fast, so it would have tried to hide, it wouldn't just run away. It would probably have tried to slide under something, and the spoon might have done that, too. None of the other items would fit under doors, or down ratholes, or anywhere awful, but the spoon could be *anywhere*.

The end table had fairly long, thin legs—it could probably move pretty quickly. The bench's legs were shorter, but straight and strong, and it had a longer . . . body? Well, it was a body now. Those two might have run for it, in which case they would probably have headed east on Wizard Street.

If they'd taken the right turn when Wizard Street crossed the East Road, they could have run right out the city gate by now.

Except that if they had gone east, Kilisha should have seen some evidence of it, and she had not.

Well, then, perhaps they went west.

The couch and the coatrack had short, curving legs; Kilisha imagined them moving like short-legged dogs, dashing and dodging rather than running flat-out. They might have taken any of the corners; they might be anywhere.

The chair had decent legs, but it would be hobbled by the cross braces; Kilisha couldn't guess how it would move or what it would do.

And the dish—how could a bowl move at all?

It could roll, she supposed, but how far could it get that way?

If it were rolling, it would tend to go downhill—and that meant west, down Wizard Street toward the shipyards.

That would be the one to start with, she thought. The others might come home on their own, they might be almost anywhere, she might need to use magic to find them, but the bowl—*that* should be fairly easy to find.

And she had to find it before it was broken, or before someone decided to keep it.

She turned and headed west at a brisk trot.

Chapter Five

It was very hard to imagine a bowl rolling all the way across Cross Avenue without being stepped on, kicked, or otherwise battered, but Kilisha had found no trace of the missing dish anywhere in the first three blocks of her search, so she had to assume it had somehow managed it. Animated objects could be amazingly clever and persistent, as she well knew; they never tired, the way living creatures did, and they couldn't be distracted by hunger or other discomforts. She hurried across the broad avenue, then stopped abruptly.

She had heard something—something that might have been the sound of a spoon hitting a bowl. That wasn't a sound one ordinarily heard outside a kitchen. It was followed by a man's voice, swearing.

The oaths meant trouble. Kilisha winced, then turned, trying to locate the source.

The swearing continued, and Kilisha determined that it was coming from a little way south on Cross Avenue. She hurried in that direction.

"...stop *struggling*, blast you!" she heard, followed by the sound of something whacking flesh.

That might not be any of the lost furnishings, but it sounded like something that needed investigation, in any case. Ordinarily she might have left it to older, wiser heads than her own, but it *might* involve one of her master's pieces.

The voice was coming, she realized, from the covered entryway of a tavern on the west side of the avenue, half a block from the intersection with Wizard Street. A sort of small porch made by cutting doorways through the two sides of an immense barrel sheltered the tavern's doorway while advertising the business, and that echoing barrel had served to amplify the sounds that had attracted her attention.

It was a remarkable piece of good fortune, if that was indeed where her quarry had gone, and as she hurried toward the tavern she murmured a quick prayer of gratitude to any gods who might have been involved.

She reached the outer doorway and peered into the barrel.

A man stood there, clutching a bowl under one arm and a wooden spoon in his other hand—but the spoon was writhing about wildly, twisting and bending, slapping at the man's arm. He was holding that arm straight out, holding the spoon as far from his body as he could; presumably it had tried to strike at other portions of his anatomy, as well.

These were unquestionably the bowl and spoon Kilisha was looking for; although one wooden spoon looked much like any other, and the earthenware bowl was undistinguished, how many *animated* wooden spoons were on the streets of Ethshar on this particular afternoon?

And this man did not look at all like a wizard; he was dressed in a workingman's brown woolen tunic and leather breeches, both filled out by an overlarge belly, and he had more hair in his close-trimmed beard than atop his head.

"Hold still! I'm not going to hurt you, confound it!"

"Excuse me," Kilisha said, "but I believe that's mine."

The man started; he had plainly been too involved with his struggle to notice her arrival. Now he turned to stare at her.

"Who are you?" he demanded.

"My name is Kilisha the Apprentice," she said, her hand dropping to the hilt of her athame. "Apprentice *wizard.*"

The man stared at her a moment longer before speaking, and Kilisha was uncomfortably aware of her own rather drab and unimposing appearance. Ithanalin had the physical presence to impress his customers, and Kilisha had long known that she did not—at least, not yet; she hoped it would come with age.

"Then why aren't you in a wizard's robe?" he asked.

"Because I wasn't dealing with customers," she snapped. "I was *working*, and *those*—" she drew her dagger and pointed it at the bowl and spoon "—escaped from my master's house."

The man looked down at the bowl. The spoon was no longer struggling; it seemed to be listening.

"How do I know they're really yours?" he asked. "I found them on the street."

"I told you, they escaped."

"But how do I know they escaped from *you*? You don't look like a wizard. That dagger doesn't prove anything!"

Kilisha, who had already had far more trouble than she expected that day, and who knew much more still lay ahead, almost growled. She should have prepared . . .

No, she told herself, she shouldn't need to prove anything—but in fact, she *could* demonstrate that she was a wizard. She had a few ingredients in the pouch on her belt. She could show this troublesome person a few things. Fendel's Spectacular Illusion required dragon's blood, which was too expensive to waste like that, but she had a chip of chrysolite she could use to conjure the Yellow Cloud. . . .

But that would cover almost the entire width of the street, and hide everything for a minute or so, and he might turn and run, and she wouldn't be able to see any better than he could. She tried to think what else she had available.

Thrindle's Combustion, of course. Her free hand dropped to the pouch, and with the skill born of long practice she used two fingers to pop the lid off her vial of brimstone. She made a gesture and spoke a word, and an inch or so of the hem of the man's tunic suddenly burst into flame.

Startled, he slapped at it and quickly extinguished the flames—but to Kilisha's surprise and annoyance, he did not drop the bowl or spoon.

As he beat out the embers, she said, "Do you *really* want to argue with a wizard, a member in good standing of the Guild?" she said. "You admit those things aren't *yours*—why should you think they aren't mine?"

"Because they're valuable," the man said, frowning as he tugged at the blackened, crumbling fabric. "You're just an apprentice, you said so yourself. I found them, and I was planning to sell them. They were just lying in the street—"

"They were not," Kilisha snapped. "They were *moving*. That's how you knew they were worth stealing."

"It wasn't stealing!" the man protested, looking up as he brushed ash from his breeches. "*You're* the one trying to steal them!"

"They're mine," Kilisha said. "Or my master's, at any rate."

"Prove it! Fine, you're a wizard, but how do I know you aren't trying to steal these from the wizard who *really* owns them?"

Kilisha frowned, amazed at the man's stubbornness. How in the World was she supposed to prove it? There was no Spell of True Ownership on them, no names written on them, no distinctive marks she could point out—they were a completely ordinary bowl and spoon that happened to have parts of Ithanalin's soul in them.

"Give them to me, and I'll show you," she said, sheathing her athame and holding out a hand.

She had no way of proving ownership. Her actual plan was to simply grab them and run, and hope that she could lose the man in the streets, or at least get back to the shop before he caught her. He was considerably larger than she was, but he didn't look particularly fast or agile—and if he had any sense, he would not want to anger *any* wizard.

The man looked from her to the spoon, then back.

"Here," he said, holding it out. "I'll hold onto the bowl until you *prove* they're yours."

Kilisha hesitated for half a second, remembering the way the spoon had been writhing about and slapping at the man's arm. If she took it, and it struggled, she might still run with it, but how would she ever get the bowl? She didn't want to rely on threats; the Guild didn't approve of outright extortion.

The spoon didn't look particularly violent just now, though; it had twisted around so that its bowl was turned toward her, leaning forward as if listening to her. She took it, holding it just below the bowl.

The instant the man released it, it wrapped its handle around her wrist, bent its bowl down, and began rubbing against her wrist, like a cat asking to be petted.

"You see?" she said, struggling to hide her astonishment. "It knows me!"

"Oh," the man said, staring.

"Now, the bowl?"

Sheepishly, he took the bowl from under his arm and handed it over.

"Thank you," Kilisha said, accepting it. Seeing no harm in being conciliatory, she added, "I'm sorry about your tunic. If you ever need a little advice, or a spell at a small discount, come to Ithanalin's shop on Wizard Street."

The man mumbled something, and Kilisha turned and marched away.

The spoon was still stroking her wrist in a thoroughly disconcerting manner, and the bowl seemed to be flexing slightly. She quickly tucked it under one arm, as its previous captor had.

The spoon unwound its handle and the tip of *that* began stroking her arm. She suppressed a scream and kept walking.

She would get these safely tucked away somewhere, under lock and key, then go out after the rest of the furniture, she told herself. She trotted quickly up Wizard Street.

She had gone a block or so when she happened to glance down

a side street and noticed a coatrack standing there, in the middle of the narrow little street, with no one near it.

It was an ordinary coatrack consisting of a square wooden post mounted on four short, curving wooden legs, with two large, graceful iron hooks on each side, one set of hooks at waist level and one set level with the top of her head. It looked absurdly out of place standing out in the open, rather than in someone's front room.

"What is that . . ." Kilisha began—and then she realized that the coatrack was a very familiar one.

It wasn't moving just now, and that, combined with focusing on getting the bowl and spoon home, had been why she didn't recognize it immediately, but it was definitely Ithanalin's coatrack, the one that had stood by the front door for as long as Kilisha had lived there.

This whole furniture-collecting task might prove easier than she had expected, Kilisha thought as she turned in to the side street.

On the other hand, it might not—she had the spoon in one hand, and the bowl under the other arm, which did not leave anything completely free to carry the coatrack. She tried to pass the spoon from her right hand to her left.

It wrapped itself more tightly around her right wrist.

"Come on, let go," she said, as she tried to tug at it with her left fingers without dislodging the bowl from her elbow—which was made more difficult by the bowl's own slow movements. She told the spoon, "I'm not putting you down, I just want to use my other hand."

The spoon seemed to hesitate, then reluctantly allowed itself to be pried away.

It promptly wrapped itself around her left wrist so securely that she didn't bother holding it in her hand at all. She had to keep her left elbow at her side to hold the bowl, but now both hands were free. She stepped forward and reached her right hand out for the coatrack.

It abruptly started to life and backed away from her, removing any possible doubt of its identity.

"Oh, don't be like that," she said. "It's just me. I've come to take you home." She stepped forward again.

The coatrack backed away again, but found itself pressing up against the stone wall of a tinker's shop, unable to retreat further. It shivered, then uncurled a hook and pointed it threateningly at Kilisha.

She stopped abruptly, with the rounded end of the hook just inches from her eyes. "What are you *doing*?" she demanded. "It's *me*, Kilisha! You're part of my master's spirit trapped in a coatrack! Let me take you home, so we can restore you to your proper state."

It waved the hook back and forth in a definitely negative gesture.

Baffled, Kilisha stared at it for a moment. She hadn't really thought about the possibility that some of the furniture would actively resist capture; she had assumed that even if it was hiding, it would all have gotten over its initial panic and be willing to return home and be restored to its natural state. After all, it was all animated by Ithanalin's spirit, and surely *he* would have wanted to go home.

The coatrack, however, clearly did not agree with her theory. It was pressing back against the stone, all eight of its hooks uncurled and pointed at her.

The mirror had told her that the furniture had been frightened and did not remember whose life animated it, but she had still never expected so hostile a reception. She had thought it would be confused, a little skittish, perhaps, but no worse than that. The spoon had seemed downright enthusiastic about being recaptured, the bowl indifferent—but the coatrack plainly had other ideas.

Maybe, she thought, it had forgotten Ithanalin's prior existence so completely that it thought it was just a coatrack.

"Don't you *know* me?" she asked. "I've hung my coat on you a hundred times!"

It shuddered, and waved its hooks back and forth. No, it did *not* know her, and it was clearly upset.

"I won't hurt you," she said soothingly. "I promise! I'm just a girl; what could I do to a big strong coatrack like you? You're solid wood and iron."

That seemed to calm it slightly; it stopped twisting and shivering.

It did not step away from the wall or recurl its hooks, however.

"Come on home with me," Kilisha coaxed. "We'll take care of you, make sure you don't get caught out in the rain—it would be *very* bad for your shellac, you know."

The coatrack seemed to hesitate, then shook its upper portion no.

"Oh, come on."

Again, it said no.

"Well, I can't *force* you," Kilisha said—and as she spoke she realized that it was probably true; if the coatrack put up a fight . . .

Well, it was taller and didn't bleed or bruise, but she was far heavier, and had hands and feet—if she could get a good grip on it out of reach of the hooks, and lift it off the ground so it couldn't get any traction, she could probably carry it away, but holding on if it squirmed would be difficult. If it was able to get its hooks on a doorframe or sign bracket somewhere, she doubted she could pry it away.

And that left out the whole question of what the bowl and spoon would be doing during all this.

Fighting it bare-handed was not a good idea, and she wished she had brought some serious magic, or at least some help.

And if just capturing a coatrack was difficult, what would she do if the couch put up a fight?

Talking it into cooperating seemed the only sensible solution, but she couldn't think of what else she could tell it.

"All right," she said, "I won't rush you—you come home when you're ready. Do you remember where it is?"

It hesitated, then waved back and forth—no.

"It's just up Wizard Street. If you want to follow me, you can see for yourself."

It took a moment to consider, then nodded. The hooks curled back to their natural shapes.

Kilisha forced a smile. "Fine!" she said. "This way."

And she turned away and started for home. By an intense effort of will she managed not to look back until she was out of the side street and back on Wizard Street.

The coatrack was following her, several feet back.

She was still too dazed and upset by everything that had happened to manage a smile, but she did let out a small sigh of relief. The spoon stroked her forearm soothingly as she hurried homeward.

Chapter Six

Yara was standing in the doorway, waiting. "Oh, thank the gods!" she said when she saw Kilisha approaching.

"Hello," Kilisha replied; she waved, and cast a glance over her shoulder.

The coatrack was still there, but seemed to be hanging back, hesitant to approach. Other pedestrians were staring at it now, which Kilisha was sure was not helping.

The spoon and bowl, on the other hand, seemed very happy to hear Yara's voice; the spoon was waving its handle cheerfully, and the bowl hugged Kilisha's side.

"Are the children around?" Kilisha asked.

"They're inside," Yara said, looking past Kilisha at the coatrack.

"Good. We need to talk." She carefully didn't look back again as she walked up to the door.

Yara stepped aside, and Kilisha crossed the familiar threshold.

Ithanalin was still crouched, half-sitting, half-rising, on the floor; the mirror was still on the wall, and the rest of the room was still completely empty. Kilisha bit her lip as she looked around.

She had hoped that some of the furnishings might have found

their own way back, but obviously none of them had. There was so much yet to be done!

And it would take planning; marching out into the streets and running around practically at random had been foolish. She was a wizard's apprentice, just a year short of journeyman if all went well—not some silly child!

"Kilisha," Yara said, "is he all right?"

"Well, no," Kilisha replied, startled. "I mean, you can see that." It occurred to her belatedly as her gaze returned to Yara's worried face that maybe some words of reassurance, rather than blunt honesty, would have been appropriate.

But she was an apprentice; lying to her master's wife, no matter how comforting, was not fitting.

"Is he *going* to be all right?" Yara asked.

"I certainly hope so, but I can't promise," Kilisha replied.

"Oh, you sound just like him! What happened? Why is he like this?"

Startled, Kilisha said, "Didn't you ask the mirror?"

"I asked it questions, but it kept saying it didn't know—it didn't know where you were or when you'd be back or what I should do to help, and I gave up."

"Oh." Kilisha frowned. "Mistress, I can't take the time to explain right now—we need to get these things safely put away." She held out the arm with the spoon wrapped around it, catching the bowl in her other hand. "Could you take these?"

Hesitantly, Yara reached for the spoon—which practically jumped into her hand. It clearly liked Yara even more than Kilisha; it wrapped itself around her wrist, vibrating with pleasure so intensely that Kilisha almost thought she could hear purring.

"Oh, my heart!" Yara said, startled; she tried to drop the spoon, but it had already secured itself, and thus released it did not fall, but instead wound its way, snakelike, up her arm, sliding into her sleeve.

"Oh!" Yara said again. "I don't—"

"It won't hurt you," Kilisha said quickly. "Don't lose it! It has part of Ithanalin's spirit in it."

The spoon had now completely vanished into the loose sleeves of Yara's tunic. Yara stared at her own shoulder, then blushed.

"I think I know which part," she said. Her bodice twitched.

Kilisha did not need to ask what Yara meant. She swallowed at the thought that Yara was probably right, and she herself had had the spoon wrapped around her own wrist; that was hardly the sort of thing that ought to happen between a married master and his apprentice!

It was a good thing that the person who had picked it up on Cross Avenue had been a man, rather than a woman, or she might have had a harder time convincing anyone that Kilisha owned it. For that matter, it was a good thing that Ithanalin's preferences had been as definite as they were.

"Here," she said, holding out the bowl.

Yara accepted it gingerly. "What does *this* do?" she asked.

"I have no idea," Kilisha said. "It's got another part of his spirit, but I don't know which." She turned. "Did the coatrack come in?"

"No," Yara said.

"Blast! We need that, too." She hurried back out into the street.

There was no sign of the coatrack.

"Mistress," she called, "you keep hold of those things, but could you send the kids out here to help me?"

"All right," Yara replied. Kilisha could hear her retreating footsteps.

"Excuse me, sir," she called to a nearby pedestrian. "Did you see a coatrack go by?"

"I think so," the man answered uncertainly.

"Which way did it go?"

"Um . . . that way," he said, pointing west.

Muttering to herself, Kilisha set out back down Wizard Street.

She had gone less than a block when she spotted the coatrack, its square peak visible over the heads of the handful of intervening pedestrians.

"Stop!" she called. "Coatrack! Come back!"

The top of the coatrack vibrated at the sound of her voice, but it did not come to her; instead it stepped sideways, as if looking for an alley to hide in. It ducked behind the open door of a shop—Adagan the Witch was sweeping out, and had his door at right angles to the frame.

Kilisha let out an annoyed sigh. She turned to see whether the children had emerged yet.

Telleth was leaning out the door of the shop, looking puzzled.

"Telleth!" Kilisha called. "Come here, please!"

Hesitantly, Telleth came. Lirrin and Pirra appeared in the doorway, and Kilisha beckoned. "All of you, come here."

Kilisha glanced at the coatrack—or rather, where she had last seen it. It was now completely hidden behind Adagan's door.

She could just march over there, but the silly thing might run away again; apparently it had all Ithanalin's doubts and uncertainties. Until now Kilisha hadn't entirely realized her master had any.

With a little planning, though, it shouldn't be hard to catch. Planning ahead had always been one of her weaknesses—she usually just dashed in to confront a problem, and only figured out later what she *should* have done—hardly the proper wizardly approach.

This time, she promised herself, she wouldn't do that. Too much was at stake. She would do this properly.

She stooped down and whispered, "One of your father's spells has gone wrong—I'm sure you already realized that. Well, I know how to fix it, but first we need to capture all the escaped furniture. Do you understand?"

Telleth and Lirrin nodded, but Pirra turned up an empty hand.

"It's bad magic," Telleth said to his baby sister. "Kilisha can fix it, but we need to help."

Pirra still looked worried and uncertain, but Kilisha decided it didn't really matter whether the girl understood, so long as she did what was needed.

"Over there, behind that door," Kilisha said, "is the coatrack from beside the front door. It can move around now, and we need to get it back home. It's very shy, though, so we need to catch it."

"How?" Lirrin asked.

"Well, I was thinking that if you three got behind it in a line, and held hands so it couldn't get past you, you could chase it this way, and I could grab it and push it inside."

The three children looked at one another uncertainly.

"It may threaten you with its hooks, but I don't think it really wants to hurt anyone," Kilisha said. "It's just scared."

Telleth swallowed.

"I think Pirra should be in the middle," Kilisha said. "If she's on the end it might be able to dodge past her, since she's so small."

"That's right," Lirrin said. "Come on!"

"Wait!" Kilisha called, before Lirrin could take more than a single step.

"What is it?" Lirrin demanded. "We need to go, before it gets away!"

"Yes, you do," Kilisha said. "But make sure you go *past* it separately, without frightening it, and *then* form a line and chase it this way."

"Right," Telleth said. "Come on, then."

This time Kilisha straightened up and let them go.

They were brave children. They hadn't argued with her, or cried, or said they were scared; they had just gone to help. Yara and Ithanalin ought to be proud of them.

She wondered which piece of furniture held the wizard's parental pride.

She waited a moment, to give the children time to get into position, then began strolling toward Adagan's door. "Oh, coatrack!" she called. "Won't you come back with me?"

Adagan chose that moment to thrust his broom out the door, pushing a fair-sized heap of pet hairs and fireplace ash. He paused, startled, at the sound of Kilisha's voice, then leaned out and said, "Coatrack?"

Kilisha had been focused on the coatrack, so that this sudden intrusion threw her into complete confusion. "Uh?" she said.

"You have a boyfriend named Coatrack?" Adagan asked.

Kilisha blinked at him. "I don't have *any* boyfriend!" she said. "I'm trying to catch the coatrack that's behind your door."

The instant the words left her mouth she knew she had made a mistake. Sure enough, the coatrack bolted. She caught a glimpse of it as it tried to dash away—but then it ran into the children, who had formed their line as instructed, and all four of them—three children and an oversized ambulatory stick—fell to the street in a tangle.

"Kilisha, help!" Telleth called, and Pirra burst out crying. Kilisha ran.

Adagan, astonished, turned to watch as the wizard's apprentice grabbed for the twisting, curling wooden bar. He clutched his own broom tightly, as if he expected that, too, to make a bid for freedom.

Kilisha did not try to untangle the children; she concentrated instead on getting her hands on the coatrack, and after two or three attempts she managed to get a solid two-handed grip on it.

It struggled for a moment, but then Kilisha pulled it out of the tangle of arms and legs and heaved it up above her head, holding it at arm's length.

It thrashed wildly for a moment, then paused, as if considering its situation.

"You can't get away," Kilisha told it. "If you try, we may have to hurt you." It gave another twitch, and Kilisha said sharply, "Stop that, right now, unless you want to be chopped up for firewood!"

The coatrack straightened out into its natural shape, beam straight and hooks curled—but it was still quivering slightly.

Trembling, Kilisha supposed.

Around her, Ithanalin's three children got to their feet. Pirra was wailing, and Lirrin was trying unsuccessfully to comfort her.

Telleth glanced at his sisters, decided they were not seriously hurt, then stared gape-mouthed up at the coatrack. Then he looked at Kilisha.

"Would you really cut it up?" he asked. "I thought you needed it for the spell!"

Kilisha threw him an angry glare, and he realized he had said something wrong.

"Come on," she said. "Bring your sisters. And the minute we're all inside the house, slam the door tight!"

"Kilisha, what's going on?" Adagan asked, still clinging tightly to his broom.

"I'll tell you later," Kilisha said, as she marched back home, with the coatrack held overhead.

"Can I help?" Adagan called a moment later, but by then Kilisha was struggling to get an uncooperative coatrack through Ithanalin's front door and was far too busy to answer.

At last, though, she got the entire thing inside, still raised above her head—where it was now trying to get traction against the ceiling, to prevent Kilisha from transporting it any further into the house. It was succeeding well enough that Kilisha was afraid it would force her back against the motionless Ithanalin, knocking her and the wizard off their feet.

"Telleth!" she called without looking for the boy—her attention was focused entirely upward, on the squirming implement in her tiring hands.

The door slammed, and she heard the click of the lock. She let out a sigh, lowered the coatrack to the floor, and released her hold.

"There," she said.

The coatrack scurried away from her, toward the far corner of the room.

"You can do whatever you want," she told it, glaring and wagging an admonitory finger, "so long as you stay in this house. You belong *here,* and we're going to *need* you here later, but we don't want to hurt you, and we don't care what you do for now so long as you don't go anywhere or hurt anyone. Do you understand?"

The coatrack hesitated, then nodded its top.

"If you get out again, we *will* hurt you. We're magicians, so we'll be able to find you no matter where you go."

It shuddered, then nodded again.

"Good." She relaxed, and lowered her pointing finger. She looked around.

Yara was in the door of the back room, staring at her. The spoon and bowl were nowhere in sight.

The three children were standing behind her, just inside the door, staring up at her openmouthed. She stared back, wondering why they looked so astonished; they were a wizard's children, and they had all seen plenty of magic before. Surely, an animated coatrack wasn't *that* amazing.

"Kilisha," Telleth asked, "what's going on?"

"Yeah," Lirrin said, "I never heard you *yell* like that before!"

Kilisha sagged, then sat down on the floor with a thump.

Yara and the children would need to know, if they were going to help—and she wasn't sure she could do the job without their help. Choosing her words carefully, she began to tell them what had happened.

Chapter Seven

Kilisha was perhaps halfway through her explanation when Lirrin's remark registered properly.

She *had* been yelling at the coatrack, and threatening it—and technically, that coatrack was her *master*. She had done things an apprentice must *never* do! She stopped speaking and her hand flew to her mouth.

"You looked funny holding the coatrack," Pirra said, breaking the sudden silence.

"Yeah," Telleth said.

Kilisha threw a guilty glance at the coatrack. She would need to apologize to Ithanalin once he was reassembled, and hope he wasn't too angry.

But first she needed to collect the remaining pieces.

She glanced at Yara; the wizard's wife was standing silently, her expression worried. She had been listening to the explanation, as well. Kilisha blinked at her, then turned back to the children.

"Anyway," she said, "the magic took pieces of your father— maybe pieces of his soul, or maybe something else, I'm not really sure—and put them in all the furniture. We need to collect all the furniture back together so we can put all that back into the master, and bring him back to life."

"The furniture?" Lirrin looked around the empty room. "All of it?"

"All of it," Kilisha confirmed. "It's not *that* bad," she added, seeing Lirrin's expression. "We already got the bowl, and the spoon, and the coatrack. Now we need the couch, and the table, and the rug. . . ."

"The bench," Telleth said, looking at the empty space by the hearth.

"And the chair," Lirrin said, pointing.

"And that's *all*, isn't it?" Kilisha asked. "Just five more pieces, and we've found three already. We're almost halfway there!"

"How are you going to find them?" Telleth asked.

"I don't know," Kilisha admitted. "Do you have any ideas?"

"Ask one of Daddy's friends," Lirrin said. "One of the other wizards."

Kilisha blinked foolishly at the little girl, and for a moment no one spoke.

"Well, of course," the apprentice said at last. "Of *course* that's what we'll do! Your father was . . . *is* a member of the Wizards' Guild, so I'm sure the other wizards will be glad to help out."

Even as she spoke, she was wondering why she hadn't done that immediately, instead of wandering aimlessly through the streets looking for the escaped furniture. True, she had, through sheer luck, found three of the missing pieces, but really, what had she been thinking? She should have gone to the Guild at once! This was obviously the sort of thing that called for consulting the local Guildmaster. Especially with that stuff still bubbling quietly on the workbench; that might be dangerous, and unidentified, potentially dangerous magic was definitely Guild business.

She frowned as she tried to remember just who *was* the local Guildmaster. Ithanalin had certainly mentioned the name a few times. . . .

Chorizel, that was it. Chorizel of Wizard Street.

Just then Yara said, "I have the bowl and spoon in two of Thani's cages, the ones he uses for those pets he makes for the lords and ladies, but I don't think we have a cage that will hold the coatrack."

Kilisha glanced at the coatrack. "We should put it on a leash, then."

"I'll find one," Yara said. She turned and vanished into the back room.

Just then someone knocked at the front door.

"Oh, death," Kilisha said. "Is that a customer?" She remembered that the spell Ithanalin had been preparing had been meant for a customer, to bring a bed to life.

Lirrin had dashed to the front window at the sound of the knock, and now she called, "It's Adagan!" Before Kilisha could respond, she added, "And Nissitha."

Curious neighbors, come to see what had the wizard's apprentice chasing furniture through the streets. Kilisha sighed; she really didn't want to deal with this right now, but before she could say anything the latch released, and Telleth opened the door.

The coatrack, which had been quivering in the corner, made a dash for the open door and freedom, but Kilisha had half-expected that; she lunged and caught it as it passed. It was quick and agile, but its legs were so short that it could not actually get up much real speed.

It struggled, but she had learned from experience; as soon as she could get a decent grip she lifted it off the floor.

"Get inside if you're coming!" she called, as she hoisted the squirming thing to shoulder height. From the corner of her eye she saw Adagan and Nissitha scurry in, and then Telleth slammed the door.

She put the coatrack down again; it backed off a few steps and stood, trembling.

"You heard me talk about a leash, didn't you?" she asked.

The coatrack nodded.

"That's because we can't *trust* you," she explained. "If I knew you would stay put, I wouldn't try to tie you up, but you're just so *nervous* about everything that I'm afraid you'll run away at the first opportunity. You keep getting scared and changing your mind."

For the rest of her life Kilisha could never quite figure out how the coatrack accomplished it, but it looked sheepish.

"I promise we aren't going to hurt you," she said. "I'll see about making the leash as generous and comfortable as we can, but really, we *need* you, and we just can't let you stay loose. Do you understand?"

The coatrack seemed unsure how to respond to that.

"Well, whether you understand or not, that's the way it is," Kilisha said. "Now, could you please wait quietly for a moment while I talk to our guests?"

The coatrack essayed something resembling a bow, and toddled back to its corner. That done, Kilisha turned to face the neighbors.

Nissitha was staring at the lifeless Ithanalin; Adagan was staring at the coatrack.

"Kilisha, what's going on?" Adagan asked.

Kilisha sighed. It appeared she was going to be repeating this explanation often.

"A spell went wrong," she said, "and Ithanalin's life is spread through all the furniture from this room. I need to get it all back together so I can undo the spell, and I need to hurry, because the master had another spell cooking and I don't know what it is or what it might do."

That was the short version, but it seemed to be enough.

"What can I do to help?" Adagan asked.

"I need to find the rest of the furniture," Kilisha said.

Adagan frowned. "I don't think I can do much about that," he said. "I might be able to help calm it down when you find it, though." He glanced at Nissitha. "Can you locate any of it?"

Nissitha, startled, tore her gaze from Ithanalin and looked at the others. "What?"

"Can you locate the other furniture?" Adagan repeated.

"Oh," Nissitha said. "Uh . . . no."

"But you're a seer!" Telleth said. "It says so on your sign!"

"Yes, but I don't work for free," Nissitha said, drawing herself up proudly.

"I'm sure that Ithanalin will be glad to pay you, once he's restored," Kilisha said. "He could do a spell for you in exchange. Or if a simple one would do, *I* could do it, even if he's not restored yet."

"I am not interested in *trading,*" Nissitha said.

"Then Ithanalin could pay you in gold," Kilisha said. "I know he has money—Lady Nuvielle paid for her new pet just the other day."

"The tax collector probably got it all," Nissitha sniffed.

"The tax collector didn't get *anything,*" Kilisha said. "The animated furniture scared him off."

"I don't work on credit," Nissitha said.

"Yara could pay you."

Nissitha still hesitated, and Kilisha suddenly understood. When Nissitha had said she didn't work for free, that was just an excuse. Her first simple "no" when asked whether she could help was the real truth.

"Surely, you're willing to help out a neighbor!" Adagan said.

Nissitha turned to glare at him. "I don't see *you* doing any spells for free!"

"I don't know any that would help," Adagan said. "I can cure warts and calm fears and the like, but finding runaway furniture is beyond me."

"Well, it's beyond me, too!" Nissitha said.

"Why didn't you just *say* so?" Telleth demanded.

"She didn't want to admit it," Kilisha said quickly—she realized, a little late, that any further discussion might establish beyond question that Nissitha was a fraud, and that that would not make for a happy neighborhood. "Magicians don't like to say they can't do something, Telleth, you know that!"

"No, I—"

Adagan stepped gently on Telleth's foot before he could finish the sentence, and Kilisha threw the witch a grateful glance. He had apparently reached the same conclusion she had.

Just then Yara reappeared from the back carrying a coil of rope, and Kilisha seized the opportunity. "You three go help your mother," she said, patting Lirrin on the back of the head.

The children hurried to obey—or at least, to watch their mother struggle with the intermittently cooperative coatrack. Kilisha watched them scamper across the room, then turned back to the neighbors.

"So what will you do now?" Adagan asked quietly.

"I need to talk to Chorizel," Kilisha said.

"Chorizel?" Nissitha asked. "Why him? There are cheaper wizards on the street."

"Guild rules," Kilisha said.

Adagan nodded; Nissitha threw him a glance, then turned up an empty palm. "I don't suppose you care to explain what Guild rules have to do with this. Surely, you don't have a rule specifically covering who an apprentice should consult when her master turns himself into a roomful of furniture."

"I'm not permitted to tell outsiders the rules," Kilisha replied.

That was the truth; Guild rules forbade her explaining the Guild hierarchy to outsiders, or admitting that Chorizel was a Guildmaster. A master wizard was allowed some discretion, but not an apprentice.

Nissitha shook her head. "You wizards are all mad," she said. "It comes from working with chaos. And you've gotten it younger than most."

"We don't exactly . . ." Kilisha began. Then she stopped. There was no reason to defend the Guild to Nissitha, or explain that wizards didn't work *directly* with the chaos that underlay reality, but only with symbols that tapped into it. "I need to talk to Chorizel," she said.

"Then go talk to him," Yara called. "I have this tied up."

Kilisha turned to see that a loop of rope was now tied tight around the coatrack just below the hooks, while Yara held the other end of the line and the children stood by, ready to grab the rope if the coatrack tried to flee.

"Good," Kilisha said. "I will." She turned back to Adagan and Nissitha, and said, "If you two could please tell everyone that we're looking for escaped furniture—"

She was interrupted by a knock.

"*Now* what?" Kilisha said. Before she could object, Nissitha reached over.

Before Nissitha touched it, however, the latch sprang open of its own accord, and the door opened. Kilisha remembered that the latch, too, had been animated in the disaster. She would want to talk to it when she had a moment; it was being far too cooperative for its own good.

Right now, though, she looked to see who had knocked.

A stranger in a green and brown silk tunic stood outside. "I have an appointment with Ithanalin," he said.

"He's not here," Nissitha said; she started to close the door. Kilisha jumped to intervene, and caught the latch.

The handle wiggled under her grip, but she ignored it. "You must be the customer he mentioned!" she said.

"Yes?" the man said, tentatively.

"I'm his apprentice," Kilisha said quickly. "I'm afraid there's been an accident."

The customer was staring past Nissitha at Ithanalin, and Kilisha resolved to move her master away from the front door. "Is he—" the man began.

"He'll be fine," Kilisha said, pushing herself in front of Nissitha and blocking the customer's view of the wizard. "In a day or two. And I'm sure he'll finish your spell then. I'd do it myself, but I'm afraid I haven't learned all the necessary secrets yet. Could you tell me, please, where I can reach you when the master is himself again?"

"I live on Steep Street, near the corner of Hillside." He frowned. "What happened?"

Kilisha saw no reason to hide the truth. "A spriggan spilled the potion my master was preparing," she said. "It will need to be redone. I'm very sorry for the delay, and I'm sure my master will give you a discount for the inconvenience."

"I promised my wife—"

"I know, but really, there's nothing we can do. It should just be a couple of days."

"Who are these two?" the man asked, looking at Nissitha and Adagan.

"Just neighbors who stopped in," Kilisha said.

"That's my shop next door," Nissitha offered.

"And mine just beyond," Adagan added.

"Wizards?"

"No," Nissitha said.

"I'm a witch," Adagan said.

"Oh."

"I'll send you a message as soon as we know when the spell will be ready," Kilisha said.

The man looked uncertain. "You're sure—"

"Quite sure," Kilisha interrupted.

The man hesitated a second longer, then turned up a palm. "All right," he said. He tried to peer over her head, but Adagan shifted to block his view, and reluctantly the man turned and departed.

Kilisha released the door, and Nissitha slammed it. The latch clicked a few times, apparently annoyed, then settled into place.

"This is going to be bad for business," Kilisha said. "I'd hoped to fix things before word got out."

"You seem very certain you'll be *able* to fix them," Nissitha said.

"I am," Kilisha said.

This was not literally true. She was not certain *she* could fix the situation, but she was certain *someone* could. After all, there were hundreds of wizards in Ethshar of the Rocks; surely one of them could reassemble Ithanalin. Javan's Restorative didn't look like *that* difficult a spell, and if that didn't work, some other spell would.

How hard could it be?

But it was definitely going to hurt business, turning away customers this way.

"I need to talk to Chorizel," she said, "but before I do, could you give me a hand? I want to move my master to the back, where people won't see what's happened to him."

Nissitha grimaced. "Are you sure it's safe?"

"Oh, come on," Adagan said, stepping toward the motionless wizard.

❖

Chapter Eight

Nissitha had fled once Ithanalin was moved, but Kilisha had left Adagan there, to help Yara and the children should anyone else turn up at the door.

She wished she could have stayed herself, but *somebody* had to talk to Chorizel, and she was the only wizard on hand. She was only an apprentice, but she was still a member of the Wizards' Guild.

The sun was low in the west, brushing the rooftops as she hurried along Wizard Street. The afternoon had slipped away in capturing the bowl and spoon and coatrack, explaining the situation to everyone, and sending away the confused customer. It was the middle of Harvest, and the days were getting shorter, but it was still dismaying to realize that she must have spent *hours* on all that.

The only good side she could see was that Chorizel would probably be at home, getting ready for supper, rather than out somewhere.

Unless, of course, he had an invitation to dine elsewhere. She picked up the pace, almost running.

Chorizel did not have an ordinary shop, with a signboard and front room; instead he had a house, and the only sign that it was a place of business was a small card set in one window that read simply:

CHORIZEL

WIZARDRY

Kilisha had passed by it any number of times in the five years she had lived on Wizard Street, but had never set foot inside. She had only spoken to Chorizel two or three times in her life, all of them when she and Ithanalin happened to encounter the Guildmaster on the street and the two master wizards had made polite conversation. After the first such meeting Ithanalin had explained that Chorizel was the local Guildmaster, and their connection to the Guild hierarchy, but Kilisha had never been especially interested in Guild business, and she had never paid any particular attention to Chorizel.

Now, though, she took a moment to look over the Guildmaster's house, and to try to remember everything she could about him. It wasn't much. He was a plump old man with a ragged white beard and a tenor voice.

The house was three stories tall and unremarkable, with heavy black timbers crisscrossing their way up to a steep slate roof. The plaster filling between the beams was yellow, and decorated with finely painted red flowers surrounded by twining green vines. The windows were tall and narrow, the leading between panes simple. Because of the street's slope the front door was at the top of a stoop, two steps at one side, three steps at the other. The stone doorframe was carved into the likeness of two doglike creatures sitting on their haunches, facing one another, their impossibly tall ears supporting the lintel.

Kilisha mounted the steps, looked for a bell-pull or knocker, and seeing none she rapped on the door with her knuckles.

The carved dog-things opened their stone eyes and looked at her.

"What is your business here?" the left-hand creature asked, in a hissing, grating, and thoroughly inhuman voice.

Kilisha was mildly impressed; most of Ithanalin's creations couldn't speak that clearly, if they spoke at all, and stone was said to be hard to work with. "I need to speak to Guildmaster Chorizel," she said. "There's been an accident."

"Who are you?" the right-hand doorpost asked, in a deeper, grinding voice.

"Kilisha of Eastgate," she said. "Apprentice to Ithanalin the Wise."

"Enter, then," the left-hand creature said. The latch clicked, and the door swung open.

That, she supposed, was the Spell of the Obedient Object at work—it was probably triggered by the doorpost's voice saying "Enter." These things were usually set up to make animated objects seem far more intelligent and independent than they really were.

She stepped inside and looked around.

The entry hall was fair-sized, with a lovely thick carpet on the wooden floor, a couch against one wall, stairs leading up, and closed doors on either side. It was dim, lit only by a window at the top of the stairs, and the dark wood wainscotting made it seem even darker.

A black and brownish-red rune drawn on the wall at the foot of the stairs spoke in a pleasant tenor, saying, "Please wait here." Then the brownish-red part evaporated into thick, foul-smelling smoke.

Kilisha studied the remaining portion of the rune with interest; she had never seen that particular spell before. Clearly it was a single-use spell; she could sense no lingering magic in it, even with her hand on the hilt of her athame. She did not actually *touch* the rune, with either her hand or her dagger, any more than she had touched that bowl on Ithanalin's workbench; she knew better than to handle unfamiliar magic so carelessly as that.

It couldn't be a very high-order spell if Chorizel had thrown it away so casually on an unimportant visitor. She wondered whether Ithanalin knew it, whatever it was. The voice had sounded like Chorizel's own. . . .

She was still studying it when the door behind her opened and Chorizel stepped in. She turned at the sound, and bowed deeply.

"Guildmaster," she said.

"Apprentice," he replied, acknowledging the bow with a nod. "Did Kaligir send you to escort me?"

"Uh . . ."

"Then is there more news?"

"*More* news? Guildmaster, I am here on behalf of my master, Ithanalin. . . ."

Chorizel frowned, and for the first time Kilisha noticed that there were two more people behind him, a man and a woman, looking over his broad shoulders.

"Ithanalin?" he asked. "What does *he* have to do with any of this?"

Kilisha blinked in confusion. "Any of what, Guildmaster?"

"The rebellion, of course! The murders! The usurper!"

For a few seconds Kilisha wondered whether this entire long day was actually some ghastly, confusing nightmare. "What rebellion, Guildmaster? What murders?"

Chorizel put two fingers to his forehead and rubbed, staring at her. "You haven't heard?" he asked.

"Heard what?"

Chorizel glanced at the door, and the man behind him hurried over and pushed it shut.

"Last night in Ethshar of the Sands," he said, "a mad magician named Tabaea led a mob from the Wall Street Field to the over-lord's palace, chased Ederd and his lords out, and declared herself empress of Ethshar."

"What kind of magician?" Kilisha asked, as she struggled to absorb this information.

"We don't know," the woman at Chorizel's elbow said. "She has an enchanted dagger—it's probably wizardry, but it's possible it's sorcery or demonology or something new."

Kilisha tried to go over everything Chorizel had said, to make sense of it. "If she's in Ethshar of the Sands, why are *you* concerned, Guildmaster? That's a hundred leagues away!"

"Not quite sixty, really," Chorizel said. "And she's murdered wizards, including Guildmaster Serem. That makes it the Guild's business. Not to mention she's declared herself empress of the entire Hegemony of the Three Ethshars, not just the one city."

"Oh," Kilisha said. No other response to this astonishing news really seemed appropriate. Murdered wizards? Empress of the Hegemony? The three-overlord system had been in place for over two hundred years, and the idea of someone trying to disrupt it simply made no sense. And who, other than the Guild itself, would dare to kill wizards?

"Kaligir has been conferring with Telurinon, Serem's successor," Chorizel said. "We're all supposed to meet with Kaligir to discuss the situation. I thought he'd sent you to fetch us."

"Oh," Kilisha said again—though she had no idea who Kaligir, Telurinon, or this murdered Guildmaster Serem might be. "No," she added, "he didn't send me."

"Then why *are* you here?"

That was the cue Kilisha had been waiting for; words spilled out of her mouth so quickly they almost tripped on one another.

"My master Ithanalin has had an accident, he tripped over a spriggan in the middle of a spell and it spilled all over him and now his life force is in our furniture and it's escaped and I need help collecting it all and using Javan's Restorative to put him back together."

Chorizel stared down at her for a moment. "Is he alive?" he demanded.

"Well, technically, yes," Kilisha said.

"Is he in any immediate danger? Will he die if we don't help you?"

"I don't *think* so . . ." Kilisha began, hesitantly.

"Then it can wait. Weren't you listening, girl? Ederd IV has been overthrown, and Serem the Wise has been murdered!"

"But—"

"But nothing. You go on about your business, apprentice, and come back when we've settled matters with this usurper."

"There's another spell involved...."

"What spell?"

"I don't know. It's cooking on the master's workbench."

"Can it wait?"

"I don't know."

"Well, it will have to. We can't spare the time."

"But the furniture—"

"*Blast* the furniture! Go away, child!" He thrust a pointing finger toward the door, and the man who had closed it a moment before swung it open.

Kilisha stared at him.

"Come on," Chorizel said, ignoring her. "Kaligir is waiting." He led the others toward the street.

Kilisha stood at the foot of the stairs, staring helplessly, as the three marched out of the house.

"You know better than to stay in a wizard's home unwanted, don't you, apprentice?" Chorizel called back over his shoulder.

"Yes, Guildmaster," Kilisha said. Reluctantly, she followed them out, and pulled the door closed behind her.

She stood on the stoop for a moment, watching Chorizel and his two companions striding westward down Wizard Street. Then, frustrated, she turned her own steps back toward Ithanalin's home.

She was still on her own, it appeared. She would have to find the remaining furniture herself. She did *not* want to wait—this political disaster in Ethshar of the Sands might last for months, and a delay like that would ruin Ithanalin's business, prolong her apprenticeship, and leave the poor children without their father for much too long, not to mention that that brown mixture might explode or start spewing poison or something. And the furniture might wander off where she would *never* find it, or get itself smashed somehow.

She couldn't afford to wait. She had to find it *somehow*.

She tried to think of some way to use one of the spells she already knew, but nothing came to mind. She didn't know any divinations; she didn't think Ithanalin knew any to teach her, though she resolved to take another look through his book of spells.

She might be able to spot some of the furniture by levitating up to where she could see half the city at a time—but only if it was still out in the open, and not hiding under someone's porch roof.

Or perhaps she could make the furniture come to her, or at least stay where she could find it. Just last month she had learned Javan's Geas, and that could be used on someone who wasn't present. If she put a geas on each piece of furniture she could, at least, prevent it from doing stupid or dangerous things—the geas could not compel anyone to do something, but only *not* to do something. Javan had been one of the finest research wizards in history, but his geas wasn't an especially powerful or versatile one.

And, she remembered, it required knowing the victim's true name.

What was a couch's true name—Ithanalin's Couch? Or if it held a part of Ithanalin, would *his* true name work?

She didn't *know* Ithanalin's true name. Only a fool of a wizard would trust his apprentice with such knowledge. A major reason many wizards used pompous, made-up names like Ithanalin or Chorizel was so their true names would not be known.

And of course, exotic names also helped the mysterious image that wizards cultivated to attract business.

She wondered whether even Yara knew Ithanalin's true name. It seemed unlikely. Ithanalin wouldn't have wanted to tell her, and Yara wouldn't have cared.

And besides, if Kilisha put a geas on the furniture, the geas would still be there when Ithanalin was restored, and he would probably not be pleased at all to learn that he could no longer leave the city, or whatever.

Javan's Geas was out.

Eshom's Oenological Transformation, Fendel's Accelerated Corruption, the Spell of Perpetual Sharpness, Gilad's Blemish Removal, Cauthen's Remarkable Love Spell—she knew plenty of spells, but she couldn't see how *any* of them would help—

She stopped dead in her tracks, just in front of Adagan's shop. Cauthen's Remarkable Love Spell.

"Oh, no," she said.

The idea was ghastly—but she couldn't get rid of it.

Cauthen's spell created a potion containing some trace of one party—a hair, a drop of sweat or blood, almost anything. When someone drank the potion, the person who had provided that trace ingredient would fall in love with whoever drank it.

If she were to find a few loose threads or splinters from the rug or the couch or the bench, and make the potion, and drink it, then the furniture would fall in love with her, and seek *her* out— but the idea of making Ithanalin in *any* form fall in love with her . . .

"Oh," she said, smiling as a sudden pleasant realization dawned.

She didn't need to drink the stuff. Yara could drink it. Ithanalin *already* loved her—though apparently the furniture did not, or it would have returned by now.

But the spell could *make* the furniture love Yara, and want to please her. The furniture would seek her out, and if she told it to stay in the house, it would stay in the house.

Then all that would be needed was Javan's Restorative.

Kilisha smiled broadly and hurried for home.

Chapter Nine

Mare's sweat, hair from a stallion's tail, water, red wine—the other ingredients of Cauthen's Remarkable Love Spell, assuming she had remembered them all correctly, were not difficult. It was finding bits from the furniture that would be tricky. Kilisha bent down and peered at the bare floor of the front room.

The coatrack was tethered in the corner; Yara and the children were nowhere in sight, but Kilisha could hear faint thumpings and rattlings from somewhere in the back as the family went about its everyday business.

Kilisha's business, right now, was getting Ithanalin back together. As his apprentice, it was her responsibility. Cauthen's Remarkable Love Spell might be what she needed, and to perform the spell she needed to find some tiny fragment of the missing pieces.

The daylight was fading rapidly, and Kilisha did not want to bother finding a lamp or candle; she pricked her right index finger with her athame and quickly spoke the incantation for the Finger of Flame.

A flame leapt up from her fingertip, and she stretched her hand until the flame burned at its maximum height of almost a foot. It was brighter than a candle, not quite as good as a well-trimmed lamp.

It also wouldn't last very long—after four or five minutes she would need to put it out if she didn't want blisters and burns—but it gave the light she needed to look around, and it reassured her that yes, she *was* a wizard, someone who knew real magic.

It occurred to her that she could have used this, instead of Thrindle's Combustion, to demonstrate her abilities to the man with the bowl and spoon, and avoided damaging his clothing—but she hadn't thought of it at the time, and he had been so annoying that she was just as happy to have ruined his tunic.

She held up the flame and looked around.

Ithanalin hadn't let Yara dust or sweep in here, and since the accident Yara had been far too busy with other concerns to worry about it, so the floor was dusty—but which dust came from the furniture? She held her hand down low, then knelt to see better.

She supposed she could use all of it, and see what happened. After all, what harm could it do? The walls and ceiling weren't animated; if they fell in love with Yara, they wouldn't do anything.

But then she noticed a long black hair curling across the planking. That probably came from Lady Nuvielle, she realized. And the flake of black paint might be from the toy dragon Ithanalin had made her. Allowing the Lady Treasurer or her pet to fall in love with Yara did not seem like a good idea.

So she would indeed need to be careful, picking and choosing.

A bit of faded blue thread was surely from the rag rug; she recognized the color. She picked that up with her left hand and clutched it carefully as she thought.

Could she use the spell on more than one target at a time? She didn't remember whether Ithanalin had said anything about that when he taught it to her, back in Rains. She had been far more interested in observing its effects on her brother Opir, who had volunteered as her test subject, and his girlfriend Kluréa, who had drunk the potion.

Kluréa was Opir's *former* girlfriend, now—she had been offended by the results of the experiment, and by some of Opir's comments after he drank the last of the four required doses of the antidote.

Kilisha frowned. She hoped that this wouldn't cause any sort of strife between Yara and Ithanalin—but why should it? They were an old married couple with three children, not a pair of teenagers.

Well, not an *old* married couple, really, but they had been together perhaps a dozen years, maybe a little more. Surely that was long enough that their marriage could survive a love potion or two.

Still, she decided that she should read over the spell carefully and see whether there were any complications she might have forgotten. Clutching the blue thread carefully, she hurried into the workshop.

Her own book of spells was up in her attic room, but Ithanalin's was still here on the shelf above the bench where she had left it. She was beginning to feel the heat of the flame burning on her finger, and she didn't want to rely on the oil lamp under the brass bowl, so she lit a candle and snuffed the spell before climbing onto a stool and hauling down her master's book.

She uncovered it and began looking through the pages. Cauthen's Remarkable Love Spell was near the front of the volume; she read over the description and notes carefully.

It was very much as she remembered—mare's sweat and stallion's hair, water and wine. The notes said that it worked on a single individual, and that the wizard must be careful that none of his own hair or sweat fell into the mixture; if Ithanalin had mentioned that when he taught Kilisha the spell, she had forgotten it.

She didn't think he had mentioned it.

A single individual—well, the rug probably counted, but she wouldn't be able to get everything at once, even if she found more threads or splinters. Ithanalin was a single individual before the accident, but somehow she doubted that would make the spell work on all the furniture simultaneously.

She might be able to do each piece sequentially, starting with the rug. She read on.

Then she frowned.

There was a catch, one she hadn't remembered, if she had ever known it. The spell took effect when the subject *saw, heard,* or *smelled* the intended love-object. For the rug to be lured home, it would need to see, hear, or smell Yara.

That might be manageable, but it did make the whole idea seem less promising. Kilisha decided to put it aside for the moment and consider other possibilities. She carefully tucked the blue thread into one of Ithanalin's countless glass vials for safekeeping, then turned back to the book.

She hesitated. Should she be using her *own* book of spells?

But all her spells would be in here, and there might be others she could use, as well. She would need Javan's Restorative eventually.

Unless she hired someone else to do it—but *she* wanted to do it, to show Ithanalin that she was a better wizard than he thought, ready to learn those animation spells and become a journeyman.

And there might be something else in here she could use to find the missing furniture, something simple. Ithanalin had always said that he didn't know any divinations, but there might be *something* that would serve.

She flipped to the front of the book, then began turning pages.

Here were all the familiar spells she had studied over the past five years: Eknerwal's Lesser Invisibility, Fendel's Elementary Protection, the Spell of the Spinning Coin, the Iridescent Amusement, Thrindle's Combustion, the Lesser Spell of Invaded Dreams. . . .

She paused at that, considering the possibility of sending dreams to the escaped furniture, coaxing it to return home, but then she remembered that most magically animated objects didn't really sleep, and didn't dream. Those that rested at all merely went dormant, rather than truly sleeping.

She couldn't be sure that was the case in this instance, since these had been animated by a botched spell rather than a standard one, but it seemed likely. She turned the page to the next spell.

Fendel's Infatuous Love Spell wouldn't be any better than Cauthen's Remarkable—and in fact, it wouldn't be possible, since it had to be performed while the target was asleep.

Lugwiler's Dismal Itch, the Prismatic Pyrotechnics, Tracel's Adaptable Potion, the Yellow Cloud, and on and on and on.

Really, she thought as she passed the fiftieth spell, it was amazing just how useless most of her magic was in this situation. Cauthen's Remarkable Love Spell was looking better all the time.

She turned a page and found Kandif's Spell of Warning; she frowned thoughtfully at that. That was quite possibly how Chorizel had known she was in his front room. It ensorcelled a specific place—usually a room of a house—so that the wizard casting the spell would know instantly if anyone entered it over the next three days. If she put that on a place where the missing furniture might go . . .

No, she would be told every time *anyone* entered the chosen place, and if it was a public place that might be every five minutes. She wasn't even sure animated furniture counted as "anyone" as far as the spell was concerned; an ambulatory table might *not* register.

The Spell of Impeded Egress would be useful for holding the furniture once it was captured—anything that had been enchanted with it would be unable to find an exit from wherever she put it. It was really just a simple, highly specific confusion spell, and Ithanalin would have no trouble performing the countercharm once he was restored. She glanced at the door and debated whether she should bother to cast it on the coatrack, or the spoon and bowl—but they were already confined. She decided not to take the time.

The Spell of Optimum Strength might be useful if she had to pick up the couch and carry it back home, as she had the coatrack. The catch there was that the spell took three hours to prepare and only lasted perhaps half an hour, but if she made it up in a batch of Tracel's Adaptable Potion, she would have the spell ready to use instantly, seven times over.

Tracel . . . it might be useful to have Tracel's Levitation ready, too. And Varen's Levitation, as well.

She wished she knew a really *good* levitation spell, so she could fly properly. Tracel's would let her rise to any altitude and descend safely, but once airborne she had no way to move forward except to let the wind blow her, or to catch onto nearby buildings; its main virtue was that it was a really easy spell to learn, and she had known it for years. Varen's was a little better, as it let her walk on air, or pick up other objects and leave them floating in midair, but the ascent and descent were slower and required more space, and while it was nearly as quick, the spell was much trickier to perform.

Using a levitation spell to get a few hundred feet in the air for a good view of the streets, to see if she could spot any of the furniture, really might be a good idea. She would have to try that in the morning; the light wasn't good enough now. The furniture had probably all found shelter by now, but if any was still wandering about in the open, in the city's streets or courtyards, she might be able to spot it.

She wished she had thought of all this much sooner. She really did need to learn to think these things through more quickly. If she had popped up to three or four times rooftop height as soon as she knew what had happened, instead of dashing off almost at random, she might have recaptured more than just the bowl, spoon, and coatrack.

Of course, she couldn't have done it instantly. The problem with all of these spells—Tracel's Levitation, Varen's Levitation, and the Spell of Optimum Strength—was that they required preparation time and specialized ingredients. Putting them in Tracel's Adaptable Potion would make them all easily portable and instantly available, but the potion itself needed a full day to cool after preparation.

She didn't remember just how long Varen's Levitation took; not long, but longer than drinking a potion. Tracel's Levitation only took about eight or ten minutes, but still, it wasn't exactly convenient to carry a rooster's toe, a raindrop caught in midair, and the rest of the ingredients around in her pouch.

And the Spell of Optimum Strength took *three hours* to prepare.

Out of all her fifty-three spells, though, those were the only ones she could see any possible use for in pursuing and capturing escaped furniture. Light spells and pyrotechnics and protective runes just weren't going to help.

She turned another page in Ithanalin's book, past the last spell she knew, and found herself looking at the Spell of the Obedient Object.

This was the one Ithanalin had promised to teach her. She read the description.

It would enchant an object so that it would obey a single command when a specified condition was met—for example, a bell might be enchanted to ring whenever the wind blew from the east.

Perhaps, she thought, she could enchant the furniture to come back home when she spoke Ithanalin's name. . . .

But then she saw that the wizard casting the spell had to touch the object with his or her athame to complete the enchantment. If she had the furniture where she could touch it, she wouldn't *need* to enchant it!

This was all horribly frustrating. She read on.

Fendel's Familiar, the Servile Animation, Ellran's Immortal Animation—she couldn't see how those would help, even if she could perform them, and glancing through the instructions she doubted she could. Ellran's took *two days* of exacting ritual, and about two dozen ingredients ranging from things as prosaic as salt to items as exotic as the mummified left wing of a carnivorous bat.

(Actually, she was fairly certain Ithanalin had the mummified left wing of a bat in the drawer just to the right of where she sat, as she had used it in learning the Spell of Stupefaction, but she didn't know whether it was from a *carnivorous* bat.)

The Creeping Darkness—she shuddered at the description of that one. Thrindle's Instantaneous Putrefaction sounded downright disgusting. Fendel's Soothing Euphony might help if she had to calm panicky furniture, but she looked at the list of ingredients and despaired of performing it successfully without considerable practice.

It didn't seem, she concluded, as if Ithanalin himself knew any useful spells in this situation. Cauthen's looked better all the time.

"Have you found anything?"

Kilisha jumped, and turned to find Yara standing in the doorway.

"I'm not sure," Kilisha said. "I did have an idea, but I'm not
sure it will work." She hesitated, then added, "I'd need your help."

"What is it?" Yara asked.

"I could cast a love spell on some of the missing furniture, so
that it would fall madly in love with you at the slightest glimpse,
or the sound of your voice. I was thinking that if I did that, and
you were to walk along Wizard Street calling out for it, it would
follow you home."

"What if it's not on Wizard Street?"

"Then you'd have to keep looking," Kilisha said. "But it's the
best I can do with the magic I have."

"Couldn't we hire someone else? Pay someone for a divination?"

"Well, I suppose," Kilisha admitted. "But that would be expensive, and it would be rather embarrassing for the master, don't
you think? I think we should try to fix things ourselves first. We
can always hire someone later."

Yara looked unhappy and uncertain.

"It's pretty late to be hiring anyone tonight, in any case," Kilisha said quickly. "Why don't we try it my way? And if it doesn't
work, in the morning you can hire someone."

"All right," Yara said, frowning. "But right now your supper's
ready."

Kilisha blinked at her, then realized that yes, she was hungry.
She had been so distracted that she might as well have had an
enchanted bloodstone in her pocket, but now that Yara mentioned
it . . .

"After we eat, then," Kilisha said, hopping off the stool.

❖

Chapter Ten

Yara insisted on putting the children to bed before trying any magic. While Kilisha gathered the ingredients for
Cauthen's Remarkable Love Spell and began the preparations, Yara
was upstairs, telling the three little ones the next installment in the
ongoing and highly unlikely adventures of Valder of the Magic
Sword, talking steadily while she brushed out their hair. As Kilisha
worked she could sometimes hear Yara's voice, very faintly,
through the ceiling.

Ithanalin's bottle of mare's sweat was almost empty, its contents slightly congealed and amazingly malodorous, but Kilisha
thought it would be sufficient. The stallion's tail hair came from a
bundle of a dozen or so wrapped in blue tissue. The red wine came
from Yara's pantry, rather than the wizard's workshop, and the
water from the courtyard well out back.

And the faded blue thread came from the floor of the front
room, of course.

When the story finally reached a good stopping point Yara
tucked the children under the blankets, kissed them good night,
and came downstairs and into the workshop, to find Kilisha well
into the incantation. The liquid mixture had begun to glow faintly,

and Kilisha could feel the magic shimmering in the air. It felt *right,* just the way she remembered it, and one of the things that made her a promising wizard was her instinctive feel for the flow and shape of wizardry. That was one of the Guild's secrets; most people believed that wizardry was an entirely mechanical process of assembling ingredients, reciting words, and making gestures, and that this somehow tapped into the chaos beneath the surface of the World and forced it into a specific action, but actually the process was a good deal more dynamic than that. A talented wizard could *feel* when the magic was working properly and when it wasn't, and could sense when a gesture needed to be altered, an incantation slowed or hurried, without any conscious understanding of why the change was necessary. A *really* good wizard could even sense whether other ingredients could be substituted, other words spoken, or the very nature of the spell somehow altered—that was how new spells were discovered.

Such wizards, wizards who could safely change spells as they went, were very rare. The ones who were able to devise multiple useful spells were little short of miraculous. Someone like Cauthen or Thrindle, let alone a one-of-a-kind genius like Fendel the Great, would be remembered for generations through the spells he created. During the Great War the military rulers had tried to force wizards who did not have this incredibly precious natural ability to develop new spells through trial and error, and had wound up with dozens of dead wizards and a good deal of damage to the surrounding landscape—but legend said Fendel could casually invent a new curse or transformation on the spot, and have it work almost every time.

Kilisha doubted she would ever reach anything near that level, but she could feel when a spell was going well, and she knew this potion was going to work exactly as intended.

Yara knew better than to interrupt a wizard in the middle of a spell, so she settled onto one of the stools by the workbench and watched as Kilisha chanted and wove a pattern of magical energy in the air with her athame.

That pattern wrapped itself around the vial that held the potion and gradually shrank inward, until at last it passed through the glass and into the liquid within. As Kilisha spoke the final word of the spell, a triumphant *"Ahmwor!,"* she raised her dagger high, and the potion flashed pale blue.

Before the flash the liquid had been murky and dull red; after the flash it was sparkling pink.

The magic in the air was gone. Kilisha's athame felt like any other knife in her hand, and holding it over her head felt slightly ridiculous. She dropped her arm and sheathed the blade, then turned to Yara.

"It's ready," she said.

"Should I drink it now, or later?" Yara asked uncertainly.

"It doesn't matter," Kilisha said, picking up the vial. "It won't spoil, and once you drink it, it will take effect whenever the rug next sees you or smells you or hears your voice, whether that's five minutes from now, or five years."

"So this will make the rug fall in love with me, and want to come back home?"

"That's the theory, yes." She held the vial out.

Yara didn't take it. "What if the rug can't find its way home?"

"Well, then the theory won't work," Kilisha said, lowering the potion.

"But if it does work, then once the rug's back here, you'll break the spell?"

"Um . . ." Kilisha frowned. "Well, actually, I can't. Not for a rug. The cure is to drink virgin's blood, and a rug can't drink *anything*. But I can break the spell once Ithanalin's restored." She hesitated, then admitted, "It takes four days, though, one drink of blood per day."

"I don't want a rug in love with me, Kilisha. I had enough trouble with that spoon."

"It's not the same thing," Kilisha protested. "The spoon was lustful; this spell will make the rug devoted. It's a *good* love spell, it's not like the Spell of Aroused Lust or Fendel's Infatuous Love Spell."

Yara still hesitated.

"Mistress, I learned this spell by testing it on my own *brother* and his girlfriend!"

"Your brother isn't a rug. And I doubt his girlfriend kept him out of her bed while the spell was in effect."

"She probably didn't—but honestly, she *could* have if she wanted to, just by asking him to sleep elsewhere. Ithanalin *already* loves you, probably just as much as this spell would make him love you, it's just that it all wound up in the spoon or somewhere instead of spread through all the furniture!"

"I don't know . . ." Yara said.

Kilisha was sure that the longer Yara waited, the more reasons she would find to not drink the potion. "Mistress," she said, "I thought you'd want to be the one to drink this, but you don't *need* to. *I* could drink it—"

She didn't have a chance to finish the sentence.

"Give me the vial," Yara said.

Kilisha obeyed, and Yara drank it down in a single gulp, then blinked in surprise.

"It's sweet," she said. "I thought it would taste foul."

"Love is sweet," Kilisha said. "At least, that's what the master told Kluréa," she added hastily. "I wouldn't know, myself."

Yara swallowed again, licked her lips thoughtfully, then asked, "Now what?"

"Now you need to roam about the streets calling out, so that the rug will hear your voice and fall in love with you and follow you home."

"Tonight?"

"Whenever you please—but the sooner the better, surely. We don't want the rug to wander further away."

Yara considered that for a long moment, then said, "Not to-night. In the morning. It's been a very long day." She glanced over at Ithanalin, sitting motionless in the corner. "I'm sorry, dear," she said. "I'm too tired. I'm going to bed."

With that, she turned away.

Kilisha stood by the workbench and watched her go.

It *had* been a long day, but Kilisha was still too wrought up to sleep. Performing the love spell had been satisfying, almost re-laxing. She looked at the shelves of ingredients, the jars and boxes and bottles, and wondered whether there was some other useful magic she could perform before going to bed.

Tracel's Adaptable Potion.

The thought struck her so suddenly and strongly that she won-dered whether it might be magical in origin. Perhaps some benign god was sending her a message, or some powerful magician some-where had decided to advise her. . . .

Or perhaps it was just her own mind.

Whatever the source, she thought it was a good idea. If she made up some potions, so as to have a few spells available instantly, they might be useful in the furniture hunt; she had thought about that earlier, but had then been distracted by Cauthen's Remarkable Love Spell.

Varen's Levitation, Tracel's Levitation, the Spell of Optimum Strength . . . which should she prepare? The potion spell would produce seven doses of any one spell.

Well, she could do it three times, couldn't she? It would mean staying up very late, but right now she didn't see that as a problem. And if she got tired after one preparation, or two, she could stop then, and leave until later to decide which spell the potion would contain. She wouldn't need to perform the second part of the spell, when she actually put the chosen spell into the potion, until to-morrow night, after the brew had cooled for twenty-four hours.

She would need water and wine again, and her athame, and human blood—she could use her own, and in fact that might en-hance the potion's effectiveness. She would need powdered goat's hoof—Ithanalin had a jar on the shelf to her right. A pot, and a fire—those were right at hand, as well, as the glow from that mys-terious brass bowl reminded her. A raindrop caught in midair for Tracel's Levitation, a rooster's toe, a seagull's feather. . . .

Humming quietly, she set about gathering the ingredients, thinking idly that it was good to have a fully equipped wizard's workshop here at hand, and that when she was a journeyman she would have a harder time getting what she needed for her spells.

Blood and water and wine were easy enough, but some of the other things were not so readily found.

There were suppliers, like Kara of Kara's Arcana, and Kensher Kinner's son, and the notoriously expensive Gresh, but the supplies would cost money, and she would need to earn that money by selling spells, and she would need supplies to perform the spells. . . .

Well, it must be possible, or there wouldn't be so many wealthy wizards in the World. She would have plenty of time to worry about it once she had completed her apprenticeship.

By the time she finished the first batch the little oil lamp she had used was sputtering; she fetched oil from the pantry and refilled it, then topped off the one beneath the brass bowl for good measure, then paused.

The house was dark and silent; Yara and the children were asleep upstairs, and Ithanalin, behind her, was still lifeless and inert. Every room but the workshop was dark and still; the coatrack was motionless, and the spoon and bowl were quiet in their cages.

Kilisha peered through the door of the parlor at the draped front window; the light from the street outside that seeped in around the edges was faint, and no sound at all reached her.

It was late. She was not sure just *how* late. She hesitated, wondering whether she should go to bed.

Somewhere out there, in the silent darkness, were several pieces of her master's essence. Furniture could be scratched, broken, smashed, burned, stolen. The sooner she recovered it all, the better.

She started on the second batch of Adaptable Potion.

By the time she finished the third and final batch and extinguished the little lamp, she was sure midnight had come and gone, and she was exhausted. The possibility of making a fourth batch occurred to her, but was promptly dismissed—she couldn't think of a fourth spell that would be worth the trouble. She carefully set the three simmering pots at the back of the workbench, guarded by an ironwork fireplace screen, then lit a candle from the still-burning oil lamp beneath the brass bowl.

Candle in hand, she glanced around the parlor, and said good night to the coatrack; it rattled in reply.

She looked at Ithanalin on her way back through the workshop and said, "I'm doing my best, Master."

And then she found her way up the kitchen stairs to her own little bed in the attic.

Chapter Eleven

The following morning Kilisha slept later than usual—which is to say, the sun was up before she was. The air was still cool and damp and the shadows were still long and dark when she came downstairs to the kitchen and found Yara feeding her offspring their breakfast.

"There you are!" Yara said, looking up from chopping salt ham into bite-sized pieces for Pirra. "I was beginning to wonder whether you had been spirited away by demons, or gone off on some silly errand."

"I was up late making potions," Kilisha said.

"*More* potions?"

"Yes." Only after a second's pause did Kilisha realize she had forgotten to add "Mistress."

Yara didn't seem to notice. "This love potion—how did you say it works?"

Kilisha sighed. "The instant the rug sees you or hears your voice, it will fall hopelessly in love with you. Then it should follow you home, and we can capture it."

"And then you can restore my husband?" She gestured toward the door to the workshop.

"No," Kilisha said, "we'll still need the bench and the table and the couch and the chair."

"And how are you going to get those?"

"I don't know yet."

Yara frowned. "I don't like this, Kilisha."

"I don't either!" Kilisha burst out. "I'm doing the best I can to restore the master, but it isn't easy!"

"Well—" Yara began.

"Wizardry is dangerous," Kilisha interrupted. "Everyone knows that. You knew it when you married Ithanalin, and I knew it when I signed up to be a wizard's apprentice. Spells can go wrong, and that's what happened, and it's not my fault! I wasn't even here, and that's because the master *ordered* me not to be here. We should be glad this is something that can be fixed, that he wasn't killed outright or turned into an ant and stepped on, or something. I'm doing what I can to fix it, but I'm just an apprentice, and I don't know very much magic yet, and Guildmaster Chorizel was no help at all!"

Yara seemed to accept this outburst with equanimity; she did not shout back, but merely said calmly, "I know spells can go wrong. This certainly isn't the first time Thani's had something bad happen. I'm not blaming you."

"I'm sorry, Mistress," Kilisha said.

"It's just that this *is* the first time a spell's gone wrong and Thani hasn't been here to fix it himself," Yara explained. "It worries me."

"I understand," Kilisha said, remembering what she had heard about a previous incident, one that had occurred when Ithanalin's first apprentice, Istram, had been nearing journeyman status, when Lirrin had been a baby and Pirra not yet born.

That mishap was why Yara did not allow her husband to cook. Until then Ithanalin had been very fond of cookery, and had reportedly been quite good at it—but after he accidentally got something magical into the gravy and turned his children into tree squids and his apprentice into a platypus, Yara had forbidden him to ever prepare food again. Ithanalin had turned them back without undue difficulty—perhaps, Kilisha thought, by using Javan's Restorative, just as she intended to do, though no one had ever told her the specifics. Still, Yara had pointed out that Ithanalin had had a fork in his hand and a bite of gravy-soaked meat halfway to his mouth when the first transformation took place, and if he'd been a few seconds quicker in eating *he* would have been changed, as well. That would have made it all much worse. A squid or a platypus couldn't have reversed the spell.

And this time it *was* worse. Instead of two tree squids and a platypus all right there in their own kitchen there were half a dozen pieces of animated furniture scattered around the city, and instead of an experienced master wizard ready to undo the spell there was a mere apprentice.

"You talked to Chorizel?" Yara asked.

"Yesterday."

Yara considered this for several seconds, then asked, "Did you talk to Kaligir?"

"No," Kilisha said, startled that Yara knew the name Chorizel had mentioned. "Who *is* Kaligir?"

"He's the senior Guildmaster for the entire city," Yara said. "Didn't Thani ever tell you that?"

Kilisha hesitated, trying to remember whether Ithanalin had ever told her this. It was rather annoying that Yara, who was not a wizard, often knew Guild secrets that Kilisha did not—but then, Yara was a wizard's wife, and the Guild didn't expect wizards to marry fools. Naturally, Yara would have picked up a few things over the years, and would have the sense not to mention them to outsiders.

It occurred to Kilisha to wonder whether wizards who *did* marry fools had to enchant their spouses to keep secrets. She hoped she would never have to do anything like that.

And she glanced sideways at her mistress, wondering whether Ithanalin might have enchanted Yara. Perhaps Javan's Geas?

Whether he had or not was irrelevant at the moment, though.

"I don't think he said anything about Kaligir," Kilisha said. "He told me Chorizel was our Guildmaster."

"He is. But Kaligir is the next level up, if Chorizel isn't helpful."

"Chorizel was going to talk to Kaligir about something. And someone named Telurinon was involved."

Yara stopped chopping, and carefully put the knife aside, out of Pirra's reach. Then she looked at Kilisha.

"Do you know who Telurinon is?"

"No," Kilisha admitted.

"Do you know what they were talking about?"

"About a usurper who's been killing wizards in Ethshar of the Sands."

"No wonder they're busy," Yara said. She glanced at the workshop door. "Do you think this assassin might be responsible for what happened to Thani?"

"No," Kilisha said. "He tripped over a spriggan while he was working a spell, that's all."

"Then the Guild won't help us. At least, not until this person in Ethshar of the Sands has been dealt with."

"I know," Kilisha said. "I asked yesterday."

"Then how do I lure the rug, again? And what can I do about the other furniture?"

"Just walk around the city and let your voice be heard," Kilisha said.

"Do I need to call to it? I'd feel foolish calling, 'Here, Rug, come home now!' "

"No, you don't need to say anything in particular; it just needs to hear your voice."

"And the other furniture?"

"Let's get the rug first."

Yara nodded. Then she turned to Pirra.

"After breakfast," she said, "we're going to take a walk down to Norcross Market, and I want you to do something special. I want you to run away from me, as if you were a bad little girl who didn't know any better. I'll shout at you, and then you come running back. Can you do that?"

"Yes, Mama," Pirra said, puzzled.

"It's part of the magic Kilisha's doing to help your father. I need to have something to shout at. I may sound like I'm mad when I do it, but I'll just be pretending. All right?"

"All right," Pirra said.

"And we may go some other places, too," Yara said.

"I found the spoon and bowl on Cross Avenue, and the coat-rack in an alley between Wizard Street and the East Road," Kilisha offered helpfully.

"We'll take Cross Avenue down to Norcross, then. Eat up, children."

"Can I shout for the rug, too?" Telleth asked.

"No," Yara said, "you didn't drink the potion last night. But you can keep an eye out for all the missing furniture."

Telleth smiled, and Lirrin said, "Me, too!"

"You, too," Yara agreed. Then she looked at Kilisha. "Will you be coming, or do you have more magic to work?"

"Magic," Kilisha said hastily.

Actually, she had no idea what she intended to do, but accompanying Yara and the children to the market did not appeal to her. Surely there was *something* more useful she could be doing!

She had the feeling there was something she had intended to do, but she could not think what it was. The three Adaptable Potions needed to be completed, but she could not do that until evening, a full day after she began them. Hunting furniture through the streets at random didn't seem like a useful idea.

If the love spell succeeded in luring the rug home, then perhaps she could use it again on the others, if she could find splinters or threads or flakes of varnish from the other pieces—but she wasn't going to waste time working on that until she saw whether or not it worked on the rug.

Perhaps she could practice Javan's Restorative. After all, it was a fairly difficult spell that she had never before attempted; trying it for the first time with her master's life in the balance was not exactly prudent.

That, she decided, was an excellent idea.

"I'm going to practice the spell that will restore the master, once we have all the furniture back," she said. "I want to be sure I know it."

"Oh," Yara said. "That's very sensible. Pirra, don't put the ham in your nose, put it in your *mouth*."

"In fact, I think I'll start now," Kilisha said hastily.

"You haven't eaten."

"I'll eat later."

"Pirra!"

Kilisha escaped to the workshop.

At first she was pleased to be back in the familiar room, but then she noticed the crouching shape of Ithanalin. He seemed to be glaring at her.

"I'm working on it," she said, though she knew he couldn't hear her. "Really I am."

He said nothing, of course. She turned away from him, and looked at the still-bubbling goo in the brass bowl.

It was thicker, and didn't smell as savory anymore; she hoped it wasn't going to do anything disastrous. It had shown no signs of supernatural activity since that one clear chime, but it had to be some sort of magic—her athame had reacted, and there had been the chime, and what *else* could it be? Ithanalin hadn't done any non-magical cooking since the squid gravy incident.

She needed to restore Ithanalin before this stuff, whatever it was, did something dreadful. She looked up Javan's Restorative in her master's book once more, and began gathering the ingredients for the spell.

She had already found most of them—peacock plumes, incense, athame. . . .

She turned back to the kitchen. "Mistress Yara?" she called.

"Lirrin, put that down! Yes, Kilisha?"

"Could you stop by the herbalist and get jewelweed? I need . . . oh, I don't know. A bag or a jar or a bundle or whatever it comes in."

"Jewelweed?" Yara stuck her head through the door. "What's jewelweed?"

"I have no idea," Kilisha admitted, "but the spell calls for it."

"Is it expensive?"

"I don't know."

"Hmph. Well, I'll see."

"Thank you."

Yara withdrew, and Kilisha looked around at the drawers and shelves and cabinets.

Ithanalin might already *have* jewelweed tucked away somewhere. It wasn't an ingredient in any of the spells Kilisha had learned as yet, but presumably he might have kept a supply on hand in case he ever wanted to perform Javan's Restorative.

Where would it be, then?

Kilisha began exploring the workshop, with special attention to the less-familiar areas—though she was not foolish enough to open anything with a visible rune or seal on it. Unless jewelweed had some very special properties, she couldn't see why Ithanalin would have put magical protections on it.

She had gone through perhaps half a dozen drawers, and was sneezing uncontrollably at some fine gray powder she had stirred up when a sticky drawer finally popped open, when Yara and the children trooped past her and out the front door.

Wiping her nose on the back of her hand, Kilisha blinked her watering eyes and stepped into the parlor to make sure they were safely on their way, and that the door had been closed behind them.

The coatrack rattled enthusiastically at the sight of her, and the door latch popped open.

"Stop that," she said. She had forgotten that the latch, too, was animated; she would need to be careful to include it in the spell when she attempted Javan's Restorative on her master. She crossed to the door and was about to close it when someone knocked on the frame.

Startled, she said, "Mistress?"

"Open, in the name of the overlord!" a deep male voice said.

Astonished, Kilisha opened the door a crack and peered out.

A guardsman in full uniform—red kilt, yellow tunic, gleaming helmet and breastplate—was standing there, one fist resting on the doorframe as he looked her in the eye. Her own gaze dropped, and that was when she saw the big leather pouch on his belt, the overlord's seal prominently displayed on the flap.

A tax collector.

Well, that was no surprise, really; the one who had come yesterday had not managed to collect what Ithanalin owed.

"My master isn't in," Kilisha said.

"You're an apprentice? A wizard?"

"Yes, sir."

"Then I'll speak with you, if you'll let me in."

Kilisha blinked in surprise. "I–I don't think I'm allowed to pay the taxes. . . ."

"That's not why I'm here." The soldier hesitated, then said, "Well, it's not the *only* reason I'm here, anyway. Could you let me in, please?"

Puzzled, Kilisha opened the door and moved aside. The guardsman smiled and stepped into the parlor. He looked around at the almost-empty room, and at the coatrack leashed in the corner.

"I see the furniture isn't back," he said.

"No," Kilisha said. "You're the tax collector who was here yesterday?"

"Yes. My name's Kelder."

"I'm Kilisha."

"You said your master isn't in? But he's all right?"

"Well—not exactly."

"He looked sort of frozen yesterday."

"He was. A spell went wrong."

"I thought so, when all that furniture came charging out. Will he be all right?"

Kilisha hesitated, then admitted the truth. "He will be if I can get all the furniture back."

"Ah. Well, that's why I'm here. When I left here yesterday, I followed the furniture—I thought maybe it wasn't supposed to be running loose like that. It split up, though, and I lost track of some of it, but I did catch a chair and a bench."

"You did?" Kilisha's face lit up. "Where are they? Do you have them with you?"

He shook his head. "No, I couldn't manage both of them—they squirm." After dealing with the coatrack, Kilisha could sympathize. "I had some of the other guards help, and I cornered them, and they're locked in a storeroom."

"Where?"

"In the shipyards, near Wargate High Street."

Kilisha blinked. "The shipyards? How did they get *there*?"

"They ran," Kelder said dryly.

Chapter Twelve

After explaining that she couldn't leave the house until her mistress returned from shopping, Kilisha escorted Kelder to the kitchen, where she questioned him for the better part of an hour—and answered a few of his questions, as well, though she didn't go into detail about exactly what spell had gone wrong, or how, or why she needed the furniture back before she could restore Ithanalin to full mobility.

Kelder told her that when the door had opened and he had stepped inside, it had seemed as if the entire roomful of furniture was charging at him. He had stepped back and lifted his truncheon—guards did not ordinarily carry swords or spears when on tax-collection duty—and had shouted for the furniture to stop, but it had ignored him.

A few pieces had run out the door, and he had run after them, and the rest had all come rushing after him, and he had been afraid he would be trampled. He had retreated a few yards east on Wizard Street.

The furniture had all headed west, in a pack; he wasn't sure whether it was all trying to get away from him, or what. He had followed, a bit warily.

The faster pieces had galloped down the three blocks to Cross Avenue, leaving the slower—the rug, the coatrack, and what he called "the little stuff"—behind. The coatrack had been the first to change course, when it turned up an alley to the north; Kelder had hesitated, and almost lost sight of the main group, whereupon he decided to let the small slow ones go and concentrate on the bigger pieces, which were presumably the more valuable and more potentially dangerous or disruptive.

The street had been almost deserted—after all, a tax collector had been at work—and most of the people who saw the furniture also saw him in hot pursuit, and stayed out of the way. The furniture had therefore made its way unimpeded around the corner onto Cross Avenue northbound, then left again onto East Road.

"They stayed together?" Kilisha asked.

"Mostly," Kelder said. "For a while."

In fact, they had split up at the fork where the East Road bore right and Low Street bore left. There the couch had taken the East Road, and the chair and bench headed southward down Low Street, toward the shipyard.

"What about the table?" Kilisha asked. "Or the rug?"

Kelder had lost sight of those well before reaching the fork, he explained. There were only the three left by then, and he had followed the pair of smaller pieces. They had dodged westward again on Wargate High Street, but he had finally caught up at the corner of Shipyard Street, and with the help of some other guards had cornered and apprehended both. He had then locked them in a materials shed and gone to report to his superiors.

"Why didn't you come back here yesterday?" Kilisha asked.

"Because I wanted orders first. I went to my captain, and he sent me to the tax commissioner, who sent me back to the captain because this didn't have anything to do with taxes, and then he sent me to see a wizard named Zorita, and she sent to to see someone named Kaligir, only I couldn't get in to talk to him because of some sort of emergency meeting, and then I got orders to go back to Wargate because there was talk about calling out the entire guard to march off to Ethshar of the Sands because someone's thrown the overlord there out of his palace. . . ." Kelder sighed. "I only got here this morning because the captain was too distracted to object when I said I was coming."

"I couldn't get to see Kaligir either," Kilisha said.

"Who *is* Kaligir?" Kelder asked.

"Oh, he's an official in the Wizards' Guild," Kilisha said, realizing she might have been on the verge of saying too much. "It doesn't matter. What matters is that you can show me where some of my master's furniture is, and help me get it back here where it belongs!"

"Then you do want it back?"

"Of *course* we do! The spell was a mistake; we'll put everything back the way it should be as soon as we collect all the pieces."

"I don't know where all of them are. I see you've caught the coatrack. . . ."

"And we have the bowl, and the spoon, and the latch, and the mirror. And my mistress is out looking for the rug right now. As soon as she gets back, we can go get the chair and the bench."

Kelder looked uneasy. "I can't stay very long," he said. "I need to report back to the captain."

Kilisha started to reply, then stopped at a rattling sound from the front. "Could you wait here a moment?" she asked. "It's probably just the coatrack, or a customer—I'll tell him we're closed, if it's a customer."

"I can't stay much longer," Kelder reiterated, but he remained seated.

Kilisha smiled and rose and hurried through the workshop to the parlor, where she found someone pounding on the front door and calling, "Open this door this instant!"

It was Yara's voice.

The coatrack was pacing back and forth nervously at the end of its leash, but Kilisha barely glanced at it as she dashed to the door and tried to open the latch.

It wouldn't budge.

"Just a moment!" she shouted through the door.

"Hurry!" Yara called.

Kilisha was puzzled by her urgency—and by the latch's reluctance. Previously it had seemed all too eager to open when nobody wanted it to, but now it was stubbornly refusing to let Yara in. She slapped at it, hard. "Open up!" she demanded.

She could see the mechanism hesitate.

"Kelder!" she called over her shoulder. "Do you have something that can break a latch? Just snap it *right apart,* so the little metal pieces spill out on the floor?"

The latch opened, the door swung in, and Yara stumbled across the threshold, her three children clustered about her legs, and a burlap-wrapped bundle in her arms.

"There!" she said, pointing back out at the street.

Kilisha leaned to one side and looked around the door, past her mistress.

Ithanalin's parlor table was standing in the street, pawing the hard-packed dirt with one wooden leg.

"The table!" Kilisha exclaimed. "How did you find the *table*?" Then she noticed the large, squirming bundle that lay atop the table—a multi-colored bundle of braided rags. "*And* the rug!" she said happily.

The rug, the table, the coatrack, the latch, the bowl, the spoon, the mirror, and Kelder had the bench and the chair. Unless she had forgotten something, that only left the couch!

"Bring it in!" she said, gesturing.

Yara was already halfway to the workshop door, and ignored her, but Telleth heard and started back toward the door.

He didn't get very far, though, because at the sound of Kilisha's voice the table trotted up to the door; Kilisha and Telleth had to step aside to avoid being bumped as it marched into the house.

The tangle of rug was squirming more than ever as it went by, and Kilisha realized it was *squeaking,* as well. There was something *in* there, she realized—it wasn't just the rug, but something *wrapped* in the rug. "What have you got there?" she asked.

The rug hesitated.

Telleth slammed the door, trapping the table in the house, and Kilisha called to the latch, "Lock up tight, please! I think our friend the rug has something he doesn't want to escape."

She wondered what it could be; had there been some other object in the room that got a part of Ithanalin's essence? One of the children's toys, perhaps?

The latch clicked solidly into place, and the rug unfolded, draping itself across the tabletop and revealing its prize.

The captive straightened up and stood there blinking at Kilisha, and she realized at once what it was.

It stood perhaps nine inches in height, naked and sexless, with sagging, dull green skin. It was roughly man-shaped, but with spindly, twiglike limbs, a bulging potbelly, and an oversized head, with immense pointed ears, bulging pop-eyes, and a gaping, lipless, froglike mouth.

A spriggan.

And she thought she knew *which* spriggan, and why the rug had caught it.

"You're the spriggan that tripped my master, aren't you?" she asked.

It blinked woefully at her, and nodded.

"The rug must have my master's urge for revenge," she said.

The spriggan blinked again, then spread its spindly arms. "Don't *think* so," it said, in a voice that sounded oddly familiar. Kilisha wondered whether she'd spoken to this particular spriggan before. It might have been hanging around the place for days or months.

"Well, why *else* would it capture you?" Kilisha demanded.

The spriggan turned up an empty palm. "Don't know," it said. "Not have rug's thoughts."

That seemed very peculiar phrasing for a spriggan—the little idiots usually didn't consider anyone else's thoughts. And that voice sounded more familiar than ever; it was exceptionally deep for a spriggan, almost human in tone. . . .

"Oh, no," Kilisha said.

"Not have rug's thoughts," the spriggan said dolefully, shaking its head. "Not have table's thoughts. Only have little bit of thoughts."

"Of *Ithanalin's* thoughts, you mean?"

"Yes, yes. Sprigganalin, me. Rest is scattered."

Kilisha clapped her hand over her mouth. Telleth looked up at her. "Did Dad turn himself into a *spriggan*?" he asked.

"Not entirely," Kilisha said, her words muffled by her fingers.

"That looks like the same one that was here yesterday," Kelder said from behind her.

"Yes, yes!" the spriggan said, nodding. "Saw you at door."

"It's the same one," Kilisha agreed, turning to see the soldier had come up behind her, far more quietly than she would have thought possible.

"Who's that?" Telleth asked, looking at Kelder. No one answered; everyone else's attention was still focused on the spriggan.

"Should I kill it?" Kelder asked, raising his truncheon.

"*No!*" Kilisha and the spriggan shouted in unison. "I need it alive for a spell, to restore my master," Kilisha explained quickly.

"The *spriggan*?" Yara said, emerging from the workshop behind Kelder. At the sound of her voice the rug humped itself up and slithered off the table, falling to the floor in a heap and knocking the spriggan off its feet.

Kilisha sprang forward and caught the spriggan before it, too, could tumble off the table. She called to the children, "Find me a cage or a rope or something! We can't let this escape."

Telleth hurried to obey and tripped over the rug, which was straightening itself out and starting toward Yara; Kelder caught the boy before he could fall.

Yara let out a yelp at the sight of the rug climbing over her son's legs and coming toward her; she backed into the workshop. The table was dancing back and forth nervously, obviously confused by all the excitement, and the coatrack had squeezed itself trembling back into its corner, its hooks extended in every direction.

Kilisha clapped her hands to her head at the sound and confusion and sudden motion, forgetting that she held the spriggan in one of them; the feel of its leathery little body against her ear was supremely disconcerting, and it was all she could do to stop herself from flinging the little creature away headfirst.

"Lirrin, help your brother get that rug off his feet, would you?" Kilisha said.

Lirrin and Pirra both hurried to Telleth, who was now kicking wildly as Kelder held him off the ground and the rug struggled to untangle itself. Before either girl could touch it, though, Telleth gave one final kick that sent the rug flying; it soared free and landed on the floor several feet to the side, where it skidded across the planking for another foot or two before it managed to stop.

Telleth stopped kicking, but not until he had thumped one bare foot into Pirra's chest and knocked her to the floor, where she sat and wailed. Lirrin hurried to her sister's aid as Kelder carefully lowered the chastened boy to the floor.

"I'm sorry, Pirra!" Telleth called. "I'm sorry!"

Kilisha was too busy watching the rug to pay much attention to the children. The floor covering had recovered quickly from its fall, and was now humping itself up, inchworm fashion, and crawling toward the workshop door. Kilisha turned to see Yara staring in horror at the approaching object.

"Stay back!" Yara shouted, holding out a hand to fend the rug off.

The rug stopped dead.

"See?" Kilisha called. "It *loves* you, and will do what you tell it!"

"Love you, yes!" the spriggan squeaked in a high-pitched parody of Ithanalin's voice.

The table danced over and bumped against Lirrin from behind, and the coatrack thumped against the wall.

"*What is going on here?*" Kelder bellowed. That made the three children cower, the table dance, the coatrack rock wildly from side to side, and the rug skitter sideways, while the spriggan squirmed wildly in Kilisha's grasp.

A sudden inspiration struck her. "Kelder," she asked, "do you have something you use to tie people up if you arrest them? Restraints of some kind?"

"I have a cord," he admitted. He reached into the big pouch on his belt and pulled out a length of rope.

"Here," Kilisha said, holding out the spriggan. "Start with this."

"Why?" Kelder asked suspiciously.

"I need it to restore my master," Kilisha said.

Kelder did not look convinced, but he looped the cord around the spriggan's wrists and tied a quick knot. Kilisha smiled.

"The ankles, too," she said. "They're tricky."

Kelder grumbled, but tied the spriggan's legs, tugging the knot tight.

When he was done, Kilisha carefully set the little creature on the floor. "There," she said.

The spriggan promptly pulled both hands out of the loops, then bent down and pulled at the cord around its ankles. The knots fell apart, and the rope dropped away. It stood up.

"Not *like* rope!" it said.

"How did you *do* that?" Kelder demanded, reaching for the spriggan with one hand and the discarded ropes with the other. The little creature danced aside, out of his grasp.

Kilisha didn't say a thing, but her eyes widened as she realized what had happened. She had seen such a demonstration before, years ago, when she had scarcely begun her apprenticeship.

One of the little-known aspects of wizardry was that a true wizard could not be held by physical bonds if he could touch the hilt of his athame. He didn't need to hold it, or cut anything, or use any sort of spell—simply touching it would cause his bonds to fall away.

Just as the spriggan's had.

Which, she theorized, meant that the spriggan now held the piece of Ithanalin's soul that had been in his athame. Or perhaps it had received his magical talents, including whatever it was that gave an athame that particular ability.

Kelder had recovered his ropes, but the spriggan had eluded

him and he was kneeling on the parlor floor, grabbing for it.

"Spriggan!" Kilisha called. "Hold still!" She remembered whose fragmentary self she was speaking to, and added, "Please."

"Not like rope!" it squeaked.

"I know," Kilisha said. "We won't tie you up, I promise."

"We won't?" Telleth asked, looking at her in surprise.

"No, we won't," Kilisha said.

Kelder looked up and growled, "Speak for yourself."

"Kelder, we *can't* tie it up. It's impossible."

Kelder stopped grabbing at the spriggan and looked at her. "Why is it impossible?" he demanded.

Kilisha hesitated, unsure what to say—she *couldn't* explain about the spriggan being like an athame; the true nature of a wizard's athame was a Guild secret, and she could be killed for revealing it.

Finally, as Kelder and the children stared at her expectantly, she simply said, "Magic."

Chapter Thirteen

It took some time to sort everything out, but in the end Kilisha was satisfied.

The dish and spoon had been moved the previous night from their cages to solid, securely locked boxes in Ithanalin's bedroom—Yara had said it made her nervous having them watching her from the cages—and they were still there. The coatrack was leashed in the corner of the parlor. The end table was securely tied to the kitchen table. The rug was rolled up and tied—*it* hadn't absorbed any athame magic—and tucked away in the pantry.

Yara and the children had retreated to the rear portion of the house, where Lirrin and Pirra were playing a sort of tag with the animated table.

Kelder had seated himself on the floor, blocking the front door, and Kilisha sat facing him, blocking the door to the workshop.

And the spriggan was sitting cross-legged between them, unbound.

"Tell us what happened," Kilisha said.

"Don't want to," the spriggan said.

Kilisha sighed in exasperation. "I know we can't tie you up," she said, "but there's no reason we can't hurt you!"

The creature squealed and covered its head with its hands.

"I don't *want* to hurt you," Kilisha quickly added, "but it's very important you tell me what happened yesterday."

The spriggan sniffed, slid its hands down to its face, and peeked out between spread fingers.

"Not hurt?"

"If you answer all my questions, I won't hurt you."

"Soldier hurt?"

"He won't hurt you, either—*if* you answer my questions."

"Will answer, yes."

"Good." Kilisha adjusted her position, then asked, "What happened yesterday?"

"Was here," the spriggan said, dropping its hands. "Had fun, watching magic, but knew wizard not want spriggans, so when wizard came out, spriggan hid under rug, yes?"

"Yes, I understand," Kilisha said.

"Wizard *stepped* on rug!"

"So the mirror told me."

"Ran out, rug slipped, wizard fell, said bad magic words, wizard's thoughts go *everywhere*."

Kilisha glanced uncomfortably at Kelder. She hoped he wasn't really following this.

"Some thoughts hit spriggan, more knife than wizard, all mixed up. Spriggan ran, ran, ran. Too mixed. Remembered stepping on *and* stepped on."

"That must have been confusing," Kilisha said.

The spriggan nodded. "So ran," it said. "And rug chased after, and table."

"They were chasing *you*? That's why all the furniture ran off?"

"Don't know *all*," the spriggan said. "Rug chased spriggan, table followed rug. Others, don't know."

"They probably just panicked," Kilisha said.

"Yes, yes! Very scary!"

"So then what?"

"Ran a long time. Got tired. Got caught. Rug wrapped up spriggan—but then rug not move! Not crawl while wrapped on spriggan, no!"

"The rug couldn't move without letting you go?"

"Yes, yes!"

"So what did it do?"

"Rug *waited*. Table just stood. Very boring. No fun." The spriggan stuck out its surprisingly long and forked tongue at the memory.

For a moment Kilisha wondered how the rug had been able to hold the spriggan when a securely tied cord could not, but then she realized this was clear proof that the rug was *alive*, possessed of a partial soul and not just a sort of magical machine; athame magic did not work on being held by a living person, only on any sort of inanimate binding.

That didn't explain how the rug had gotten the spriggan back home, though. "Then what?" Kilisha prompted.

"This morning rug hear wife's voice, get excited. Tug at table until table push rug and spriggan against wall, then push up between table and wall until on top. Then rug slap table to tell it where to go, and we run run run after wife!"

Kilisha smiled. It would seem that Cauthen's Remarkable Love Spell had done its job, and yielded not just one of the escapees, but three. The love spell had apparently inspired the rug to find a way to get home with its captive.

"And here we are," she said.

"Here, yes yes."

"And you'll *stay* here?" Kilisha asked. "I know we can't tie you up—will you stay here until I get everything ready to restore my master?"

"Don't know," the spriggan said, cocking its head thoughtfully to one side. "Is fun?"

Kilisha grimaced. "Don't you want to be put back the way you were?" she asked.

"Don't know," the spriggan repeated.

"It wouldn't be so confusing," Kilisha offered helpfully.

"You'd be *you* again, an ordinary spriggan. And Ithanalin would be himself again."

"Don't know. *Like* wizard. *Like* magic."

Kilisha didn't like the sound of that at all.

"Like *you*," the spriggan added.

"Then do what I ask, and stay here."

"Mmmmmmm. . . . Maybe," the spriggan said.

Kilisha decided that would have to do. If the spriggan *did* escape she would just have to capture it again. At least now she knew that she needed it, that a part of Ithanalin's soul had wound up in the little nuisance.

A cage or box *might* hold the spriggan, but somehow she doubted it. Spriggans were very good at getting through locked doors even without an athame's magic.

Perhaps the rug could be convinced to wrap it up again—but Kilisha really hoped that it wouldn't come to that, because even with the love spell she didn't trust the rug completely. There was a possibility it might either get bored and free the spriggan at an inopportune time, or accidentally smother the creature. She had no idea how vulnerable spriggans might be to asphyxiation.

For now, she intended to just rely on the creature's self-interest.

It had been a good morning so far. She had Ithanalin's body, and the rug and table and bowl and spoon and coatrack and latch and spriggan, and most of the ingredients for Javan's Restoration. She still needed the chair and bench and couch, and jewelweed, whatever that was.

And Kelder had locked the bench and chair in a storeroom near the shipyard.

She had finally remembered her intention to levitate above the city and see if she could spot the missing furniture, and she might still do that later to locate the couch, but fetching the bench and chair seemed more immediately helpful.

Carrying them by herself might be something of a challenge—she could use the Spell of Optimum Strength, even if the potion wasn't ready, but they might struggle, and it might take two trips, which seemed a waste of time—and besides, this soldier Kelder knew where they were and she didn't.

"Kelder," she said, "can you help me bring the bench and chair home?"

"Of course," the guardsman said.

"Then let's go," Kilisha said.

"Do you want to bring anything? Any magic spells?"

"Oh!" Kilisha paused; she realized she hadn't thought about that very hard. She considered for a moment.

Tracel's Adaptable Potion wasn't ready, and since she would have Kelder along to help carry, it didn't seem worth taking hours to work the Spell of Optimum Strength—and what other magic did she have that would be useful in carrying furniture? She could think of only one really useful thing to bring, and it wasn't exactly a spell.

"Just a minute," she said, running back to the kitchen.

A moment later she returned with a coil of rope slung on her shoulder. "Let's go," she said.

Kelder looked curiously at the coil. "Is that magic?" he asked.

Startled, she looked up at him. "No," she said, "it's *rope.*"

"Oh." He stood, looking slightly foolish, as Kilisha pushed past him and opened the front door; then he followed her out into the street.

The morning was wearing on; the sun was high overhead as the pair of them set out toward the waterfront. Kilisha had closed the shop door securely and ordered the latch to behave itself, but all the same she was slightly worried about it, and not really surprised at all when, after they had gone no more than two blocks, the spriggan came running up beside her.

"Like you!" it said. "We have fun!"

Kilisha looked down at it and sighed.

Kelder looked as well, and stopped walking. "Shall I catch it for you, and take it back?"

"No," Kilisha said. She already knew that spriggans were expert at getting in and out of places—their ability to turn up in the workshop at inconvenient times proved that. And *this* spriggan had an athame's magic, making it impossible to bind; it was probably smarter than the average spriggan now that it held a portion of Ithanalin's intelligence, and might well have a bond of sorts with the animated latch on the front door. The chances of keeping it restrained against its will, even with cages and the Spell of Impeded Egress, were amazingly poor—and if she tried to confine it and it escaped, it would be that much more reluctant to be recaptured.

She would just have to rely on its common sense and the fact that it *liked* her.

She grimaced. Relying on a *spriggan's* common sense? Had she gone mad?

No, she told herself, she had simply not been given any better options.

"Fun!" the spriggan said.

"Your legs will get tired if you run after us," Kilisha suggested.

"Don't care. We have fun!" It grinned an impossibly wide and foolish grin.

The silly creature was clearly determined to accompany them, rather than staying sensibly at home. Kilisha glanced at Kelder. "I don't suppose it could ride in your pouch?"

Kelder looked at her, at the spriggan, at his pouch, then back at Kilisha. "No!" he said. "That's the overlord's property. I keep important things in there; I can't have a spriggan playing with them!"

"All right, all right," Kilisha said. "It was just a suggestion." She looked down at the spriggan. "Would you like to ride on my shoulder? You can hold onto my hair to keep from falling off." That would keep it within her reach.

"Ooooooh!" the spriggan said, eyes widening. "Ride is *fun*! Yes, yes!"

Kilisha stooped down, and the spriggan ran up her lowered arm to perch on her shoulder. It grabbed a healthy handful of hair and shook it, like the reins of an oxcart.

"Ow!" Kilisha protested, as she straightened up. "Not so hard."

"Sorry, sorry!"

The creature did not *sound* the least bit sorry, but Kilisha did not argue. "Lead the way," she told Kelder, ignoring the stares of the other pedestrians.

Kelder led.

Half an hour later he stopped at the door of an ugly brick structure on Shipyard Street. "This is it," he said.

Kilisha tried the latch. "It's locked," she said.

"Of course it is," Kelder agreed. "I didn't want them getting out."

The spriggan, which had been tugging with one hand at the coil of rope Kilisha carried while its other hand remained tangled in her hair, looked up. "Get out?" it said.

"Yes, there is furniture in there we didn't want to get out," Kilisha said.

"More furniture?" The spriggan shuddered. "Didn't like rug and table. Got *squeezed.*" It pulled its hand out of the loop of rope.

Kilisha tried to turn her head far enough to look at the creature, but it was pressing up against her ear, making this impossible.

"But they're other pieces of the same person!" she said.

"Other pieces of *wizard,*" the spriggan corrected her. "Sprigganalin is spriggan *and* Ithanalin. Spriggan doesn't like furniture."

"Is that why you followed us?"

The spriggan buried its face in her hair, and she could feel it nodding.

"We need to find the foreman," Kelder said, pointedly ignoring her conversation with the spriggan. "He's the one with the key."

"*You* don't have the key?" Kilisha asked, startled.

Kelder looked at her, equally startled. "I'm a guardsman assigned to collect taxes for Lady Nuvielle—why would I have a key to a shipyard storage shed?"

"Because you put my master's animated furniture in the shed!"

"It's still not my shed," Kelder said. "You wait here; I'll find the foreman."

"Which foreman?" she asked.

"Arra the Carpenter," Kelder said, pointing at the nearest hull. "He should be in there."

Kilisha looked at the mud, the rickety-looking walkways and their utter lack of handrails, and the large, dirty workers. She took a good whiff of the stench of mudflat.

"Go ahead," she said. "I'll wait here."

Kelder glanced at her, then spread an empty hand. "As you please," he said. He crossed the street, looked hesitantly at the steep, rocky slope that separated the street from the shipyards, then started trudging down the road toward Ramp Street, the nearer of the two ramps that led down into the yards themselves.

Kilisha turned and looked out across the shipyards, hundreds of yards of muddy tidal flat spread out at the foot of the steep drop-off on the other side of Shipyard Street. The flats were covered with wooden frameworks of one sort or another. Some were the partially built hulls of new ships, suspended on wooden frames over muddy ditches; others were the cranes and scaffolding used to construct those hulls and put masts and decking into them; and still others were the wooden walkways and bridges connecting everything, keeping the workers up out of the worst of the mud. Assorted sheds and huts were scattered among the frames, and dozens, perhaps hundreds, of muddy workers were moving about, hauling ropes and timbers and metalwork hither and yon.

The whole thing stank of sawdust, seawater, and rotting vegetation. When a spring tide came in the entire flat would be awash, most of it no more than ankle deep, but the channels cut beneath the hulls would fill; completed ships could be lowered, released, and if the workers were quick enough in catching the tide, floated down the broad canal known as the Throat and out to the sea.

If a storm surge came sweeping in through the Throat the solid hulls and scaffolding would survive, and most of the walkways, but the huts and loose pieces would all be washed away; that typically happened once or twice a year. When the Lord Shipwright's budget allowed, magical warnings or protections prevented any serious loss of materials or men, but in bad years the shipbuilders just accepted the risks as part of doing business.

Of course, anything really important or valuable was stored outside the shipyard proper, in the sheds and warehouses lining the outer side of Shipyard Street, well above the high-water line.

Kilisha counted four ships abuilding; one had masts up, two were solid hulls, and one was still little more than an oaken skeleton. Kelder appeared to be heading directly for the nearest, a solid but mastless hull.

She was still watching him when she heard a thump on the door of the shed.

Chapter Fourteen

Kilisha leaned close to the locked shed door and called, "Is anyone in there?"

Another thump sounded, but no one answered her. She knocked on the door and called again, "Is someone in there?"

A series of thumps was followed by what sounded like a high-pitched giggle.

"What's going on in there?" she called. She glanced after Kelder, but he had apparently not heard anything; he was already at the corner, starting down the long, curving ramp into the shipyards.

Kilisha frowned, then leaned over and put her ear to the door.

Thump, thump, rattle, another giggle, and then a squeaky voice shrieked, "Fun!"

"Oh, no," she breathed.

There was a spriggan in the shed. She looked quickly at her own shoulder, and was reassured to see Sprigganalin, as it called itself, still perched there, clutching a hank of her hair.

"*Hai!*" she said. "How did one of you get inside there?"

"Spriggan inside?" The spriggan blinked at her, and grinned broadly. "Oh, fun!"

"*Not* fun," Kilisha said angrily. "I think the furniture is trying to stomp it to death."

"Oh, stomping not as easy as you think! We go in and help?"

"The door's locked," Kilisha reminded it. "And besides, we don't want to let the furniture out yet."

"Not?"

"Not."

"But—"

Something slammed heavily against the door, and Kilisha was certain she heard a high-pitched shriek.

"Oh, death," she said, putting a hand on the door. It still felt solid, but she was sure something had rammed it, hard, from the other side.

It was probably the bench, she thought.

"Open door?" the spriggan on her shoulder asked.

"I told you, it's *locked*," Kilisha growled.

"We unlock it, have fun! Spriggans like fun."

"We don't have the blasted *key*," Kilisha said, exasperated.

"Don't need key," the spriggan said, as it released her hair and scampered down her arm.

"What?" She stared down at it, frozen in astonishment.

"Don't need key," the spriggan repeated, as it wrapped its legs around her wrist and leaned down toward the lock.

"What are you *doing*?" she demanded—but she left her hand where it was. She couldn't risk flinging the spriggan aside, and losing a bit of Ithanalin's soul.

"Open lock!" the spriggan said, thrusting a long, thin forefinger into the keyhole.

Kilisha stared, and suddenly saw the solution to a mystery. Here was how spriggans kept getting into the house, no matter how careful she and Yara and Ithanalin were about closing shutters and locking doors. The spriggan's fingernail was a natural lockpick, and the creatures apparently had an instinctive understanding of locks—or at least of how to open them.

The spriggan wiggled and twisted its finger, grimacing, its huge pointed ears flexing as it concentrated on its task—and then the lock clicked open.

"Blood and death," Kilisha swore, still staring.

The spriggan paid no attention as it slid the latch aside and gently pushed the door open.

Something suddenly rammed the door from the inside again, and Kilisha started back as the heavy wooden slab slammed against the frame, then bounced open. The spriggan on her wrist clung harder and whooped with excitement.

"Hello?" Kilisha called, peering into the dark interior of the shed.

She was answered by the pounding of half a dozen wooden feet and the squeaking of not one, but *several* spriggans.

"Oh, no," she said. She pushed the door open and stepped in.

The interior of the shed was dim and dusty, the only good light coming from the door behind her, but she could see well enough to make out immense coils of rope stacked to the ceiling along one side, and boxes and shelves of black ironmongery along the other.

Unfortunately, one stack of ropes had toppled over, and three boxes of ironmongery had broken open, their contents scattered across the floor.

The familiar straight chair from Ithanalin's parlor stood in one far corner, tipped at an angle, two of its four legs braced against a coil of rope; it was rocking back and forth, plainly trying to dislodge a spriggan that clung, squealing, to its back.

And the heavy oaken bench was standing in the middle of the floor, quivering while four spriggans sat on it; the spriggans were grinning broadly. The bench had obviously been what had rammed the door, and Kilisha guessed it had been trying to knock the spriggans off.

"Ride! Ride!" one of the spriggans called happily, slapping the bench.

"Get off!" Kilisha shouted back. "It's not your bench!"

The nearest spriggan looked up at her in wide-eyed surprise. "Not?" it asked, in an amazingly sincere tone.

"No, it's not," Kilisha said angrily, stepping forward and reaching for the spriggan.

The spriggan already clinging to her wrist squealed, and she stopped. She didn't want to dislodge it; she *really* didn't want to lose track of which spriggan was which. They all looked very much alike, and while she *thought* she could recognize the individual she wanted, she was not sure of it.

She reached out with her other hand, caught Sprigganalin, and tried to pry it loose, to return it to her shoulder.

Sprigganalin clung more tightly, keening at this abuse.

"Get back on my shoulder, damn you!" she shouted.

The keening stopped abruptly. "Shoulder?" it asked.

"Yes, my shoulder!" Kilisha said. "So I can use my hand!"

"Fun!" the creature said, releasing its hold and scurrying back up her arm.

She let out a growl of exasperation, then reached for the spriggans on the bench.

They all crowded away from her toward the far end of the bench but did not jump off. She stepped to one side, to go around the bench and grab them.

The instant she stepped to the side, though, and was no longer between the bench and the door, the bench bolted.

"*Hai!*" Kilisha called, staring stupidly as the thing charged past her, its four legs churning, its wooden joints creaking, and all four spriggans still clinging to it. "Come back!"

The bench paid no attention, but dashed out into the sun, pivoted on one leg, and galloped westward along Shipyard Street.

Kilisha took one look at the chair, then ran to the door and screamed, "Kelder!" at the top of her lungs.

Several men in the shipyard turned and watched as the bench ran away, but Kilisha did not see anyone in the yellow tunic and red kilt of a guardsman. She hesitated; if she ran after the bench the chair might escape. And the bench was heading westward, into Hillside and the Fortress district, while almost the entire city lay in the other direction; if it didn't double back it would reach the seaside cliffs in a few blocks, and she could corner it there.

But it *could* double back, or turn up a side street, or throw itself over the cliff. . . .

But the chair was behind her.

She whirled, dove for the chair, grabbed it up, hoisted it over-head with the squealing, giggling spriggan still clinging to its back, and ran for the door. She promptly whacked the chair into the lintel, almost throwing her off her feet; she was not tall, but even so, the doorframe was not meant for the combined height of a woman and a chair.

The spriggan on the chair squeaked and fell off, hitting the floor with a thump; the spriggan on her shoulder squealed, "Fun!" and grabbed a double handful of hair while digging its toes under the coil of rope she still carried.

"Damn," she said as she regained her balance. She lowered the chair and tried again, and this time made it out onto Shipyard Street.

The bench was still in sight, well around the curve to the west, the four spriggans still riding it and shrieking happily. Kilisha raised the chair over her head again and ran after it.

The chair finally overcame its surprise and began to wave its feet feebly, joints creaking. Kilisha ignored that and ran.

The street was not crowded, and both she and the bench easily dodged the occasional passerby, leaving various men and women standing there, staring after her. Kilisha called out, "Stop that bench!" but no one reacted in time.

The gap between the bench and herself narrowed briefly, then widened again as the bench picked up the pace and Kilisha could not. In fact, she began to slow; running while carrying a chair over one's head was surprisingly tiring.

"Kelder!" she called again. She kept moving, alternately run-ning and trotting.

The bench had passed two intersections without turning, but she could see it was nearing the fork where Shipyard Street con-tinued straight ahead, leaving the curving side of the shipyards and continuing up the hillside toward the Fortress and the coastal cliffs, while Old Seagate Street curved down to the left, toward the Throat and the Fortress Docks.

Old Seagate Street remained open to one side, overlooking the shipyards, though tall old houses replaced the storage sheds on the other side; Shipyard Street beyond the fork was lined with housing on both sides.

The bench slowed, and for a moment she thought it was going to stop and give her a chance to catch up, but then it seemed to make its decision and went charging on up Shipyard Street, up toward the Fortress.

If she followed, in a few moments she would be out of sight of the shipyards and Kelder would be unable to spot her—but, she asked herself, what did that matter? She had the chair, even if it was starting to squirm a little, and she could catch the bench soon enough, she was sure—especially if she could get some passing pedestrian to help her. She had rope to tie the bench and chair together, once she had them both cornered, and then she could lead them both home. She didn't really *need* Kelder.

At least, she hoped she wouldn't need him.

She charged onward, in pursuit of the bench.

Chapter Fifteen

Two blocks past the fork Shipyard Street began to curve to the left, the better to follow a fold in the terrain. The bench was still two and a half blocks ahead of her; by the time she passed the fork it was vanishing around the curve, out of sight.

And there were no other people around to call on for help; the street was, just for the moment, deserted. She strained to run faster, ignoring the whooping and babbling of the spriggan on her shoulder, and the twisting and kicking of the chair she carried above her head.

The chair and the spriggan did not slow her as much as the street itself did; it was sloping up steeply by the time she passed the third cross street, so steeply that along either side stone steps were provided. The earthen center was intended primarily for wheeled vehicles, not pedestrians; in dry weather, such as the city had experienced for the past two sixnights, it was suitable for walking, but in wet weather, when the dirt turned to slick mud, the steps were needed.

By the time she reached the first steps Kilisha could not see the bench.

Two blocks later Shipyard Street ended in a T with Steep

Street—and Steep Street lived up to its name; it was *all* stone steps, with grooves cut into them for cart wheels. To the right Steep Street continued up the hill toward the Fortress; to the left it dropped down toward the Fortress Docks.

Kilisha stopped, panting, the chair still over her head, and looked both ways.

She did not entirely understand how the bench, with its short legs and cross braces, could move so fast, or how it could negotiate the steps of Steep Street, but it seemed to have done so; she could not see it in either direction.

She stood in the middle of the trapezoidal patch of level pavement where the streets intersected and slowly turned, left to right, in a full circle.

She saw narrow houses, so black with centuries of smoke that she could not tell whether they were wood, stone, or plaster between the heavy wooden beams. The figures on their carved cornerposts were worn down to facelessness, and their chimney tops thrust up crookedly above sagging gables; a few had shopwindows displaying jewelry or fine fabrics. She saw the gray stone steps of Steep Street leading up the hill, kept clean and worn smooth by rain and passing feet, curving to the left so that she could not see to the next intersection.

She turned past the upward-bound street.

On the corner stood a larger house, gargoyles leering over the cornice, and almost unreadably worn runes carved deep into the lintel spelled out ARMORER. She doubted that any armorer still lived or worked there; to the best of her knowledge all the armorers still operating were based in Wargate, near the parade ground. Presumably this house dated back at least to the end of the Great War.

Then, past the corner, came Shipyard Street, back the way she had come, tumbling down the hillside away from her, houses and shops on either side; the bench could not possibly have gotten past her in that direction.

Then the other corner, occupied by a shuttered house of no great distinction.

And finally, the other side of Steep Street, narrow stone steps curving down to the right, dropping away so steeply that a level gaze looked into third-floor windows half a block away.

Somewhere on this street lived that man who had wanted his bed enchanted, but she had no idea which house might be his, or whether that had anything to do with why the bench had come this way. Had some shred of Ithanalin's memory guided it here, seeking out that customer? Could the bench possibly be heading that way? It didn't seem likely. Ithanalin had presumably known where the man lived, and the bench might remember that, but why would it want to go there? It wasn't a bed, and it surely knew that.

The customer had said he lived near the intersection with Hillside Street, and she was fairly certain that was farther up the slope—but did that mean anything? She saw no one, no sign of movement, no sign of the bench in any direction. She could hear distant voices as the city went about its business, and the faint hissing of the sea breaking over the rocks below the cliffs, but nothing that gave her any clue to the bench's whereabouts.

"Damn," she said.

"Not fun?" the spriggan on her shoulder asked.

"No," Kilisha said. "No fun at all." She realized that her arms, legs, and feet were all sore, and that she was still holding the chair over her head. She lowered it, and set it carefully on the pavement.

She looked down at it for a moment, not releasing her hold, and then did the obvious thing. She sat down, taking the weight off her feet.

The chair did not react at first; it seemed as inert and lifeless as any ordinary chair. She looked down past her hip at the edge of the seat, wondering whether she had somehow done something to it, perhaps inadvertently broken a part of the spell. Her sheathed athame might have brushed against the wood when she sat down, she thought; might that have triggered something?

Could it possibly be that simple to restore Ithanalin's life to its rightful place?

And then the chair abruptly lifted her up an inch or so, then dropped back.

"Oh!" she said, startled by this proof that the enchantment had not been broken.

"Ooooooh!" the spriggan replied.

Kilisha had no time to respond to that; the chair was moving, and she was too busy clinging to the seat to say anything more.

It moved with an odd rocking gait that felt horribly unsteady, but was not actually bumpy or uncomfortable. It carried her to the west, to the upward-bound side of Steep Street, up to the base of the first step.

Perhaps the bench and chair really *were* trying to deliver the customer his spell, even though it had all gone wrong? Kilisha blinked, and brushed hair from her eyes as she tried to think.

Then the chair paused, and tentatively lifted one leg, straining and creaking as it tried to gain purchase on the step.

Kilisha was fairly certain that if she had not been sitting on it, holding it down, it would have been able to manage the step. As it was, however, it was rocking backward threateningly, on the verge of tipping over backward and spilling her out onto the granite pavement.

"*No,*" she said. "Don't you dare."

The chair hesitated, then lowered its probing leg.

Then it turned suddenly, and before Kilisha could protest it trotted across to the downward half of Steep Street.

"No, wait!" Kilisha called; she was sure that if it tried climbing down it would send her tumbling down those steps.

The chair hesitated.

"Do you know where the bench went?"

The seat seemed to quiver slightly. She could not interpret that as a useful answer.

"Tap a leg once for yes, twice for no," she said. "Do you know which way the bench went?"

The chair tapped twice. Kilisha sighed.

Then a thought struck her. Spriggans were drawn to wizardry. Presumably that meant that they could *sense* wizardry, and the bench was enchanted. She turned her head and stared at the spriggan on her shoulder.

"Oooh!" it said. "Pretty eyes." It grinned.

Kilisha blinked again. No one had ever told her she had pretty eyes before, and she wondered whether it was the spriggan half of the creature's personality, or the Ithanalin half, that had spoken.

But it didn't matter. "Do *you* know which way the bench went?" she asked.

"Oh, yes!" it said happily. "Down, down down! With spriggans."

She was sure, now, that Hillside was farther up; then it *hadn't* been looking for Ithanalin's customer. Winding up on Steep Street had just been a coincidence. "Why didn't you say so sooner?" she demanded angrily.

"Didn't ask," the creature replied.

"Augh!" She had no intention of riding the chair down the steps of Steep Street; she got up, carefully keeping a solid hold with one hand. She looked down the slope and reached to pick up the chair again.

Her muscles ached at the very thought.

"No," she said—and then she belatedly remembered that she *had* come equipped. She reached up and slid the coil of rope from her shoulder.

As she snugged the first knot down tight against one of the two slats in the seat back she prayed to whatever gods might be listening that none of the essence of Ithanalin's athame had wound up in the chair.

Her prayers appeared to have been answered; a moment later one end of the rope was securely tied to the chair, the other end wrapped around her wrist, with no indication that the chair could escape as the spriggan had.

She set the spriggan on the seat of the chair and said, "Ride there for a while; my shoulder's tired."

"Yes, yes!" the spriggan said. "Ride chair."

The chair did not seem happy with this; it tried to pull away, but Kilisha tugged on the rope.

"It's just for a little while," she said. "It won't hurt you; you share the same soul." Then she straightened up and looked down Steep Street.

The bench had had plenty of time to build up a lead by now, but she didn't see where it could have gone. Two blocks down Steep Street would bring them to Old Seagate Street and the foot of the cliffs. If it had doubled back to the east Kelder might well have seen it and caught it; if it had turned west again the road wound its way up to the Fortress in no more than a quarter of a mile. She set out down the steps at a steady trot, trailing the rope behind her.

The chair hesitated, then followed, keeping a comfortable slack in the line.

Half a block from the corner Steep Street straightened out, and she could see the ocean ahead, sparkling in the afternoon sun. She smiled at the sight; then her smile vanished as a horrible thought struck her.

What if the bench had dived off into the sea?

It couldn't drown, not being capable of breathing in the first place, but she would *never* find it if it were underwater!

And that assumed the waves hadn't pounded it to bits against the rocks, and the tide hadn't swept it out of reach of land.

Well, she told herself, she would just have to hope it hadn't done anything so foolish. Even if it thought it would survive a plunge into the sea, salt water would ruin its finish, and surely it would realize that.

She crossed the intersection with Straight Street, pausing just long enough to glance in both directions. Straight Street was not level, but it *was* straight; to the right she could see right up the slope to the east door of the Fortress, the massive structure's gray stone walls blocking out the western sky at the end of the street. To the left she could see down past houses and shops and ware-houses into the shipyards.

She saw a few people going about their business on the ship-yard side, but no ambulatory bench. She continued on down Steep Street without stopping—until she heard a sudden clatter behind her and felt the rope go slack.

She turned to see that the chair had tumbled down several steps, dumping the spriggan. The little creature now yelped, "Sorry sorry sorry!"

Kilisha couldn't be sure what had happened, but she supposed the spriggan had moved at the wrong time and thrown the chair off balance on the steep steps. She hurried back up and righted the chair, petting it on the back.

"There, there," she said. "I'm sorry. These steps must be hard for you!"

The chair tapped a leg, just once.

Then she looked for the spriggan, and spotted it two steps up.

"Hop back on," she said, gesturing toward the chair.

"Don't want to," it said, thrusting out what would have been its lower lip if spriggans had actual lips. "Too bumpy!"

Kilisha glared at it. "Get on the chair!" she growled.

The spriggan took a step back, but crossed its arms across its chest and said, "No."

Kilisha glowered, hoping that Ithanalin wouldn't remember any of this when he was restored to himself.

"All right," she said. "Get back on my shoulder, then." She held out her arm.

The spriggan cheered up instantly and hurried up her arm, settling comfortably on her shoulder, one hand clutching her hair. Once it was securely in place she once again headed down Steep Street, being careful not to go fast enough to overbalance the chair again.

The odd little party reached the corner of Old Seagate Street without further incident. Kilisha hurried across to the far side, where the land dropped away to the sea.

At the moment the tide was mostly in, so most of the rocks at the foot of the fifteen-foot drop were partially submerged. Waves were breaking noisily across the exposed stone, sending plumes of spray into the air, and a few stubborn tufts of seaweed washed back and forth across the broken rock.

If the bench had plunged down there it would have landed on rocks, not open water. It might have survived such a fall and scrambled on to open water, but Kilisha doubted it would have any reason to . . .

And then a thought struck her. The bench was *wood*. Heavy oak, yes, but still wood. It wouldn't sink to the bottom, out of sight; it would *float*.

She shaded her eyes and peered out to sea, and saw no sign of a drifting bench or anything like one. She could see ships at the piers of Seagate, and another at sea rounding Seagate Head, and in the distance beyond the headland, almost lost in haze and spray, she thought she could see the masts of more ships docked in Southport—though those last might have just been her imagination.

But she didn't see the bench.

She looked down Old Seagate Street, where it wound its way down the rocky verge toward the Fortress Docks and the shipyards; for once the curvature of the road favored her, so that she could see past the two docks and almost to the Throat. A crowd of men was hauling on ropes, securing a barge to the nearer of the docks, and a few other people were watching this labor, but she did not see the bench.

A guardsman was coming up the street past the docks, the mustard yellow tunic and blood red kilt unmistakable even at this distance, but she wasted no time trying to determine whether this was Kelder or someone else. She turned the other way, to where Old Seagate Street zigzagged up the rocky slope toward the Fortress.

The cliffs loomed above her, and the Fortress loomed above the cliffs. From her current position most of it was hidden behind the shops and warehouses that lined the inland side of Old Seagate Street, but the southern end thrust out from behind the other buildings, a sheer wall of sunlit gray stone that seemed to tower impossibly high into the western sky.

She did not see the bench—but because of the twisting course of the street, that did not mean much. The bench could easily be somewhere around one of the several curves.

She turned to the spriggan on her shoulder. "The bench went

that way, up toward the Fortress, didn't it?" She had to shout to be heard over the crashing of the waves.

"Don't know," the spriggan said.

"Why don't you know?" Kilisha demanded.

"Just don't," the spriggan said unhappily. "Don't smell it, don't feel it."

Kilisha hesitated, and threw a glance down the slope. That guardsman was still approaching, striding toward her quickly, and it did look like Kelder. The bench was probably farther up the hillside, and she ought to pursue it—but she couldn't be *sure* it had gone that way, rather than ducking into a shop or alley, or dodging around a corner somewhere.

And she was so far behind it now that another moment's delay could scarcely matter; she waited for the soldier where she was.

Chapter Sixteen

What happened?" Kelder demanded as he came within earshot. "How did you get the door open?"

"The spriggan did it," Kilisha shouted back, struggling to be heard over the pounding of the surf. "They can pick locks with their fingers!"

Kilisha did not hear Kelder's reply to that, but she was fairly certain she wasn't meant to; he appeared to be cursing vigorously. When he had finished he called to her, "Well, that explains a few things, doesn't it?"

"Yes," she agreed, "it certainly does."

"So the furniture got out, and you chased after it and caught it?"

She started to nod, then realized what he had said. "I caught the *chair*," she said. "The bench is still missing."

"Oh, for . . ." He began cursing under his breath again, and by the time he had completed this round he had reached her side. He looked along the rope to where the chair was pacing back and forth across the bottom two steps of Steep Street, then asked, "Do you know which way it went?"

"I think it went up that way," she said, pointing. "I followed it up Shipyard Street and down Steep Street, but I lost its trail. If you didn't see it go back down toward the shipyards, then it must have gone up."

"So it would seem," Kelder said. "Now what? Do you have some magic we can use to track it and capture it?"

"I didn't bring any magic," Kilisha admitted.

This was not literally true; she had her athame, and the pouch on her belt, much smaller than the elaborate one Kelder wore, held the ingredients for a few very minor spells. However, it was quite true that she had not brought any magic that would help in their present situation. She could see no way to use Fendel's Spectacular Illusion or Thrindle's Combustion in finding an escaped bench.

Kelder looked at her. "I thought wizards *always* carried magic," he said.

"I'm just an apprentice," Kilisha said, annoyed.

"Still . . ."

"Fine, I should have brought a few useful spells, but I didn't, all right? I do have *some* magic, but nothing that will help."

"All right, all right." He looked around. "You think it went that way?"

"I think so, yes." She looked at the spriggan on her shoulder. "Do you think so?"

"Don't know," the spriggan said.

"You can't tell?"

"Can't tell," it confirmed.

"You're asking spriggans?" Kelder said. "How would *it* know?"

Kilisha turned to him angrily. "They can sense magic," she retorted.

"Can they? Well, why don't we ask that one, then? Maybe it's got a more sensitive nose." He pointed up Steep Street.

Kilisha turned, and saw that indeed another spriggan was descending Steep Street, apparently headed directly for the enchanted chair.

"Where'd *you* come from?" Kilisha said. Then a thought struck her. "Maybe it's one of the ones that was on the bench!"

"There were spriggans on the bench?" Kelder asked.

Kilisha had been about to run up the steps toward the spriggan, but then she thought better of it; that might scare the newcomer away. Instead she gave the rope a gentle tug.

The chair clambered down a step so that two legs rested on Old Seagate Street and two on the bottom step of Steep Street.

The spriggan came bounding down the steps happily, ignoring the two humans who were maneuvering into position on either side of the chair. It jumped from the steps onto the chair seat—and Kilisha jerked the rope, tipping the chair up so that it wobbled wildly on one leg.

The spriggan slid from the polished wood and landed face-down on the hard-packed dirt. Kelder dove for it, and managed to grab one splayed foot before it could scramble away.

The guardsman sat up on the street, the front of his tunic smeared with dirt, his tax collector's pouch twisted around to his left hip, and the spriggan dangling from his hand, squirming wildly.

Kilisha hurried over and demanded, "Were you riding our bench?"

"Let go let go let go let go!" the spriggan yelped, still struggling.

"Answer the lady's question!" Kelder rumbled.

The spriggan stopped wriggling and turned to look at him, then decided to cooperate. "Rode bench, yes!" it said. "Fun ride. Bouncy, fast, bouncy, and fast, then got bounced off."

"Where'd the bench go?" Kilisha asked.

The spriggan twisted its head to stare solemnly at her. "Don't know names," it said.

"Point."

The spriggan hung down from Kelder's hand and slowly turned its head back and forth, taking in the scenery.

"World upside-down," it said. "Makes head hurt, thinking directions this way up."

Kelder grabbed the creature around the chest with his other hand and turned it over, releasing his hold on its foot.

"Better!" the spriggan squeaked, as it looked around again. "Came *that* way!" It pointed back up Steep Street. "Around corner."

"You mean the bench was on Straight Street?"

"Street was straight," the spriggan said uncertainly.

"Did it go *up* the street, or *down*?" Kilisha asked. Kelder tightened his grip warningly.

"Up!" It was plainly relieved to be able to answer this one.

"Good," Kelder said. He lowered his hand.

"Don't let it—" Kilisha began, but it was too late; Kelder had released the spriggan, and it had promptly dashed away, down and across Old Seagate Street, toward the rocky shoreline.

"—go," she finished. She sighed, then beckoned to Kelder. "Come on."

Kelder got to his feet and looked around for the spriggan, but it had vanished from sight. He brushed off his tunic, straightened his belt, and followed Kilisha as she climbed back up Steep Street, tugging the chair behind her.

Ten minutes later they had crossed Fortress Street and the dry moat and neared the top of Straight Street; the huge red doors of the Fortress loomed before them, tightly shut, a spear-wielding guardsman to either side. The chair seemed reluctant to go anywhere near these two men, and hung back at the end of its rope.

There was no bench in sight.

The soldiers were looking at them with interest; Kilisha supposed they were wondering what a tax collector and fellow guardsman was doing here, and how he had managed to get his clothes so dirty.

And, she supposed, they could see the chair. People out walking a chair on a leash were not a common sight in Ethshar of the Rocks.

"Hai!" she called. "Have you seen an animated bench running loose? Seats two, with a humped back?"

"That way," the right-hand guard replied, pointing north with his spear. "We wouldn't let it too close to the door here—you understand, in case it had some sort of dangerous spell on it, an explosive rune or something. We had to chase it away three or four times before it gave up."

"Did it have any spriggans on it?" Kilisha asked. If it had still had one or more to dislodge that might help locate it.

The guards exchanged glances. "I didn't see any," the left-hand guard replied.

"Excuse me for asking," the right-hand guard said, "but what's going on? I expect our captain will want a proper report, what with all this fuss about the usurper in Ethshar of the Sands. Did *she* send this bench?"

"No," Kilisha said. "Nobody sent it. An animation spell went wrong, and it ran away from home. It's harmless, so far as we know."

"It seemed to want to get into the Fortress."

Kilisha turned up an empty palm. "I don't know why," she said. "It can't talk, so we don't know much about its thinking. We don't know why it ran away in the first place, let alone why it came here."

"Fun!" the spriggan on her shoulder suddenly piped. Kilisha resisted the temptation to punch it.

"Well, it did seem to want to get in, so maybe it went to try the other door," the left-hand guard suggested.

"Thank you," Kilisha said with a curtsy. "We'll try there."

"Is that chair . . . I mean . . ." The left-hand guard pointed down the street, along the rope.

"That's from the same ruined spell," Kilisha said.

"Should we know who *you* are?" the right-hand guard asked, looking at Kelder.

"Kelder Goran's son of Sixth Company, on tax duty," Kelder replied. "I was the one who interrupted the animation spell, and I can't collect the wizard's taxes until it's fixed."

Kilisha doubted this was true—Yara could probably pay the taxes—but didn't say anything to contradict it.

"Which wizard?" the guard asked.

"Ithanalin the Wise," Kilisha said. "I'm his apprentice."

"Ah." The soldier straightened up, raising his spear into position. "Well, good luck, then."

A sudden thought struck Kilisha. "If the bench did get inside—well, maybe we should look in the Fortress."

"It didn't get inside," the guard said. "*Nobody* gets inside today without special permission, because of the usurper."

"Oh," Kilisha said. "Then we'll check at the other door. Thank you!" She curtsied again, then turned away.

They made their way back out across the bridge over the moat and turned left onto Fortress Street, toward the north door.

As they walked Kilisha looked first to the left, where massive jagged revetments rose up from the moat guarding the Fortress grounds, then to the right, where the mansions of the older noble families stood. The contrast was not as striking as one might have expected; these old homes were themselves forbidding structures of blackened stone, nothing like the glittering palaces the wealthy merchants and newcomers to the overlord's court had built themselves over in Highside.

She could see no openings in the mansion facades, no alleyways where the bench might have concealed itself—but on the other side, might it have fallen down into the moat? If it had been turned away at the north door and had still wanted to get into the Fortress, crossing the moat and finding an opening was the only other possible route. She crossed to the left side, paying out more line so that the chair could continue down the center of the street; when she reached the curb she paused to lean over the iron railing and peer down into the ditch.

The bottom of the moat was lined with a thin layer of black mud and debris, and she could see a few discarded odds and ends—a woman's hair clip, a wooden doll's crudely carved arm, a boot with the sole torn away. There was no bench in sight, nor did she think there was anywhere one might hide.

"What are you doing?" Kelder asked, stopping a few feet away while the chair wandered aimlessly about the street, the rope swinging back and forth as it moved.

Kilisha looked up from the moat to answer Kelder's question, and suddenly there it was, just around the curve of the street, clearly visible through the railing—the bench!

There were no spriggans clinging to it; it had apparently finally managed to dislodge them all. It did not seem to be in any great hurry; instead of the headlong dash she had seen before it was ambling along Fortress Street at no great speed, just inside the railing, heading directly toward them.

"There it is," she hissed to Kelder.

"I see it," he hissed back, crouching.

"Bench!" Sprigganalin shrieked.

"*Augh!*" Kilisha said, her left hand flying up and stopping just short of grabbing the spriggan by the throat. "*Shut up!*"

The bench had stopped dead at the sound of the spriggan's voice; it seemed to be wary, but it wasn't fleeing.

Yet.

"Circle around," Kilisha whispered to Kelder. "Get behind it."

"Right," he said, veering sideways across Fortress Street, while Kilisha stayed close to the railing.

The bench turned, keeping its front toward Kelder. "I think it recognizes him," Kilisha whispered to the spriggan.

"You bet!" the spriggan said cheerfully—and loudly. The bench abruptly swung back to face Kilisha.

It didn't like spriggans, Kilisha thought. That was why it had gone charging off, trying to dislodge them. If the spriggan kept talking the bench might run away again, frightened off by the sound of its voice.

For the present, though, its attention was focused on her and the spriggan, and Kelder was circling around it. He was on the far side of the street, creeping along the front of an ancient stone mansion, his eyes fixed on the bench.

"Do you think it sees us?" Kilisha asked the spriggan.

She knew perfectly well that the bench knew where they were—though "see" might be the wrong word, since it had no eyes. Just how animated objects perceived their surroundings was a mystery even to the wizards who created them; when customers asked, the universal reply was simply, "It's magic." She was just hoping to keep the furniture confused, unsure whether to flee, by asking foolish questions.

Kelder was now safely north of the bench, moving away from the facade toward the center of the street; if the bench tried to run he should be able to grab it. Kilisha slid her hand along the iron rail and took a step forward, around the curve to where she could look at the bench without the railing between them.

"Why, hello there, bench!" she said. "Do you remember me? You used to stand in the parlor of my master's house."

The bench took a step back. Kelder moved across the street behind it, getting ready to lunge. Kilisha slid farther along the railing.

The bench backed away another longer, faster step, then started to run—but Kelder was coming up behind it, so it changed direction quickly, trying to double back south, past Kilisha.

That was exactly what Kilisha had hoped for. She ran northward *past* the bench, then cut east, across the street.

And the bench ran into the rope strung between Kilisha's hand and the chair.

The impact was enough to jerk Kilisha's hand painfully, and the chair toppled over completely and lay thrashing in the dirt.

Kilisha wasted no time in racing around behind the bench, encircling it in the rope, before it could step over the rope or slide under it. The chair was dragged up against the bench, entangling the two pieces so that neither could move freely, and allowing Kilisha to spiral in, wrapping the rope around them both and tying them together.

"There," she said, satisfied with her performance. She called to Kelder, "Now, sir, could you give me a hand?"

A few minutes later the bench was tied securely to one end of the rope, the chair to the other, and Kilisha held the center in both hands, leading the reluctant furniture back down the hillside toward Wizard Street.

Sometimes the two pieces cooperated, and sometimes they didn't; holding them was often a struggle, and more than once Kilisha had to call for Kelder's help in holding onto the rope. She almost wished she *had* used the Spell of Optimum Strength. By the time they got safely back to Ithanalin's shop they were exhausted—but more of the furniture was back where it belonged, and Kilisha was pleased.

❦

Chapter Seventeen

Kilisha did not trust the bench and chair; they had put up too much of a fight. The chair seemed glad to be home, running around the parlor like a puppy rediscovering familiar surroundings, but all the same, Kilisha made sure the door was closed and locked before she let go of the rope for even an instant.

And she didn't untie either piece at first; instead she looped the rope around the door latch and left Kelder to guard it while she went to make more permanent arrangements. The line holding the coatrack was tied to a lamp bracket, but somehow Kilisha doubted that would be strong enough to hold the bench; she wanted to find something that would be.

Yara had heard the noise of her return, and the thumping and rattling as the bench and chair moved around the parlor; she met Kilisha in the workshop, worried by the racket but eager to know what was happening.

"I got them, Mistress," Kilisha explained, pointing. "Kelder had them locked up, and I stupidly let them out, but we followed them and caught them again. Now we need to tie them up so they won't get away again, but I'm not sure how to do it."

"Them?" Yara peered past her into the parlor.

Kelder waved cheerily at her, and Yara retreated slightly.

"The chair and the bench," Kilisha explained. "We still need to find the couch. And right now I'm trying to think what we can tie these two to. I don't want them in the workshop; they might break things or spill something."

"I don't want them in the kitchen, either, or anywhere upstairs," Yara agreed. "They belong in the parlor."

"But there's nothing solid to *tie* them to in the parlor!"

"Oh." Yara considered for a moment, then turned up a palm. "I'm sure you'll think of something. I'd best go tell the children what's happening."

"Yes, Mistress," Kilisha said, suppressing a sigh. She looked around the workshop, but inspiration failed to strike.

From the doorway, Kelder said, "I overheard. Really, they should be secured to the house itself, if there's any way to do that."

"I don't see any way," Kilisha said. "Not in the parlor."

Kelder turned and gazed critically about, then suggested, "You could run a rope out the door and back in a window, then tie the furniture to both ends, making a loop. That would hold them."

"But then we couldn't close the door or the window," Kilisha said, stepping up to him and pointing.

Kelder, startled, looked at the front door and realized she was right.

"The barracks doors generally don't fit their frames that well," he said apologetically. "There's room enough for a rope underneath most of them."

"The barracks isn't the home of a respectable wizard," Kilisha retorted.

"This time of year, you could leave the door open—"

"No," Kilisha said instantly. Keeping the captured pieces in the house was quite enough to worry about with the door securely closed.

"Well, then, I don't know."

"I'll think of something," Kilisha said. "Can you stay for a little while longer, and help out? We still need to secure these, and find the couch."

"A little while," Kelder agreed. "Not all afternoon."

"The afternoon's already half gone," Kilisha said.

"Well, I can't stay for the entire other half! I do have my duties, you know—including collecting the tax on this house."

"I told you earlier, I don't have anything to do with that," Kilisha said. "You'll have to talk to Yara."

"Then I'll need to talk to Yara. Maybe I can do that while you find the missing couch."

"I don't . . ." Kilisha began, intending to say she didn't know how to find the couch, but then she remembered her earlier plan— levitating up above the city and looking for it from the air.

This was clearly a good time for that, while the daylight was still bright and the shadows not yet too long or deep. She could float up and look down at the streets and chimney tops . . .

And a sudden inspiration struck her.

"You talk to Yara," she said. "Hold onto that rope, don't let the furniture escape. There's something I need to do. It should only take a few minutes."

"What?"

"I've figured out how to tie them to the house, and maybe I can find the couch at the same time. You hold them and talk to Yara. It shouldn't take more than half an hour, at most."

"Well . . ."

"Thank you!"

With that, without giving Kelder any more time to protest, she dashed through the workshop to the kitchen, and on through to the scullery at the back of the house.

There was another coil of rope, as she had remembered, hanging by the door there; she snatched it up, then looked around.

Yes, the big axe was still there. Kilisha had never seen Ithanalin use it; just once she had seen Yara whack off a pig's head with it, when the household was expecting an important dinner guest and wanted the freshest possible meat, and Yara had been sufficiently distressed with the resulting mess that she had announced she would never do it again. Usually the axe simply sat unused in the corner, gathering cobwebs.

It should do perfectly. Kilisha picked it up, then almost dropped it again upon discovering how heavy it was. She hefted it up onto a stone bench, then tied one end of her new rope securely around the axe handle.

Now it was time to levitate.

She hesitated. Which spell should she use?

Tracel's Levitation required a rooster's toe, a vial containing a raindrop caught in midair, her athame, and a few minutes of ritual. It would allow her to rise straight up to whatever height she chose—but it would provide no horizontal movement unless she allowed herself to drift on the breeze. A single word would then lower her gently back to earth.

Varen's Levitation called for a silver coin, a seagull's feather, a lantern, and again, her athame and a few minutes of chanting and gestures. It would let her walk up an invisible staircase in the air, then walk on air, and then descend again—but only once each. She could not ascend, then go level, then ascend again.

Neither set of ingredients was at all onerous; the raindrop was the only remotely difficult item, and ever since Ithanalin had first taken her on as an apprentice one of her duties had been to collect a few drops from every storm. There was a rack of tightly stopped vials in a drawer in the workshop, and while some of the captured water had undoubtedly managed to evaporate by now, she was sure there were at least half a dozen still available for her use. She wouldn't be using up anything especially precious with either spell.

Nor was either one particularly difficult. Varen's was definitely a higher-order spell than Tracel's, requiring a more agile set of fingers and some more esoteric vocabulary, but both were well within her own abilities. Tracel's ascent was faster and less tiring, since the user simply rose like a bubble instead of walking up the air, but the horizontal element of Varen's was very useful. . . .

And it was that horizontal component that decided her. She needed to place the axe and rope. It would have to be Varen's.

Coin, feather, lantern, athame. . . . She ambled back to the workshop, the coil of rope on one arm and the axe clutched in both hands, as she reviewed the spell.

"What are you doing with *that*?" Kelder demanded from the parlor door. "I thought you needed them intact! If you just wanted them smashed, we could have done that at the shipyard."

Startled out of her reverie, Kilisha looked down at the axe, then up at Kelder. She could hear the bench thumping, and see the rope in Kelder's hand jerking with its movements.

"No, no," she said. "It's not for that. We *do* need them intact. I would never hurt them!"

The thumping stopped.

"Then why do you have that axe?" Kelder demanded.

"Not to smash anything," Kilisha said. "You'll see."

"Do you—"

"Could you hold this for a moment?" Kilisha interrupted, holding out the axe. "I need to work a spell."

Kelder blinked at her. "I thought you . . . you said earlier you didn't have any magic."

Kilisha stared at him in surprise. "I said I didn't have any *with* me!" she said. "This house is *full* of magic."

"Oh," Kelder said. "Of course. I'm sorry. I mean, I know you're a wizard's apprentice, but you don't *look* like a wizard."

"Why do people keep saying that?" Kilisha said. "What does a wizard look like?"

"Like that," Kelder said, pointing at the covered shape of Ithanalin in the corner.

"Like a middle-aged man? You know there are female wizards, and wizards of all ages."

"Yes, but you look so . . . so . . ."

"So ordinary?"

"So sweet," Kelder said. "Wizards are supposed to have a little meanness to them."

Kilisha was struck momentarily silent by this astonishing statement, then managed, "I think you're thinking of demonologists or warlocks, not wizards."

"Wizards, too," Kelder said. "Not as much as the others, true, but a little. Witches can be sweet, sometimes."

"So can wizards," Kilisha said. "Not that I am, myself. Ithanalin's sweet, but I have too much of a temper."

Kelder started to reply, then thought better of it. "What do
you want me to do?" he asked.

Relieved to have the conversation back on its intended course,
Kilisha thrust the axe at him. "Hold this while I work a spell," she
said.

"Right," he said, taking the axe.

Once free of her burden, Kilisha turned to the workbench and
tried to get her thoughts back to the business of magic. Coin,
feather, lantern . . .

It was only after she had the ingredients on the bench and had
begun the ritual, placing the coin inside the lantern and magically
impaling it with the seagull feather, that she remembered a drawback to Varen's Levitation, as compared to Tracel's. She would
need to carry the lantern with her, which would be inconvenient;
it would make it that much harder to position the axe and rope.
Tracel's required no such burden.

For that matter, if she had used a potion for Varen's, then it
wouldn't need the lantern, either—the potion in her belly would
have been an adequate substitute. Unfortunately, the potion
wouldn't be ready until late that night, and she did not want to
put this off any longer.

She continued, using her athame to weave magic into the air,
and a moment later she turned from the workbench, the lantern in
her hand and her athame back in its sheath on her belt.

Kelder had watched this all from the doorway, of course; she
knew no one could resist the temptation to watch a wizard at work.
Most spells were actually quite boring for a nonparticipant to ob-
serve, but wizardry had such an air of secrets and mystery built
up around it—built up deliberately by the Guild—that people
would always watch for a few minutes.

"Give me the axe and open the front door," she said, holding
out her free hand.

Kelder handed her the axe, puzzled. He tried to hand her the coil of rope, too, but she had no hands left to take it, and she let it drop to the floor.

That didn't matter; it was tied to the axe at one end.

"Open the door," she repeated, standing where she was.

She *had* to stand where she was; from now on each step she took would carry her higher into the air.

"The rope . . ."

"Don't worry about the rope, so long as it's tied to the axe. Just open the door." She took her first step, keeping it as long and low as possible.

Her foot came to rest perhaps two inches off the floor.

Kelder didn't notice; he had turned to obey.

"Hold the furniture," she said, as she began walking forward, still making her steps as long as possible.

She crossed the parlor in half a dozen stretching steps, taking her almost three feet upward; she had to squat down on empty air to get through the door.

Once past that obstacle, though, everything was easy. The air above the street was open and unlimited. She smiled, and began marching upward.

Chapter Eighteen

Kilisha had not been able to get the coil of rope arranged properly while she held the axe and lantern, so now, as she walked up into the air, it trailed behind her as she rose. The line gradually unwound from Kelder's hand. The soldier stood in the doorway of Ithanalin's shop, watching her climb.

A few people on the street turned to stare or point at her, but no one said anything to her or made any move to interfere. A levitating magician was only a mildly unusual sight here on Wizard Street, after all.

She paid little attention to the observers, except to wish that she had thought to wear something under her skirt. After all, they weren't really interested in looking at *her*—she was completely ordinary-looking, and knew it. They were just looking at her magic, at the ability to rise up into the air. That they might catch a glimpse under her skirt was merely a small bonus for the young men among them.

The first time she had tried this spell and gone walking about over people's heads that aspect of the situation had occurred to her very suddenly, and she had been as utterly mortified as only a fourteen-year-old girl can be and had almost dropped the lantern in her desperation to rearrange her clothing; only Ithanalin, levitating beside her, had prevented a fall by grabbing her hand before she could release the lantern's handle.

Now, a little older and wiser, she felt only a mild regret that she had not remembered that people might be looking up at her from beneath. She ignored it, and concentrated on the task at hand—or tasks, rather, as she had two purposes in her ascent.

Given the nature of the spell, she decided to start with the one that required greater altitude—searching for the couch. That meant hauling the heavy axe and dangling rope that much farther into the sky, but it really seemed the safer, more sensible approach. She heightened and shortened her stride, climbing upward.

It was really remarkable how very solid the air felt beneath her feet. She needed merely to place a foot as if on a stair, and the stair would somehow *be* there, invisible but quite firm.

Magic, she thought, was wonderful stuff; at times like this she loved being a wizard.

Of course, she thought as she glanced down along the trailing rope, it was also very *dangerous* stuff; if she released her hold on the lantern for even an instant those sturdy steps beneath her feet would suddenly once again be nothing but empty air, and she would plummet to the hard-packed earth thirty feet below. From this height the fall probably wouldn't kill her, but it would not be pleasant—and she intended to go much higher than this. She was level with most of the rooftops now, higher than some, and could see perhaps half a mile along Wizard Street, but most of the city was still hidden.

Magic was dangerous, yes—she was up here in the first place because Ithanalin had discovered that.

She tightened her grip on the lantern and marched onward and upward, passing gables and chimneys; the sharp sea breeze whipped her hair and skirt about her as she cleared the obstructing buildings. Below her the end of the rope finally rose out of Kelder's reach and began wiggling back and forth, squirming like a snake, as the winds caught it and played with it.

The axe really was heavy, and the climb was long; she wondered whether she should have used the Spell of Optimum Strength, or some other endurance spell, before beginning her ascent.

That would have taken too long, though. She sighed, and continued climbing.

She could see across the shops and houses and courtyards to the north and south now, to the East Road to the north and the tangle of smaller streets to the south. In the slanting light of late afternoon the gray slate of the steeply angled roofs looked black on the eastern slopes and pale on the west, so that each block of housing looked like a gigantic loop of herringbone. She carefully noted the distinguishing features of Ithanalin's shop, so that she could find it again on the way down—the shape of the chimney pots, the slightly asymmetrical gable that she knew was the niche where her own bed lay, and so on; four houses from the west end of the block and seven from the east.

The buildings were not what she was up here to look at, though; once she was sure she would recognize her home she forced herself to focus on the spaces between the houses, the streets and courtyards.

A red velvet couch ought to stand out even in the shadows, she thought. Most of the people in the streets wore brown or gray or black or white or blue or green; very few were dressed in red. And a couch would be horizontal, where pedestrians were vertical.

The couch was nowhere to be seen in the long visible expanse of Wizard Street, or in the courtyards on either side.

She climbed higher, turning her steps to the right and spiraling upward, until she could see the blue of the reservoir to the northeast and the red-and-gold banners of the Arena to the south, flickering in the wind. She rose still higher, until the looming gray mass of the Fortress and the twin towers of Eastgate were visible. The people below her looked like little more than dots now; she slowed her ascent but did not stop, because she knew that once she stopped she could not rise any farther.

Beyond the Arena, far to the southeast, she could glimpse the parade ground in Wargate; to the west lay the shipyards, just as she had seen them earlier that day. Market lay beyond the reservoir, and Farmgate beyond that.

And at last she stopped; if she went any higher she thought she might well miss something as small as a couch. She stood in midair and looked down past her bare feet; the wind tore at her hair and tunic, and her skirt flapped like a ship's pennant. The dangling rope was writhing and coiling madly below her.

She frowned. She had probably, she decided, come too high after all. She could move horizontally, as long as she didn't change altitude or release the lantern, and hadn't needed to come up this far.

She shuddered at the thought of dropping the lantern; a fall from this height *would* kill her, beyond question. At least the chill of the wind kept her hands from getting too sweaty and weakening her hold!

She shifted her grip on the axe and began walking westward; that was the direction Kelder said the couch had gone before he lost sight of it. It had fled up the East Road, toward the Fortress.

The bench had been headed for the Fortress, too—was there something there that had attracted the furniture, perhaps? Before she had thought that perhaps the attraction was Ithanalin's customer on Steep Street, but the bench had definitely aimed for the Fortress, instead.

That was the original heart of the city, of course. Ethshar of the Rocks had begun as a military outpost during the Great War, at the extreme western limit of Old Ethshar's power, and a watchtower had been built atop the cliffs on the headland. The watchtower had been expanded gradually over the long years of conflict, and then finally torn down and replaced with the Fortress—a massive stone complex dominating the coastline and serving as the headquarters for the entire Western Command. It had been surrounded only by camps at first, but gradually a few other buildings had appeared, and the city walls had been built to protect the camps.

And then, after hundreds of years of fighting, the war ended. General Gor declared himself overlord, and the tents and huts were replaced by houses and shops, the Arena and Baths were built, the shipyards converted from building warships to freighters . . . but in the subsequent two hundred and thirty years Lord Gor and his heirs had never seen any reason to move themselves or their government out of the Fortress.

The Fortress was the largest and oldest building for fifty leagues in every direction; perhaps it had somehow accumulated some sort of magical attraction that had affected the furniture.

Kilisha didn't find it very attractive, though, as she walked over the East Road toward it. It was a huge, ugly gray mass. In most of the city, homes and businesses were decorated with carvings and paint, but the Fortress walls were flat slabs of blank stone, the windows—and only the upper floors *had* any windows—simple unadorned rectangles.

The top, largely invisible to anyone but a magician, was a little more interesting than the sides; the battlements were mere elevated walkways surrounding a stone courtyard where Kilisha could see guardsmen marching in formation. There were guards posted along the ramparts, as well, which seemed foolish in a city that had been at peace for more than two centuries.

But then she remembered that a usurper had just driven out the overlord of Ethshar of the Sands. Perhaps the walls had not always been manned, but were now guarded against this Tabaea and her followers.

In any case, the Fortress guards were not her concern. She was trying to find the couch.

She could see nothing the right shade of red anywhere along the East Road, nor in the Fortress rooftop courtyard, nor on Wizard Street. The streets and alleys of Hillside, the district surrounding the Fortress, were so steep and tangled that she could see very little of what might be on them.

The other high hill in the city was Highside, to the northeast of Hillside, and that was dominated by the mansions of the city's wealthiest families; there she could see into not just streets and courtyards, but gardens and plazas. Instead of being crowded together, as the homes were throughout most of the city, the mansions of Highside were elegantly placed amid lawns and fountains and flowers, all behind high fences and walls—but from her present height the fences and walls were meaningless. She glanced in that direction—and froze.

Red! The deep, rich red she remembered. . . .

She leaned forward, peering down, and then snorted at her own foolishness. That was a rose garden. And over there was a flower bed of something else nearly the right color.

The couch might be there somewhere, of course, perhaps under the willows, or in one of the pergolas or gazebos, or simply behind a mansion, where she couldn't see it from her present position.

And that was in the open terrain of Highside. Beyond it, to the west, to the north of Hillside, lay the mazes of alleys and passages of Bywater. That had been a fishing village supplying food to the troops during the Great War, and the city had absorbed it but had never straightened out its tangled streets. Upper stories of the older structures there were often cantilevered out, shading the street beneath; it was said that in some neighborhoods lovers could hold hands by leaning out the upstairs windows on either side of the street. If the couch was beneath one of those overhangs . . .

And beyond Bywater was Northshore, and then Cliffgate, and then eastward along the city wall Northgate and Northmark, to Farmgate in the northeast corner. Then Eastgate and Eastside and Wargate and Newgate, and the New Quarter in its own little walled-in area outside the original wall, and in the south end Grandgate and Southgate, and closer in Southport and Southside and Bath and Arena and Crafton and Seagate and Norcross and Lakeshore and Center City and Northside and the Merchant Quarter, each district a tangle of streets and buildings and courts.

The city was just too large for one person to search, even from the air, without some sort of guidance.

For *one* person.

She would need to find help. All those districts, all those streets and houses, were full of people, and surely *someone* must have seen where the couch went. If she really wanted to find the couch she would need to enlist the aid of as many of those people as she possibly could, and keep on asking until she found someone who knew where it had gone.

Either that, or she would need to find some magic that would locate the fugitive furniture.

She sighed. It would have been so much simpler if she had spotted it from up here—but she could see no sign of it.

She took another step, but this time let her forward foot sink below the other, beginning her descent.

Her other task remained to be done, of course, so the spell hadn't been a total waste of time, and she would also keep looking on the way down, in hopes of catching a glimpse of the couch, but her earlier high hopes had vanished. Her steps were heavy as she marched down the air.

A flicker of movement in an alley caught her eye at one point, but appeared to be merely a dog; other than that she descended without incident until she was walking just a dozen feet above Ithanalin's own roof, the rope trailing across the slates.

And here she slowed, spiraling in carefully toward the chimney that vented the parlor hearth. While still holding the lantern she caught up the dangling rope across her forearm, working it across until the free end hung down just a few feet. She twisted and maneuvered it, working intently until that loose end slid down into the open chimney.

She smiled, and quickly began feeding the line down the flue as she continued to walk in slowly sinking circles around the opening.

Finally the entire rope was hanging down into the chimney, just inches below her; she reached down and dropped the axe into place across the opening.

Now all she had to do was go back into the house and fish the bottom of the rope out of the fireplace. As long as the knots held, anything tied to that line was going to stay in the parlor. No bench or chair or couch could possibly pull that axe down the chimney!

That done, she raised the lantern high as she marched out over the street and back down to earth.

Chapter Nineteen

By suppertime Yara had paid Kelder the household's tax and the guardsman had gone about his business, though he promised to stop in later to check on the situation—he said he still felt partially responsible for Ithanalin's condition. Kilisha had secured the table, chair, bench, and coatrack in the parlor with various cords and leashes tied to the rope in the chimney, had taken the rug from the pantry and packed it into a solid box, and had then moved the locked boxes containing the dish, spoon, and rug into the workshop, to have them all in one place. The latch was still firmly attached to the front door, and the mirror still hung in its accustomed place on the parlor wall. Ithanalin's body was in the workshop with a sheet draped over it, so that any visitors would not see what had happened—and so Kilisha wouldn't feel as if her master was watching her whenever she tried to do any magic.

The spriggan was unsecured, and that worried the apprentice, but she saw nothing she could do about it while the athame's magic resided in the creature and its fingernails served as lockpicks. Any cords used to bind it would fall away uselessly, and any attempt to lock it into a box or closet would hold it only for the few seconds it needed to spring the lock. Asking the rug to hold it might work, but she didn't really feel as if she could trust the rug unless Yara kept an eye on it, and Yara had better things to do with her time.

Perhaps if they found a box that relied on bolts and bars too heavy for the spriggan to work, or arranged so it couldn't reach them . . .

But spriggans were much stronger than they looked, and in-humanly flexible, and she really couldn't be sure anything could hold it. Better, she thought, to avoid antagonizing it and to instead rely on the fragment of Ithanalin's personality it held. After all, she might well need its active cooperation during the restorative spell.

The dark brown goo on the workbench was still simmering over the oil lamp, and Kilisha still had no idea what it was; she had asked the spriggan and received merely a turned-up palm and "Don't remember" as a reply. The mixture's savory smell had turned to a sort of burned odor, then that had faded away, leaving a faint sourness in the air. Kilisha was fairly sure that it was no longer fit for whatever it had been intended to do or be. Still, she could see nothing sensible to do but leave it where it was. Thinking it the safest course she had refilled the lamp when it burned low, her hands trembling in case that altered the spell and triggered some catastrophe, but nothing untoward had happened.

She had not yet had a chance to practice Javan's Restorative; the pursuit of the chair and bench, and the levitation to look for the couch and put the line down the chimney, had eaten up most of the day, and besides, she still had no jewelweed. She could not attempt the spell until she had all the ingredients.

Of course, she also did not yet have the red velvet couch. That was the only piece of furniture still missing.

She had *most* of what she needed to restore her master, though, after less than two full days. She was reasonably pleased with her-self as she sat at the kitchen table with the children, eating the boiled supper Yara had prepared—but still, every so often she glanced uncomfortably at the empty seat at the head of the table.

"Is Dad going to stay petrified very long?" Lirrin asked, as she reached for the spiced green beans.

"I hope not, sweetie," Yara said, glancing at Kilisha.

"He's not really petrified," Kilisha said. "He isn't stone, he's just . . . well, deanimated."

"Is he going to stay that way?" Telleth asked. Where Lirrin had sounded worried, Telleth sounded belligerent.

"Not if I can help it," Kilisha said. "I still need two more things before I can bring him back to normal."

"What are they?" Lirrin asked.

"I still need something called jewelweed for the spell," Kilisha explained. "I don't know what it is—a plant of some kind, I suppose. There might even be some in the workshop, but I can't tell."

"We can get that from an herbalist, I'm sure," Yara said. "Or from Kara, if it's something only wizards use."

"Who's Kara?" Lirrin asked.

"Kara's Arcana, on Arena Street," Kilisha said.

"That's where Dad gets lots of his stuff," Telleth explained to his sister.

"I want Daddy back," Pirra said, clearly on the verge of tears.

"We all do," Yara said quickly. Then she turned to Kilisha. "Jewelweed?" she said. "You know, I said I don't know what it is, but I think I remember it now. It has white flowers, and the leaves have healing properties, if I remember correctly. We can find that."

"I'm sure we can," Kilisha agreed.

"You said you need two more things. What's the other one?"

"The red velvet couch from the parlor."

"Do you know where it is?"

"No." Kilisha shook her head. "It ran off to the west, with the other furniture, and Kelder chased it, but he lost track of it. I tried to spot it—I levitated up several hundred feet and looked at all the streets and courtyards I could, but I didn't see it anywhere. I think I'll need help finding it."

"Who's Kelder?" Pirra demanded.

"The soldier who was here today," Kilisha explained.

"Oh," Lirrin said. "There's a boy across the back court called Kelder; I thought maybe you meant him."

"There are a *lot* of people named Kelder," Yara remarked.

"Is the soldier going to bring Daddy back?" Pirra asked.

"No," Kilisha said. "We need a spell to do that, not a soldier. But maybe he can find the velvet couch."

"Can I help look for it?"

Kilisha smiled. "Maybe," she said. "*Anyone* who can help find it is welcome, as far as I'm concerned. We'll all start looking in the morning, shall we? And we'll ask all our friends and neighbors to help."

"Couldn't we look tonight?" Telleth asked. "The torches are bright, and a couch is too big to hide in holes or anything."

"I want Daddy back," Pirra said.

Kilisha looked at Yara, who said, "We might look a little. But it probably isn't anywhere on Wizard Street, and I don't want to go too far in the dark."

"Kelder said he last saw it on the East Road," Kilisha said. "It's not on the street now, at least it wasn't when I was looking a couple of hours ago, but it might have ducked in somewhere."

"The East Road?" Yara said. Kilisha nodded.

"Headed for the *gates*?" Lirrin asked, horrified.

"No, no," Kilisha said quickly. "Headed *west* on the East Road, toward the Fortress." The idea that it might have doubled back eastward, or turned north or south and headed for one of the gates, was not a pleasant one—but she couldn't rule it out. Maybe she hadn't spotted it from the air because she hadn't looked outside the walls. . . .

She would want to check on that tomorrow, if the couch didn't turn up. She would ask the guards at the gates.

At least nobody was likely to have not noticed an animated couch, or forgotten seeing it.

"It's in the Fortress, then?" Telleth asked.

"Oh, I don't think so," Kilisha said. "How would it get inside?"

"Through a door!" Pirra said.

"The doors were closed," Kilisha said. "We were over there today, and it's all closed up tight because of some trouble in Ethshar of the Sands. The couch might be *near* there—it was headed in that direction—but how could it have gotten inside with the guards there and the doors locked?"

"Oh."

That ended the conversation for a time, and the five of them ate in silence. A few minutes later Kilisha took a final gulp of small beer, then pushed back her chair. "I need to finish that potion I was making," she said as she rose. "I thought it might help catch the escaped furniture."

"I thought you said you just need the couch and the jewelweed," Yara said.

"I *do* just need the couch and the jewelweed," Kilisha agreed. "But I didn't know that when I started the potion last night."

"Then why are you finishing the potion?" Telleth asked.

"Well, partly because it still might be useful in finding and catching the couch," Kilisha said, "but mostly because if I don't, who knows what could happen? Unfinished spells can go wrong, the way the master's did."

"You mean *you'd* turn into a statue?" Pirra asked, her eyes widening.

"Maybe. Or something else entirely might happen. You never know what might happen when magic goes wrong. They say there's a place in the Small Kingdoms where there's a pillar of fire a hundred feet tall that's been burning for a hundred years because somebody sneezed while doing a spell. And some people say that spriggans come from a magic mirror spell that someone did wrong, which is why they started turning up suddenly just a few years ago."

"And Dad accidentally turned Lirrin and me into tree squids once," Telleth said. "Right here in the kitchen." He grimaced, and added, "It felt really *weird*."

"Exactly. And he turned Istram into a platypus, as well. The master has always told me how very important it is to be careful with magic, and never leave a spell unfinished, so I'll be finishing the potion tonight."

"What about that stuff on the workbench, then?" Telleth asked. "The brown stuff in the bowl. Isn't that an unfinished spell?"

"Yes, it is, but I don't know what kind," Kilisha said, frowning. "I don't know *how* to finish it, and I want to bring the master back to life as quickly as possible so *he* can deal with it!"

"How did *you* know about that bowl?" Yara asked, glaring at Telleth. "Have you been snooping in your father's workshop?"

"I just *looked!*" Telleth protested. "I didn't touch anything! I didn't even *breathe* on it!"

"Well, don't even *look* unless Thani or Kilisha says it's all right!" She looked up from her son to the apprentice. "Is there anything we can do while you're finishing the potion?"

"I suppose it's too late to get the jewelweed," Kilisha said. "The herbalists will be closed by now. But if you can think of any way to find the couch, that would be good."

"I could ask around," Yara said thoughtfully. "Maybe buy a divination from one of the neighbors?"

"If you think it's a good idea," Kilisha said. "I don't have the money for one." Before any of the children could speak, she added, "And I don't know any myself."

"Thani never liked divinations," Yara said. "He said that people always want to argue if they don't like the answers they get."

"He's probably right," Kilisha said.

"So he never learned any," Yara said. "He said he could always buy one if he needed it."

"Well, if he were animate right now, he could."

"I'll talk to some of the neighbors," Yara said. "You finish your potion."

"Yes, Mistress," Kilisha said, bowing her head politely before she headed for the workshop.

A few minutes later, as she gathered the materials to complete her potions, she glanced uneasily at the bowl on the lamp; it was still simmering. She sighed.

It would certainly simplify matters if Yara did hire a magician who could find the couch by magic, but Kilisha had doubts about the idea. At least for wizards, divinations and other information spells tended to do strange things when enchanted objects were involved—which was another reason Ithanalin had never liked them. Some of them would answer the question asked, but in the most useless way possible—for example, if a wizard asked, "Where is the red velvet couch that stood in Ithanalin's parlor?" the answer might be, "In the Hegemony of the Three Ethshars," or "In a house," or "Seven feet to the north of a purple drape." Learning to phrase questions so as to obtain useful answers was as tricky as learning the actual spells, so that wizards who did divinations often had no time to learn much of anything else.

Kilisha suspected that they would do better to question neighbors, or to offer a reward, or even to interrogate spriggans, who seemed to roam everywhere in the city and who could clearly "smell" wizardry, than they would to buy a divination.

And when they *did* find the couch, however they managed it, she wanted to be better prepared than she had been that afternoon in pursuit of the bench. Catching the bench in the rope and then dragging the bench and chair home had been difficult and exhausting.

That was where these potions came in, and why she was so eager to finish them. She had misled the master's family slightly; while it was certainly true that neglected spells could go spectacularly wrong, the Adaptable Potion was flexible and relatively harmless. She could have left it unfinished for at least another day or so without harm, and simply leaving it entirely uncharged would probably have been safe.

Probably. She had never actually done it, or spoken to anyone who had. When she was first learning to make the potion she had always charged it with *something*, even if it was just the Iridescent Amusement.

This time, though, she wanted a levitation potion.

Tracel's Levitation would work only on the person who cast the spell—or drank the potion, in this case. Whoever drank the potion could then rise to any height she desired, and stay there, drifting on the wind, until she spoke the word that broke the spell and lowered her gently to the ground. That might be useful for getting a good look around, seeing over obstructions, and that sort of thing, but she couldn't see how it would help capture or transport a couch. She still intended to make it anyway, since it was easy and she had three batches of potion brewing, but she didn't really expect to use it.

Varen's Levitation, which she had used that afternoon, took two forms. The wizard who cast the spell could walk on air as if it were solid, ascending or descending by using the air as a staircase, as she had done—that was one form, the one she had usually practiced when learning the spell. Having that in a potion would mean having it instantly available, and not needing to carry the damned lantern.

The other form was to cast the spell on an object, and a wizard who did that could then place an object of any size in midair, and it would remain there. She would need to get her hands on the couch to use it, and she would be unable to lift it higher than she could reach, or move it once it was levitated, but it would certainly be a way to immobilize the couch. Then she could fetch a wagon, roll it underneath, release the spell, tie the couch down, and cart it home.

Of course, she would need to lift the couch to use Varen's Levitation on it, and that was where the Spell of Optimum Strength came in. *That* spell gave the subject immense strength for perhaps half an hour—not infinite, by any means, but the most strength a person of that size and build might ever have had without magic. Kilisha knew that she could lift about four hundred pounds when enchanted with Optimum Strength—and she knew the couch didn't weigh anywhere near that much.

So if she found the couch, and it did not want to cooperate, she would drink the strength potion, then Varen's Levitation, and then she would pick up the couch and hang it in midair.

It would be simple.

She just needed to find the couch first.

She hummed quietly to herself as she set up the first batch of potion and began the final preparations.

She had Tracel's Levitation finished and was beginning Varen's when Yara leaned through the doorway and called, "I'm going out. The children are upstairs; would you put them to bed if I'm not back in time?"

"Of course, Mistress," Kilisha replied. Yara disappeared back into the kitchen, and the apprentice reached for the silver coin and a bundle of seagull feathers.

The levitations were the quick, easy part, of course; the Spell of Optimum Strength took hours. That was the challenge in the evening's work. All the same, all three potions were long since finished and the children secure in their beds when Yara finally returned; Kilisha had been waiting at the kitchen table and was half-asleep herself when the back door finally opened and her mistress stepped in.

"Damn them all," Yara said.

Kilisha blinked in confused surprise. "Damn who?" she asked.

"The wizards," she said. "I talked to a dozen of them—Heshka the Diviner, Anansira the Sage, Virinia of the Crystal Orb, Istha, Onoli, Tirin—everyone I could think of and find at home. None of them knew anything about the missing couch, and none of them would try to find out. They wouldn't help *at all*."

"They wouldn't?" Kilisha blinked again.

"Some of them don't do divinations, some of them wouldn't do them for anything magical, and the *good* ones were all too busy on this blasted project of Kaligir's, trying to figure out what this beggar-queen Tabaea is doing in Ethshar of the Sands. They said maybe when they've done everything they can for the Guild. *Damn* the Guild!"

Kilisha's eyes widened, and her sleepiness vanished. "Don't *say* that!" she gasped. "You're a wizard's wife; you know better than that!"

Yara snorted. "I'm not sure of that right now," she said. "I told them we had a half-finished spell simmering here, and they didn't care, they still had to do their spells for Kaligir. I hope whatever that stuff is, it blows up and turns Kaligir into a toad!"

"Don't say that," Kilisha repeated. "The divinations probably wouldn't have worked anyway. We'll find the couch ourselves tomorrow; don't worry about it. I couldn't do anything more tonight anyway—I'm exhausted, and we don't have the jewelweed."

"I'll get you the jewelweed in the morning," Yara replied. "You had *better* find that couch!" Then she stormed past Kilisha and up the stairs.

"I will," Kilisha said to her retreating back. "I promise."

Then she got to her feet and began climbing the stairs herself, far more slowly than Yara had.

No matter how it turned out, tomorrow was going to be a very long day, she was sure.

Chapter Twenty

Kilisha had forgotten to draw the curtains or close the shutters on her garret window, and the morning light awoke her earlier than she might have liked. She had been up far too late waiting for Yara.

But she had duties, so the idea of closing the drapes and going back to sleep was discarded immediately. Instead she sighed, sat up on her pallet, and reached for her apprentice robes.

A few minutes later, dressed and brushed and with her favorite feathered hair ornament in its accustomed place, she carried the chamber pots and wastewater out to the sewers behind the house, then headed for the pump at the other end of the court to fetch the morning's supply of water, idly wishing as she went that she had managed to apprentice herself to a wizard who knew how to create water magically. She had heard of a spell called Eshom's Freshwater Spring, for example. . . .

But there was probably a catch. There usually was, with wizardry. The spell might call for some especially rare or loathsome ingredients, or require an impractical amount of time and effort for the water thus obtained. If it were really useful then everyone would use it, the way every wizard knew at least one combustion spell to avoid meddling with flint and steel.

Ithanalin had taught her one of Eshom's other spells, the Oenological Transformation, which turned water to wine, but the Freshwater Spring wasn't in her master's book of spells, so someone in the chain of masters and apprentices had presumably not thought it worth passing on. Or perhaps Ithanalin or his own master had bought the Oenological Transformation, rather than learning it as an apprentice, but at some point someone had learned the one and not the other. Changing water to wine was good for impressing people, but not really much use beyond that—the ingredients included a dragon's scale, which cost considerably more than a decent bottle of wine, so the spell didn't save any money. A single scale could be used several times before its virtue was exhausted, but not enough to make the spell a bargain.

So if someone had thought that spell was more use than Eshom's Freshwater Spring, then the Spring must have some serious drawback.

Some of the neighbors were out in the courtyard, dumping their wastes and fetching water just as she was; Kilisha waved to a few, but did not say anything beyond a brief acknowledgment of their greetings.

The earth of the court was muddy and slightly slick—apparently it had rained during the night, though the sky was mostly clear now, with just a few pink-edged clouds scudding across the brightening blue. That made the footing tricky, and she had to be careful not to spill anything.

She was still wondering what the flaw in the Freshwater Spring might be as she carried the two heavy buckets back to the kitchen. She was almost to the door when Adagan called her name from his own back door.

She nodded to him, but didn't stop until he called, "Wait a minute!" He was hurrying across the muddy kitchen yards.

Reluctantly, she lowered the buckets and asked, "What is it?"

"Did you find all the furniture? I saw you and the soldier bringing back some of it on a rope yesterday, but then you were flying around later, and I wasn't sure whether you might be looking for more."

"We've got *most* of it," Kilisha said. "Everything but the red velvet couch—you know the one I mean?"

"Yes, of course. The one Ithanalin's customers sit on for presentations."

"That's the one. I haven't seen it since it got animated. So yes, I was looking for it when I levitated." A sudden thought struck her. "Have *you* seen it?"

Adagan turned up an empty palm. "I'm afraid not," he said. "I'll let you know at once if I do."

"Yes, please. And tell anyone else you know to keep an eye out, would you? I think we'll need all the help we can get to find it."

"Of course. Do you have *any* idea where it is?"

"It was last seen heading west on the East Road, toward the Fortress," Kilisha said. "But that was two days ago. It could be anywhere."

"I suppose it took shelter during the rain last night."

Kilisha looked up, startled. "I *hope* so," she said. "Rain wouldn't be good for the finish. Or the fabric."

"No," Adagan agreed.

"I need to get this water inside," Kilisha said, picking up the buckets. "Yara will want it."

"Of course. But do let me know if there's anything I can do to help. And I'll tell everyone I know about the couch."

Kilisha nodded, and then hurried inside.

Yara was waiting, Pirra clinging to her skirt. "Any news?" Yara asked.

"No, Mistress," Kilisha replied.

"I heard your voice."

"Adagan the Witch was asking whether there was any news. I told him we still need the couch, and asked him to keep an eye out for it."

"Oh, Adagan." She glanced at the door. "What about the other neighbors?"

"I didn't speak to anyone else, Mistress."

"We should ask them if they've seen it."

"I'll do it, Mother!" Telleth volunteered from the stairs.

"We should ask anyone we can," Kilisha agreed. She glanced through the open door of the workshop, and noticed the spriggan—she *hoped* it was the same spriggan, and it certainly appeared to be from her present vantage point—perched atop Ithanalin's sheet-draped head, sitting back comfortably and drumming its heels on the wizard's right ear. "Even spriggans—if you see any today, ask them if they know where the couch is."

"Spriggans?" Yara turned and glared into the workshop. "Talk to *those* little pests?"

"They might know something," Kilisha said. "Oh, they're stupid and annoying, but they can smell magic and they can talk, so we might get a hint from one."

"*I'll* talk to them, Mama!" Lirrin called.

"I'm going to go around to all the gates," Kilisha said, "and talk to the guards to make sure the couch didn't leave the city."

Yara blinked at her in surprise. "*All* the gates? That would take all day!"

Kilisha had not really thought about that. She had been thinking of Eastgate and Farmgate, the two she had visited before, but of course there were others—Wargate and Newgate and Grandgate and Southgate and Northgate . . . was that all of them? She tried to remember the view from the air.

Oh, Cliffgate. That was all, she was fairly sure. She counted on her fingers.

Eight gates, spread around three leagues of wall. Yara was right—that *would* take all day. Kilisha sighed.

"What if it got on a ship and sailed away?" Pirra asked.

"Then the gods are being cruel and it's hopeless," Kilisha said. "But really, who would let a velvet couch on board a ship? Something that size couldn't stow away very easily."

"Maybe someone should ask down in Seagate and Southport," Telleth said. "Just to be sure."

"There are docks in Bywater, too!" Lirrin pointed out.

"Those are mostly just for fishing boats," Telleth retorted.

"Would a couch know the difference?"

"There are only five of us," Kilisha said before Telleth could reply. "We can't search *everywhere.*"

"But what if we *need* to?" Lirrin asked. "We might not find it if we don't look everywhere!"

No one had a good answer to that. After a moment's awkward silence, Yara said, "I don't want you asking at all the gates. We'll get someone else to do that. Could you make a homunculus for the job, maybe?"

"The master hasn't taught me any animations yet," Kilisha said.

"Well, I still don't want you spending the entire day checking the gates. I want you here as much as possible, in case some other spell goes wrong—you're the only one here who knows any magic."

"The neighbors—"

"I don't want the neighbors!" Yara interrupted. "I want a member of this household to be ready. I want you to stay here and keep an eye on Thani's magic and practice the spell you'll need to revive him. I was scared half to death when you were out roaming around the city yesterday; I was constantly worrying about whether that thing on the lamp in Thani's workshop was going to explode or bubble up a demon or something. The rest of us will find the couch—or you know, maybe it will come home on its own."

"It might," Kilisha admitted. After all, if it had any of Ithanalin's memories it would know this place was home.

But it had had a day and a half, and it hadn't returned yet.

"Then you'll stay."

"Mistress, I can't practice the spell without jewelweed," Kilisha protested. "I found the bench and the coatrack—I could—"

"I'll get you your jewelweed from the herbalist, right after breakfast," Yara said. "You'll stay here."

Kilisha swallowed her half-formed protest and bowed her head. "Yes, Mistress," she said.

And while she was waiting for the jewelweed, she told herself, maybe she would take another look through Ithanalin's book of spells. Perhaps she might yet identify the brown goo. Or perhaps she might find an animation she could use to create a homunculus, as Yara had suggested.

Perhaps she could make a whole *swarm* of homunculi. . . .

But no, she knew better than that. Animations were difficult, unreliable spells—that was why Ithanalin hadn't taught her any yet, and why they were so expensive, and why the World wasn't overrun with wooden servants, talking gargoyles, and self-pouring teapots.

She sighed.

"Eat," Yara ordered, serving out the last of the salt ham, and Kilisha sat down at the table to eat her breakfast.

The meal was finished and Kilisha was clearing the plates when a thought struck her.

"We might be able to find a thread or a splinter or a flake of varnish from the couch," she said.

"And what would that do?" Yara asked, as she wiped crumbs from Pirra's face. "Do you know some divination you could use, then?"

"Not a divination," Kilisha said. "Cauthen's Remarkable Love Spell. The one I used on the rug."

"No," Yara said immediately.

"Why not? It worked, didn't it?"

Yara scrubbed Pirra's face vigorously before replying, "Do you know what that rug tried to do when I was locking it up? And there was the spoon, before that. They're small enough that I can handle them, but I do *not* want an amorous sofa chasing me around the house, trying to lift my skirt or stroke my hair! No more love spells. None. Is that clear?"

"But it's really—"

"I said *no*, Apprentice!" She flung the facecloth at the empty bucket by the door.

"Mistress, I—"

"*You*, Apprentice, are a naive young virgin. I am a respectable married woman, and I am telling you that I do not want any more formerly inanimate objects enamored of me, because it's *weird*, in ways you probably don't understand. It makes my skin crawl. I've put up with a lot in twelve years of marriage to a wizard, but there are limits. Nor do I want any portion of my husband's soul to fall in love with anyone else. You will *not* use any more love spells on the couch or any of the other furniture. You won't use them on *anything* except paying customers. Is that clear?"

Kilisha had never before seen Yara direct this sort of speech at anyone except her children, but she knew better than to argue further. "Yes, Mistress," she said, as meekly as she could.

"Good. Now, why don't you check on your master, and then start practicing the spell to restore him?"

"I need jewelweed, Mistress."

"I'll go get it. Find *something* useful to do until I get back."

"Yes, Mistress." Kilisha clasped her hands behind her back and stared at the floor.

A thought struck Yara. "Actually, you can watch the children. I'll be quicker without them."

"Yes, Mistress."

A few minutes later Yara had left, bound for the nearest herbalist—which would probably be old Urrel, in the little shop on the corner of Arena Street, Kilisha thought. Yara had partially relented on demanding Kilisha care for the children; she was taking Pirra with her, but Telleth and Lirrin were still upstairs.

Kilisha came back down the stairs after ensuring that her two charges were safe, then wandered into the workshop to check on things there.

Ithanalin had not moved, of course, and the sheet was still in place, but crooked; she straightened it.

The boxes holding the dish, spoon, and rug were still where they belonged, and still locked.

The goo in the brass bowl was still simmering, but looking far less gooey, as most of the moisture had cooked out of it; she checked the oil in the lamp and added another cup. The concoction was beginning to smell somewhat foul, like sour wine, but it didn't seem to be doing anything dangerous.

She looked into the parlor, where the chair and the table were having a shoving match. "Stop that!" she barked.

They ignored her. She marched in and pulled them apart, whereupon the table ran to the far end of its tether and stood by the back wall, turning back and forth, while the chair rocked side to side in what looked like a dance of triumph. The ropes that connected them all to the line in the chimney had gotten somewhat tangled, but Kilisha decided it was not worth trying to separate them; the furniture would undoubtedly just tangle them up again.

She hoped none of the furnishings managed to damage each other; that might complicate the restoration spell.

She glanced at the mirror over the mantel, then crossed the room, stepping carefully over the ropes, and asked, "Are you all right?"

I AM AS WELL AS MIGHT BE EXPECTED, it replied.

"Have you remembered what that is cooking in the workshop?"

NO.

"Do you have any idea where the couch might have gone? We have all the other pieces."

NO.

Kilisha wondered whether the mirror might have some link to the other objects that it was not even aware of. "Did you know part of Ithanalin wound up in the spriggan?" she asked.

NOT UNTIL YOU SAID SO YESTERDAY.

Well, that would seem to indicate that no link existed. She turned away and looked at the furniture—and a thought struck her.

"Where *is* the spriggan?"

She hardly spared a glance for the mirror's I DO NOT KNOW as she dashed for the door.

Chapter Twenty-one

The front door was, to her relief, still locked—but that did not necessarily mean very much with the latch animated. The spriggan might well have escaped into the street, and the latch could have locked itself afterward.

Kilisha opened the door and leaned out, and saw only the normal morning traffic of Wizard Street; no spriggans were anywhere to be seen. She closed the door again, locked it, then hurried to the workshop.

The spriggan was nowhere in sight—but there were dozens of nooks and crannies among the shelves and drawers and clutter where it might have hidden. She peered into the most obvious openings without locating the creature.

Then she heard a thump overhead, and a faint sound that might have been a child's giggle—or a spriggan. She turned and ran for the kitchen stairs.

The dim drawing room at the top of the stair was empty, but she heard thumping and laughter from the front of the house; she hurried into the sunlit day nursery and found Telleth and Lirrin chasing a spriggan back and forth across the toy-crowded Sardironese carpet.

"Stop!" she shouted.

Telleth and Lirrin skidded to a stop and turned to look at her; the spriggan kept running and giggling, bounced off the far wall, then glanced over its shoulder and realized its pursuers were no longer pursuing. It stopped, too.

"Chase?" it said.

Kilisha glared at it.

It was the right spriggan, anyway—the face and voice were familiar. She had been worried for a moment.

"Is something wrong?" Telleth asked.

Kilisha started an angry reply, then stopped.

Really, *was* anything wrong? So the spriggan had come upstairs to play with the children; where was the harm in that? If anything, it would keep the little pest out of her way.

And Ithanalin had played with his children sometimes; he hadn't been as aloof as Kilisha's own father. The bit of his spirit trapped in the spriggan was probably enjoying this foolishness.

"No, I suppose there isn't anything wrong," she said. "I'm just worried about your father—it's got me nervous that we haven't found the couch yet, and that we still don't . . . well, I'm nervous." She looked at the children's faces—Lirrin was openly worried, while Telleth was clearly trying to hide his own concern and look grave and mature. "It'll be fine. You go ahead with your game. In fact, if you can keep an eye on this spriggan, I'd appreciate it."

"Sure!" Telleth said, managing a smile.

"Chase?" the spriggan said.

"I don't think I want to play anymore," Lirrin said; Kilisha saw the girl's face, and regretted mentioning Ithanalin's condition.

"We have fun!" the spriggan insisted. It ran up and tugged on the hem of Lirrin's tunic. She batted it away.

The spriggan danced around her hand and tugged at the tunic again.

"Stop that," Lirrin said angrily. Telleth quickly tried to grab the spriggan away from his sister, but it dodged. He ran after it.

The spriggan doubled back and ducked between Lirrin's legs.

"*Hai!*" the girl shouted; then she, too, grabbed for the creature.

A moment later they were chasing the spriggan back and forth across the room again, just as they had been when Kilisha came in. The apprentice smiled, then slipped quietly back out of the room and down the stairs.

Once she was back in the workshop, though, she stopped. What was she supposed to do here? She had no jewelweed, so she couldn't practice the Restorative, and she couldn't think of any other useful magic to do, given that her potions were all prepared and Yara had forbidden any further love spells. Yara had also ordered her to stay in the house, so she couldn't levitate again to see whether the morning light might give a better view than had late afternoon.

That reminded her to check on the potions. She found the three vials where she had left them after completing the last spell and was relieved to see that yes, she *had* remembered to label them the night before, though the labels were nowhere near as clear and neat as Ithanalin would have made them.

Each vial held seven sips, seven doses. She read the labels—OPT. STRENGTH, VAREN'S L., TRACEL'S L.—then carefully tucked all three into her belt pouch, next to her mostly empty vial of brimstone and a tiny, tightly sealed bottle that held a single drop of dragon's blood. A chip of chrysolite, necessary for conjuring the Yellow Cloud, was wrapped in a bit of rag and tucked behind the brimstone.

With the potions in there, the next time someone like Kelder asked her whether she had any magic with her she would have something better than the Yellow Cloud to use. Being able to levitate to see over the rooftops might yet be very useful in finding the couch— if she only had some hint where in the city to look for it.

She was just closing the pouch when someone knocked on the front door.

"Kelder," she said to herself. "Maybe *he* can check the gates." She hurried through the parlor, almost tripping over the bench's tether as it wandered toward the door, clearly curious about who had knocked. "I'll be right there!" she called.

The latch apparently decided that meant the new arrival was welcome, and clicked itself open. The door swung inward slightly.

"Kilisha?" a voice called—a *female* voice. Kilisha stopped, her hand just short of the latch.

"Who's there?"

"It's me, Nissitha. Nissitha the Seer."

Kilisha swung the door wide. "What can I do for you?" she asked, looking out at her neighbor and trying to display polite interest, rather than mere puzzlement, at this unexpected visit.

"Adagan told me you wanted help finding a runaway couch?" Nissitha said hesitantly.

"Yes!" Kilisha smiled hopefully. "Have you seen it?"

"Well, no," Nissitha admitted. "I was hoping you could tell me more about it—what it looks like, where it was last seen, that sort of thing."

"Oh." Kilisha's smile faded. "Come in, and I'll tell you."

Nissitha stepped in. The bench stepped aside to make room for her while the chair rocked a little closer. The coatrack cowered back into its corner, and the table moved to one side for a better view. Nissitha looked around, her eyes wide.

"They won't hurt you," Kilisha assured her.

"You said some furniture had been animated . . ." Nissitha said, her voice trailing off.

"Yes, and we've found most of it, but we still need the couch. The one that used to stand over there." She pointed.

"Oh," Nissitha said. "What did it look like?"

Startled, Kilisha blinked. "Oh, you must have seen it. It's been there as long as I've been Ithanalin's apprentice!"

"I've never been in here before," Nissitha said. "What did it look like?"

Trying to hide her astonishment that someone who lived just next door had never before been in Ithanalin's parlor, Kilisha said, "It's modest in size, enough to seat two comfortably, but three adults would be crowded. The wood is stained dark, and the front legs are carved in reverse curves, with claws on the bottom. The upholstery is red velvet, and the arms are partially upholstered as well as the back and seat. It looks almost new—Ithanalin put a preservation spell on it when Telleth first started walking, so the children wouldn't damage it."

Nissitha nodded. "And it's animated?"

"Just like the others," Kilisha confirmed, a sweep of her arm indicating the chair, bench, and table.

"Where was it last seen?"

"The tax collector followed it, but he lost sight of it on the East Road heading west, where Low Street forks off."

"So it could be anywhere?"

"I'm afraid so." Kilisha hesitated, reluctant to say anything rude, but she was puzzled by Nissitha's presence and questions. If she was a true seer, why would she need to ask all these questions? And if she was a fraud, why would she *bother* to ask all these questions? She had never before shown any signs of going out of her way to be helpful in the five years Kilisha had lived there. "Are you going to help search?"

"I thought I might," Nissitha said, with a toss of her head that sent a ripple down her lush mane of black hair.

It popped out before Kilisha could stop herself. "Why?"

Nissitha grimaced. "I don't suppose you'd believe it's just neighborliness."

"Not . . . uh . . . well, you know," Kilisha said.

"Well, it *is* neighborliness, partly," Nissitha said, "but I admit it's directed more at Adagan than at you or Ithanalin."

Sudden enlightenment burst in Kilisha's mind as a dozen scattered incidents over the past year suddenly fell together. Nissitha wasn't married; neither was Adagan, and Adagan was a handsome, charming fellow perhaps a year or two younger than Nissitha—close enough in age that the difference didn't seem significant, in any case.

Kilisha had suspected for some time that Adagan preferred men to women, but perhaps she was wrong—or perhaps Nissitha either hadn't noticed or hoped to change that. Nissitha clearly wanted to impress Adagan with her enterprise and helpfulness by finding the runaway couch.

"And it would be good advertising, don't you think," Nissitha added, "to find this couch that a wizard can't find?"

"I suppose it would," Kilisha agreed. And it really didn't matter *why* Nissitha wanted to help; *any* help was welcome. "Thank you."

"You're welcome. Now, is there anything else you can tell me about it?"

Kilisha turned up an empty palm. "I can't think of anything."

"Does it have any known likes or dislikes?"

"No."

"Is it dangerous?"

"I don't know," Kilisha admitted. "It's big and heavy enough that I suppose it could do some damage if it wanted to. It shouldn't be particularly aggressive, but I don't really know which personality traits it got."

"Can it do any magic?"

Startled, Kilisha considered that for a moment. A couch had no voice for incantations, no hands to gesture with, and the spriggan had gotten at least part of the athame's magic. . . .

"I don't see how it could," she said.

"Can it talk? Or fly?"

"No."

"Why haven't you found it? Did you try any divinations?"

"I don't know any," Kilisha said. "And all the diviners Yara asked were too busy with some big crisis in Ethshar of the Sands."

"I heard something about that," Nissitha said. "Someone's declared herself empress and led a bunch of beggars from the Wall Street Field in taking over the overlord's palace."

"You mean Soldiers' Field?"

"They call it Wall Street Field in the Sands," Nissitha said. "It's a better name, if you ask me, but the Soldiers' Field name is traditional here, so it'll probably never change."

"But there are beggars in the Fortress there?"

"Palace," Nissitha corrected. "No Fortress there. And yes, this empress invited a bunch of beggars and thieves to be her court."

"How could she do that? Why didn't the guard stop her?"

"Because she's a magician. Some one-of-a-kind freak who came out of nowhere, and no one knows what to do with her. It's a little like the Night of Madness, I guess."

Kilisha didn't remember the Night of Madness, when warlockry first appeared; that had happened seven or eight years before she was born. Nissitha would have been a little girl at the time. Kilisha had heard about it, of course; it was supposed to have been much worse in the other two Ethshars, where there were more warlocks, but even here there had been trouble.

The idea that this trouble in Ethshar of the Sands might be something similar hadn't occurred to her; she had been too caught up in Ithanalin's situation to give it much thought. "Is it really that bad?" she asked.

It was Nissitha's turn to raise an empty palm. "Who knows?" she asked. "Do you think this thing with Ithanalin and your furniture might be connected?"

"Oh, I don't *think* so," Kilisha said. "The master tripped on a spriggan and spilled a half-finished potion, there wasn't anything inexplicable about it."

Nissitha blinked. "He tripped on a spriggan?"

Kilisha immediately regretted her words, but it was too late to call them back. "Yes," she admitted.

"The great Ithanalin the Wise tripped on a spriggan?"

Kilisha sighed deeply. "Yes," she said. "I'd appreciate it if you didn't go around telling everyone that, though."

"Oh, of course, of course, I'll keep it quiet." Nissitha's grin belied her words. "So you don't know anything more about where this couch is?"

"Nothing," Kilisha confirmed.

"Then I suppose I had best go and start looking." The self-proclaimed seer tucked her skirt clear of the chair's inquisitive approach, then turned and stepped back out into the street. She called over her shoulder as she departed, "I'll let you know as soon as I find it."

"Thank you," Kilisha called after her, but she did not feel very grateful. She closed the door, locked it, and ordered the latch, "Stay locked until I tell you—"

She had not finished the sentence when a knock sounded.

"Never mind," she told the latch, as she opened it again.

Chapter Twenty-two

Kilisha stared when she saw who had knocked, but she quickly gathered at least a portion of her wits. "What are *you* doing here?" she asked.

The young man on the doorstep smiled. "It's good to see you, too, Kili."

Kilisha swung the door wide. "Come in!" she said. "I mean, I'm glad to see you, Opir, but what *are* you doing here? You know it's not permitted for family to interfere with an apprentice's training!"

"I'm not here to interfere in anything," her brother replied. "I'm here to see whether there's any truth to the rumors I've heard." He looked around, taking in the furniture as it moved about the room and the tangled ropes leading from the various pieces to the fireplace, and added, "I'd say there must be some truth in them, all right."

"What rumors?" Kilisha asked. "What have you heard?"

"That some sort of magic has run wild and started bringing all your furniture to life, and nobody's seen Ithanalin in days. He's supposed to be holed up somewhere working on a counterspell.

Or maybe he got turned into a coatrack—is that him in the corner?" He pointed.

"No," Kilisha said, not wanting to be distracted by explanations just now. "Go on."

"Or that he's been spirited away by the Empress Tabaea, or that he's secretly working for her, or that he's been transformed into *you,* and the *real* Kilisha of Eastgate is imprisoned somewhere dreadful."

"That's ridiculous."

"Is it? What did you call your toy pig when you were little?"

Kilisha stared at him. "You mean Gruntpuppy?"

Opir smiled broadly. "It's you, all right—I can't imagine you'd ever tell *anyone* you named that pig Gruntpuppy."

Kilisha shrugged. "I'd tell Ithanalin if he asked, because he's my master and I'm an apprentice—but he's never asked, and there's no reason he would." She closed the door behind Opir. "Where did you hear all these rumors?"

"From Mother, mostly. She collects them."

Kilisha blinked, then grabbed the chair and sat down. "Lock, please," she ordered the latch. The chair shifted beneath her, and she told it, "Hold still." She gestured to Opir. "You can catch the bench if you like."

Opir eyed it uneasily, then said, "I'll stand."

"Please yourself. Now, tell me more about where Mother's been getting all these stories. I mean, Ithanalin's only been . . . *gone* for about two days."

"So he *is* gone?"

"Not really." Kilisha sighed. "He's in the workshop. But he can't move—a spell went wrong and transferred his life force into all the furniture."

"So you're *sitting* on him?"

Kilisha closed her eyes and bit her lip as the chair shifted slightly. Her older brother had always had a knack for making everything she said or did sound stupid. "After a fashion," she admitted. "Mostly, though, I'm sitting on the straight chair we keep here in the parlor. It just happens to have a little bit of Ith-analin's spirit in it at the moment."

"And the bench, too? And the coatrack?"

"All of it," Kilisha said.

Opir looked around the parlor. "Where's the couch?" he asked.

"I don't know," Kilisha admitted. "That's why I haven't been able to restore him yet—I need all the pieces. I've got all the others, but the couch ran away and I haven't found it yet."

"Then why aren't you out looking for it, or working a spell to locate it?"

"Because I'm obeying my mistress's orders. I'll find it later. Now, tell me about these rumors. Where did Mother hear them?"

"Didn't you know she has spies all around here?"

Kilisha closed her eyes again and sighed deeply, then opened them. "No," she said. "I didn't know. What spies?"

"Lirrin, for one—Ithanalin's daughter. And Thetta, Heshka's wife. And Virinia's little sister Fara, and that fellow Genzer of Northmark who's been trying to court that cute apprentice of Tirin's, and the two kids who help out in Kara's Arcana, and that old woman across the court from your back door who calls herself Zinamdia, which isn't any sort of real name I ever heard of. And probably others I don't know about. You know Mother's always been fond of gossip."

"Yes, but she *used* to just talk to people in the courtyard at home, or in Eastgate Market. She didn't come all the way over here to gather news!"

"But that was before she had her youngest apprenticed to a genuine *wizard*. You're the first magician in our entire family, Kili—didn't you realize how special that makes you?"

"No, I didn't," she lied.

In fact, she knew perfectly well that it made her the object of family pride and envy. That had been much of the *point,* really, after a childhood of being utterly ordinary. She had gotten tired of being dull; she had even bored *herself,* and had begged to be apprenticed to a wizard largely so she could escape that tedium. It had worked, too.

But she wasn't about to admit that to her older brother.

"Well, you should have known," Opir said. "After Ithanalin took you on Mother boasted about it constantly for sixnights—but after a while she needed *new* things to say about her daughter the wizard, and you hardly ever came home anymore, or wrote letters. . . ."

"I don't have *time*! I'm an *apprentice*!"

"I know that," Opir said, grinning. "So did Mother. She didn't want to do anything that might interfere or annoy Ithanalin, for fear he'd send you home in disgrace—"

"He can't," Kilisha interrupted. "Guild rules. I passed the point where he could send me home when I was thirteen." She caught herself before explaining further—that once she had made herself an athame she could only leave the Wizards' Guild by dying, and if she fouled up her apprenticeship badly enough that she couldn't continue Ithanalin wouldn't have sent her home, he'd have had her killed. Somehow she didn't think she wanted her parents to hear that. She didn't think she even wanted her brother to hear it.

"Really? We didn't know that."

"Really. And you weren't supposed to."

Opir hesitated, waiting to see if Kilisha would give any details, then turned up a palm and continued. "She didn't want to cause you any trouble, but she really wanted to know what you were doing, so she started visiting along Wizard Street and the East Road. She's been doing it for years. You didn't know?"

"I didn't know."

"Oh. Well, she's been doing it, and for the past two days the gossip and rumors have just been pouring in—mostly other things, but a few about Ithanalin and you." He glanced around at the furniture, then asked, "What really happened?"

"I told you—a spell went wrong. A spriggan tripped the master as he was stirring something, and it spilled, and the spell scattered his soul into all these different pieces."

"A spriggan? So it doesn't have anything to do with Empress Tabaea and her strange magic?"

"I don't even know for certain who Empress Tabaea *is*," Kilisha said angrily. "You mean the usurper in Ethshar of the Sands?"

"That's the one. Haven't you been hearing about it? Word is that the whole Wizards' Guild is going mad trying to deal with her."

"I've been a bit distracted," Kilisha said. "And the Guild hasn't been helping me any—they're too busy with this madwoman to do anything about my master."

"Well, you can hardly *blame* them! She's taken over an entire city and killed a dozen magicians!"

Kilisha hesitated. "She has?"

"Yes, she has!"

"I've been busy. I hadn't heard the details." Actually, she realized that she *had* heard that much, but hadn't given it much thought, or remembered the specifics.

A dozen magicians? A *dozen*? If she had heard that before, she *should* have remembered it.

But she had been distracted by her own concerns.

"I'm surprised," Opir said. "I thought *all* the wizards were involved in it."

"I'll start paying attention again once Ithanalin is restored!" she snapped. "As an apprentice, my first duty is to my master, and *only* to my master. When he's back to normal I'll worry about the usurper, and do what the Guild asks, but right now I need to work on the restorative spell and get all the pieces together."

"Oh." Opir looked around the room; the coatrack backed away, the table twirled on one leg and almost toppled over, and the bench flexed itself. "You know, Mother and Father didn't send me, I came on my own. But they did tell me, since I was coming anyway, to ask whether there's anything they can do to help out."

"Is that why you came?"

"Well, and to find out what had really happened. And to find out if you knew anything about the empress; some of the neighbors were wondering whether it might be wise to flee the city until matters settle down."

"I don't know anything about her," Kilisha said. "But if you want to be helpful, there is *one* thing—maybe Mother can set her informers and spies on this. I need the couch. I don't know where it's gone—we last saw it heading west on the East Road, toward Hillside and the Fortress. If *anyone* knows where it is, I need to know, as soon as possible. There might even be a reward, though I can't promise that without talking to Yara."

"I think we can ask around, certainly," Opir said.

"Good. Now, get out of here before Yara gets back, or the children hear you—you shouldn't be here!" She got to her feet and gave her brother a shove toward the door.

"I'm going," Opir said.

Just then a crash sounded upstairs. Opir paused and asked, "What was that?"

"Lirrin and Telleth are playing with a spriggan. I should go check on them, so will you please go?"

"All right, I'm going." He glanced at the ceiling, then reached for the door.

The latch popped open before he could touch it.

"I don't think it likes you," Kilisha said, as Opir stared at the latch.

"It's alive?"

"For the moment. Now go!" She gave him another shove.

He opened the door—and almost collided with another young man who was standing on the step, about to knock.

"Istram?" Opir said.

"*Go!*" Kilisha shouted, pointing.

Istram stepped to one side, and Opir slipped past him.

"I'll tell them to look," Opir called back over his shoulder; then he marched off quickly, eastward along Wizard Street.

"What was that about?" Istram asked as he stepped inside.

"A family emergency," Kilisha said. "What can I do for you, Journeyman?"

"*Master,*" Istram corrected her. "As of last month."

"My apologies, Master Wizard. What was it you wanted?"

"I'm here to see Ithanalin," Istram said. "On Guild business."

"I'm afraid my master is indisposed just now," Kilisha said.

"Indisposed?"

"Yes."

"Indisposed *how*?"

"Just indisposed."

"Could I speak with him anyway?"

"No."

"Because he's indisposed?"

"Yes."

Istram frowned. "I don't think Kaligir will consider that an adequate explanation."

Kilisha looked puzzled. "What does Kaligir have to do with anything?"

"*Guildmaster* Kaligir is organizing our efforts against the usurper calling herself empress in Ethshar of the Sands," Istram said, drawing himself up to his full height—which was a good bit more than Kilisha's. "He wants Ithanalin's assistance, and is somewhat irked that our master hasn't already joined the Guild's meetings. I believe the Guild wants Ithanalin to make some homunculi to serve as spies in Tabaea's palace."

"She has a palace?"

"She has the overlord's palace," Istram said. "She chased Ederd out. Now, where's Ithanalin?"

"Excuse me, but hasn't anyone *told* Kaligir what happened to my master?"

Istram blinked in surprise. "Told him what?"

"Oh, this is stupid," Kilisha mumbled. More clearly, she said, "Chorizel knows what happened—I told him about it two days ago! And Yara talked to Heshka and half a dozen others last night."

"Well, the news hasn't reached Kaligir or me," Istram said. "Chorizel didn't say anything. They sent me to fetch Ithanalin, since I was the only one who'd apprenticed under him. What's happened? Where is he? Did Tabaea kill him?" He looked around the room, as if finally noticing that something was not quite as it should be.

"Tabaea has nothing to do with it," Kilisha said wearily. "He's in the workshop." She led the way across the parlor; the coatrack cowered away, and the table danced aside.

"Why is all this furniture moving? What are all these ropes for?"

Kilisha turned up an empty palm without answering and marched into the workshop, where she snatched the sheet from Ithanalin's head.

Istram stared. "What *happened* to him?" he asked.

Kilisha sighed, and explained the accident for what seemed like the hundredth time.

Chapter Twenty-three

Have you tried Javan's Restorative?" Istram asked, as Kilisha pulled the sheet back into place on her master's head. He was studying the brass bowl and its contents. The lamp's flame had turned most of the bowl's metal an ugly black by this time.

"Not yet," Kilisha said. "I don't have any jewelweed, and I don't have the red couch."

"Well, jewelweed's easy enough," Istram said, giving the simmering bowl of foul-smelling muck a final glance before crossing to one of the herb drawers. "The master always used to keep it right here."

"Yara's gone to the herbalist . . ." Kilisha began, but then Istram had the drawer open and pulled out a dried plant with white flowers and diamond-shaped leaves.

"Here it is," he said.

"That's touch-me-not," Kilisha protested.

"Same thing," Istram said. "Didn't you know?"

Kilisha was about to say that no, she didn't, when someone knocked on the front door.

"Oh, gods and spirits!" she said. Why, she wondered, had

everyone in the city decided to visit *now*? She hurried back across the parlor.

Istram set the stalk of jewelweed on the workbench and followed her. "Someone should tell Kaligir—" he began.

"I *tried* to tell Chorizel," Kilisha said, as she pushed the chair out of her path. "He insisted it would have to wait until after the usurper in Ethshar of the Sands had been dealt with." She reached for the latch, but it sprang open before she could touch it.

"Oh," Istram said. "He might have a point, at that." He stopped a few feet into the parlor, where the bench had blocked his way.

Kilisha ignored him as she peered around the door at the well-dressed stranger who stood just outside. "May I help you?" she asked.

"Is this still the home of Ithanalin the Wise?"

"Yes, it is, but I'm afraid my master is indisposed right now."

"You're his apprentice?"

"I am." She essayed a quick curtsy.

"Well, he made me a self-pouring teapot about ten years ago, and a sixnight ago my daughter broke it, and I was wondering—"

"I'm afraid he really *is* indisposed just now," Kilisha interrupted. "I'm sure that once he's himself again he'll be happy to enchant a new teapot for you. Could you come back in two or three days? I can't set a definite appointment until he's feeling better, but . . ."

She didn't finish the sentence; she was distracted by the sight of Kelder, walking up the street behind the customer, waving to her.

"Ow!"

That came from behind; she turned to see Istram fending off the coatrack. "Leave that alone!" she called. Then she turned back to the customer. "Today is the eighteenth; I'm sure my master will be well again by, oh, the twenty-second. Could you stop back then? If he's not ready right then, at the very least we'll make an appointment."

"Maybe I should just find a different wizard," the man said uncertainly.

"Well, you could do that, but as I'm sure you know, Ithanalin does the finest animation spells in the city, perhaps in the entire Hegemony. And I suspect we might be able to arrange a discount for a returning customer, especially after putting you to all this inconvenience." She smiled.

The customer ignored her smile as he realized someone was right behind him; he turned to find a large guardsman looming over him.

"I'll come back," the customer said. He slipped away and let Kelder step up to the door.

Kilisha watched the man go with mixed feelings; animating a teapot was a relatively simple and profitable engagement, but one still beyond her own abilities. She hated to see that commission walking away, possibly to wind up in another wizard's hands, but what else could she do?

"Kilisha," Kelder said. "Any news?"

"I have everything but the red velvet couch," Kilisha replied, forgetting the teapot buyer and meeting Kelder's gaze. "Do you have *any* idea where it might be?"

"I last saw it heading up the East Road toward the Fortress," Kelder said. "I told you."

"And you haven't seen any sign of it since then?"

"No."

She hesitated, then asked, "Could you do me a favor, then? Could you ask the guards at the gates, and make sure it hasn't slipped out of the city?"

"All eight gates?"

"Yes, please."

"That'll take all day."

"I know. I'm sorry, but—"

"Who's this person?" a voice asked from behind.

Kilisha started; she hadn't realized Istram was so close. She turned aside and made introductions. "Kelder, this is Istram the Wizard; he was Ithanalin's first apprentice, before me. Istram, this is Kelder, the tax collector who was at the door when the accident happened."

Both men made semipolite noises of acknowledgment; Istram's might have been intended as the words "Pleased to meet you."

After that the three of them stood in awkward silence for a moment. Then Istram said, "I should be going. I need to tell Kaligir what's happened."

"You're sure?" Kilisha asked. "I was hoping you could help me with Javan's Restorative, or figure out what that stuff on the lamp is."

"I might come back, if Kaligir doesn't need me—but I have no idea what's in the brass bowl, and you ought to be able to do the Restorative yourself, after five years of training."

"I'm sure I can, but I wouldn't mind having a more experienced wizard on hand when I try it."

"I'll see if I can, but the Guild really is keeping me busy."

"You're sure that's jewelweed?"

"Oh, quite sure. It's called jewelweed when you want the leaves, and touch-me-not if you want the seeds or flowers."

Kilisha stared up at him for a moment. "Why?" she asked.

Istram turned up a palm. "I have no idea," he said. "It just is."

"I could have told you that," Kelder said. "We use jewelweed leaves to soothe chafing—the oil's very cooling. What do you need it for?"

"The spell to restore Ithanalin," Kilisha explained. "You knew what jewelweed is?"

"Of course."

"Why does everyone know this but me?" She started to demand to know why he hadn't said anything, but then realized she had never asked him, had never mentioned jewelweed in his presence at all.

It was reassuring to have Kelder's confirmation, all the same; she didn't entirely trust Istram, though she couldn't say why. And this meant that she had all the ingredients for the spell, and Yara's trip to the herbalist was unnecessary.

That trip also seemed to be taking longer than it should, she realized. She hoped Yara hadn't run into difficulties, or had to inquire of more than one herbalist.

It seemed more likely that Pirra was distracting her, or that she was taking the opportunity to restock some of the household supplies.

"I should go," Istram said, moving around Kilisha toward the door. "I'll come back as soon as I have the chance."

"Please do," Kilisha said. Kelder stepped aside to let Istram pass.

Something thumped behind her, but Kilisha assumed it was just the furniture moving about. She asked Kelder, "Could you please ask at the gates? Maybe you could get some friends to ask at some of them; you wouldn't need to do it all yourself."

Kelder rubbed his beard thoughtfully. "I could do that," he said. "In fact, I could pass the word for the whole city guard to keep an eye open and look for your couch. We have a system for spreading urgent news."

"Oh, that would be wonderful!"

"I'm happy to do it, then. I still feel responsible for—"

He was interrupted by a scream from the workshop. Kilisha whirled.

"*Get it off me!*" Yara's voice shrieked.

Before Kilisha could react Kelder charged past her, truncheon drawn—and promptly tripped over the bench, which was running back and forth, panic-stricken, across the parlor. The guardsman managed to catch himself before he actually fell, but his rush to Yara's aid was still quite effectively interrupted.

Kilisha pushed aside the chair that was trying to nuzzle up to her, rounded Kelder and the bench, stepped over a tangle of rope, and dashed to the workshop, where she found Yara standing in the middle of the room, bent almost double, prying at the rug that had wrapped itself around her ankles. She must have come in the back way, as usual, Kilisha thought—but how did the rug get out of its box?

She would worry about that later; for now she fell to her knees, caught one edge of the rug, and tried to pull it loose.

It struggled ferociously. It was trying to climb up Yara's legs and shake off Kilisha's grip when Kelder arrived, reached down, and grabbed a handful of rug. He heaved.

Yara went over backward; Kilisha snatched at her, and managed to break her fall but not prevent it. Yara sat down hard on the plank floor.

That made it much easier to pull the rug off her legs, and a moment later Kelder and Kilisha held it by either end while it squirmed and wriggled.

"Talk to it, Yara!" Kilisha called. "It *loves* you!"

"Augh!"

"Mama?" Pirra called from the kitchen doorway.

"You just settle down right this minute!" Yara barked at the thrashing rug, wagging an angry finger.

The rug's movements stopped.

"Now, you go back in the box until we get the couch back! No more escapes! No more trouble!"

The rug sagged. It rippled its upper edge as if nodding, then went limp.

Kelder looked at Kilisha, who said, "The box is behind you." A moment later they had the rug secured once again. Kilisha fumbled with the lock.

"Mama?" Pirra called.

Yara had been sitting on the floor, her legs stretched out before her, and watching the rug's incarceration; now she turned and asked, "What is it, darling?"

"What's that spoon doing?" She pointed.

Yara turned and saw the spoon just as it reared up its handle and stretched out toward the waistband of her skirt; she let out a wordless shriek and smacked it away.

Kilisha saw, and dove for the spoon as it spun and skittered across the floor. She caught it one-handed.

"How did *that* get loose?" she demanded of no one in particular, as she got back to her feet, clutching her prize. She looked for the box that had held her first two captives.

Sure enough, its lid was wide open, flung back to one side. She looked inside.

The bowl was still there; apparently it had not been sufficiently agile to climb out the top. Kilisha dropped the spoon inside, then slammed the lid.

"Who opened these?" she shouted. "Don't tell me they *both* just managed to get themselves unlocked at the same time!"

"Maybe the spriggan?" Pirra said, pointing.

Kilisha turned her gaze to follow the girl's finger. Kelder and Yara turned, as well, until four sets of eyes were fastened on the little green creature that cowered under a corner of the workbench.

"*You*," Kilisha said. She checked to make sure the bowl and spoon were securely confined, then took a step toward the spriggan. "*You* let them out, didn't you?"

The spriggan nodded. "Fun?" it said uncertainly.

Kilisha growled and reached for it.

The spriggan, moving far more suddenly than Kilisha would have thought possible, sprang over her outstretched hand, made a right-angle turn on one foot, then dashed out through the parlor door, weaving between the bench's legs and bounding over a rope.

Kilisha followed, calling, "Lock the door!"

The latch clicked helplessly; Kelder had left the door standing open, and the latch could not reach the frame to obey. The spriggan dodged around the edge and vanished into the street.

"Oh, blood and death!" Kilisha muttered, as she narrowly avoided tripping over the ropes and catapulted herself across the parlor. She snatched the door open and ran outside.

The spriggan was heading west; she could just see it, scurrying past three startled pedestrians. She charged after it.

The three passersby stared, and one called out a question, but Kilisha could spare no time for them; she ran on, chasing the spriggan. She had to squeeze around a wagon the spriggan ran under, then dodge around a puddle the spriggan ran through, but she was slowly gaining.

"Apprentice!" someone called, and she looked up just in time to avoid running directly into a woman in green velvet. She skidded to a stop and belatedly recognized Lady Nuvielle.

"I was just on my way—" Nuvielle began.

"I'm sorry, my lady," Kilisha gasped. "No time right now!" Then she stepped to the right and dashed past the startled noblewoman.

The encounter had cost her precious seconds, and the spriggan was almost out of sight. She lowered her head and ran all-out, her skirt and hair flapping behind her. She felt her hair ornament slip out of place, falling down behind her ear, but she ignored it as she ran.

They were almost to Cross Avenue when she finally dove forward, landing flat on the dirt of the street, and grabbed for the spriggan with both hands.

Her right hand missed, but her left closed on one scrawny leg. The creature squawked, waving its arms wildly, but she held on.

"Let go! Let go!" it shrieked.

"Never," Kilisha said, closing her right hand around its plump throat. With her prize thus secured, she slid forward, tucking her elbows under her. Then she pulled in her knees, so that she was on all fours, then slowly and carefully got to her feet, keeping both hands and both eyes fixed solidly on the spriggan.

She stood in the street, aware that the front of her apprentice's robe and her hands and arms were all smeared with black dirt, aware that several people were staring at her, but with her attention focused entirely on the spriggan.

"Why did you do that?" she asked, her voice trembling.

The thought that the spriggan might have gotten away was terrifying; if that happened she would *never* be able to restore her master to life! Finding an enchanted couch or a runaway bench was one thing; those were unusual, and magical, and could be tracked down somehow. Finding *one specific spriggan*, though, in all the city, in all the *World*, a spriggan that not only had the normal stealth and idiot cunning of its kind, not only had a spriggan's innate resistance to wizardry, not only could pick locks with its fingernails, but that *could not be bound* because it held the essence of Ithanalin's athame . . .

That would have been virtually impossible.

"Do what?" it squeaked, in that voice so oddly reminiscent of Ithanalin's.

"Why did you run away?"

"You scary!"

Kilisha clamped her teeth tightly shut for a moment to keep from trembling, then said, "If you think I'm scary *now*, you should see what I'll be like if you ever try that again! You are going to *stay* in my master's house until my master is restored to life, do you hear me?"

"Sprigganalin hear fine!"

"Do you *understand* me?"

The thing's ears drooped, and its eyes widened.

"No," it said.

"Augh!" Kilisha fought a temptation to fling the idiotic little beast against the nearest wall.

Its eyes widened even further; its ears folded back.

"Listen to me," she growled.

"Sprigganalin listen!" it said, nodding desperately.

"You are going to *stay* in the house until *I* say you can go! If you *don't,* you will never have any fun ever again, I'll make sure of that! Your life will be the *opposite* of fun if you ever again set a single toe outside the door without my permission. *Now* do you understand?"

"Spriggans not real good with understanding."

Kilisha's grip on its neck tightened, and it quickly added, "But Sprigganalin stay in house! Promise, promise!"

"Good." Her hold relaxed. "You just remember that promise."

"Remember, yes!"

"Then let's go home," she said. She raised her head to get her bearings.

A good two dozen people were standing in a circle around her, staring at her.

She blinked at them, then said, "What's the matter with all of you people? Haven't you ever seen a wizard's apprentice before?"

Voices muttered, feet shuffled, and most of them turned away.

One boy, a few years younger than Kilisha, pointed and said helpfully, "You're losing your feather."

Kilisha turned her head and discovered that her hair ornament had slid down farther, and was now almost completely loose, one corner hanging from a tangle in her hair.

"Thank you," she said—but she didn't do anything about it. Both her hands were still clutching the spriggan. She just turned and began marching home, trying not to bob her head enough to lose the ornament entirely.

Chapter Twenty-four

Kelder was waiting on the doorstep. "I see you caught it," he said.

"Yes," Kilisha said, relieved to see him still there. "Is my mistress all right? Is everything else still secure?"

"Your mistress is fine," he said. "And I didn't see anything else get out."

"Good." She looked down at the spriggan clutched in her hand and wished she had some way of confining it—but she didn't. She stepped inside, set it on the floor, and released it.

Kelder watched as the spriggan promptly ran in circles, frightening the bench and chair. "There was another customer while you were out, but I told her the wizard was indisposed, and she went away," he said.

"Thank you," Kilisha said, as she disentangled the leather-and-feather device from her hair.

"I really need to go now—but I'll pass the word about your couch."

"Thank you," Kilisha repeated.

For a moment they both hesitated, as if something more was expected but neither of them quite knew what, and then Kelder

said, "Well, I'll come back if I have any news." He bowed, then
backed out the door, turned, and was gone.

Kilisha watched him go, then looked down at the ornament in
her hand and decided against restoring it to its customary place.
Instead she thrust it into the pouch on her belt, closed the door,
ordered the latch to stay closed, then wagged a finger at the spriggan and admonished it, "You stay in this house!"

The spriggan stopped running and stared up at her. "Stay!
Stay!" it said, nodding vigorously.

"Good," she said, as she straightened and marched to the
workshop.

Yara was there, peering into the brass bowl. "This looks like
overcooked beef gravy," she said, straightening up. "What is it?"

"I don't know what it is," Kilisha admitted. "It's something
Ithanalin had cooking when he was interrupted."

"Cooking? Don't you mean brewing?"

Confused, Kilisha said, "Well, *something*. Heating."

"You're sure it's magic? That Thani wasn't secretly cooking
behind my back?"

Kilisha realized that she wasn't sure of anything of the sort;
Ithanalin *might* have been cooking, and the magic her athame had
detected might have just been a minor protective spell or the like.
That would explain why the stuff in the bowl hadn't done anything
magical for two days. Telling Yara that just now, however, did not
seem like a good idea. "There was definitely wizardry there, and
it chimed once," she said.

Yara frowned. "Chimed?"

"The bowl rang like a bell without anyone touching it."

"Ah. Yes, that's magic." She nodded, then changed the subject.
"You caught the spriggan? That soldier said that that was why you
disobeyed my order to stay here."

"I caught it," Kilisha said. She was chagrined to realize that in
the urgency of pursuit she had completely forgotten Yara's orders.

"I got your jewelweed," Yara said. "You didn't say how
much." She lifted a sack as large as Lirrin.

Kilisha suppressed the urge to say anything about the absurdity of such an amount, or to mention that in fact Ithanalin had had jewelweed on hand all along. Instead she merely said, "Thank you."

"I told everyone I spoke to that we were looking for the couch," she said. "Just in case anyone sees it."

"That's good," Kilisha said.

"I told them, too!" Pirra called from the kitchen.

"Good for you!" Kilisha called back.

"Now what?" Yara asked.

"Now I practice Javan's Restorative, and we hope the couch is found soon."

"Oh." Yara hesitated, then asked, "Is it dangerous?"

"Any magic can be dangerous if it's not done well," Kilisha said, automatically quoting a statement Ithanalin had made to her countless times in the five years of her apprenticeship.

Yara recognized the words and grimaced.

"I'm sorry," Kilisha said. "I mean, he's right when he says that. I don't think this spell is going to be especially difficult; Istram thought I could do it easily enough."

"Istram?"

"Yes, he stopped by while you were out."

"And he didn't stay for lunch?"

"He's on Guild business, and couldn't spare the time."

Yara frowned. "What sort of Guild business?"

Kilisha hesitated; Yara, despite being Ithanalin's wife, was no wizard, not a member of the Guild or, at least in theory, privy to its secrets. All the same, this particular affair was hardly secret. "Something about the usurper in Ethshar of the Sands," she said.

"Oh, I heard everyone talking about that!" Yara said. "Rumors are everywhere."

"Yes, well, I don't know any details, but the Guild is studying the situation, and Istram's helping."

"Good for him. Well, I hope that when this is all over he'll come by again and stay a little longer!"

"As you please, Mistress," Kilisha said, bowing slightly, and wondering whether Yara would be glad to see her come back to visit when *she* was a wizard in her own right, rather than an apprentice.

That assumed, of course, that she ever did become a wizard—and if she didn't learn Javan's Restorative and use it on Ithanalin, that might well never happen.

"I should practice the spell," she said.

"Of course," Yara said. "I'll see to the children, and bring you something to eat in a bit."

"Thank you."

With that Yara withdrew into the kitchen and closed the door.

Kilisha hesitated, glancing at the parlor door. Ordinarily that, too, would be closed while serious magic was being practiced, but she did not want to miss any callers—especially not with the enchanted latch apparently eager to let in anyone who knocked.

And she wanted to keep an eye on the spriggan and the furniture, as well.

The door stayed open, and she turned her attention to the ingredients she would need for the spell. Peacock plumes, incense, water . . .

First she went through the motions slowly and carefully without drawing her athame or invoking any actual magic, just to get the feel of them. She recited the words until she was comfortable with their rhythms. She handled the ingredients, sensing their magical natures. She lit a candle and set her pan of warm water on a tripod above a charcoal burner, then opened a vent into the chimney so that the charcoal fumes would not poison her. She lit the charcoal and waited until the water began to steam gently.

And when it did she found a stick and snapped it in two, then placed the two pieces on the workbench.

Then, finally, she drew her athame, recited the initial incantation, and lit the block of incense.

She could feel the magic begin to gather almost immediately.

She proceeded slowly and carefully, crushing the jewelweed leaves in her hand and flinging some in the water, others onto the incense, where they flared up briefly before being reduced to flying ash. Smoke and steam and ash rose and thickened, gathering in an increasingly unnatural fashion.

After some forty minutes of this the entire room was thick with smog, and a great opaque cloud of it hung swirling over the workbench. She made the transitional gestures, completed the first chant and began the second, and with her athame clutched in both hands began to cut the cloud into the shape she wanted.

How she knew what shape to make she could not have explained; by this time the magic was as thick as the smoke. Somewhere in the back of her mind she knew that she could not possibly be breathing the air in the workshop without coughing, probably could not breathe it at all, had the magic not been flowing through her, protecting her and giving her power and guiding her hands.

She trimmed and shaped and shaved the thick gray mist, transforming it from an amorphous blob into something roughly resembling a corkscrew, and the magic was strong and easy. . . .

And the spriggan shrieked happily from somewhere near her right foot, "Oooooh, cloud!"

The athame hesitated, slipped, and suddenly it was just a knife and the vapors were just smoke and steam and she began coughing desperately, waving a hand in front of her face to try to clear the air. She staggered from the workshop into the parlor, gasping. She flung open the front door and sucked in the cleaner air of Wizard Street.

"Awww, cloud gone!" the spriggan said somewhere behind her.

Kilisha, able to breathe once again, bit her lip to keep from screaming.

The spell was ruined and would have to be started over from the beginning—and it could easily have gone wildly wrong, interrupted like that!

It *might* have gone wrong as it was. It *felt* as if it had simply dissipated harmlessly, but she couldn't be absolutely sure.

She looked down at herself, and saw two hands, two feet, her apprentice robe—everything seemed to be normal.

She wasn't the only one in the house, though. She turned.

The parlor furniture was cowering in the corners; clearly all of it remembered, on some level, what could happen when a spell went wrong.

It all seemed to be there, and undamaged, though. She closed the door, told the latch, "*Stay* closed," then made her way back to the workshop.

A look under the sheet reassured her that Ithanalin hadn't changed; then she proceeded to the kitchen, where she found Yara and the children finishing their lunch.

"What happened?" Telleth asked. "What's all the smoke?"

"A spell went bad," Kilisha explained. "That spriggan interrupted me, and I lost control."

"Did it hurt anything?" Lirrin asked, eyes wide.

"I don't think so," Kilisha replied. "I came back here to be sure it hadn't done anything to any of you."

"We're fine," Yara snapped.

Kilisha, startled by her tone, didn't reply immediately, but after a moment of gathering her wits she said, "I'll try again, then."

"Do you need to fast?" Yara asked.

"No," Kilisha said.

"Then eat first, and let the place air out. *Then* try again."

"Yes, Mistress," Kilisha said meekly. At Yara's direction she found bread and cheese and salt pork, and sat at the table. She ate quickly, but even so, by the time she had finished the air in the workshop had cleared, the smoke vanished, leaving no lingering trace.

No natural smoke would have faded away so completely so quickly. Kilisha had not expected even *magical* smoke to disappear so easily; perhaps having the spell interrupted had something to do with it.

At least no one was waving any tentacles around; she wouldn't have wanted to have to try to turn a squid back to a human.

She took a deep breath of clean air, then began the spell anew.

Distracted by Yara and lunch, she had forgotten to tell the spriggan not to interrupt. The creature made a few remarks and asked a few questions, but Kilisha simply ignored them, keeping her attention focused on the spell.

At least this way she knew the spriggan wasn't slipping out of the house and wandering away.

Yara glanced in the door at one point and caught the spriggan climbing on a stool, apparently about to grab for something; she hurried in and snatched the little nuisance up, then carried it into the parlor. Kilisha saw it all from the corner of her eye and was grateful, but refused to let it distract her.

The cloud of smoke and steam formed, ash drifting in the currents and magic thick in the air, and Kilisha shaped it as she knew it had to be shaped, twisting and carving it into a crooked helix that she guided down over the broken stick. Her eyes stung with smoke, and her hair was soaked with sweat and steam, but she could feel the magic all through her, warm and strong, strongest in her hands as she completed the ritual.

The smoke covered the broken stick, hiding it from mortal sight, but Kilisha could sense it, could see it simultaneously broken and intact as if two images were glowing on the bench before her.

And then the spell was over, the smoke dissipated with impossible suddenness, and the stick lay unbroken upon the bench.

Kilisha pushed hair from her eyes with a smoke-stained, unsteady hand, and smiled down at the stick.

She had done it! She had performed Javan's Restorative.

For the first time, she had learned a new spell without another wizard there to guide her.

She sat down abruptly on the stool, grinning broadly. She *loved* being a wizard!

As she rested, letting the outside world return to her awareness, Kilisha heard a voice from the parlor—Yara's voice, talking quietly. Yara must have gone around the outside of the house—or perhaps slipped through the workshop when Kilisha was distracted by the spell. Her attention had been so focused on her magic that that was possible.

For a moment Kilisha sat on the stool, staring happily at the restored stick and feeling pleased with herself, but then she could no longer contain the enthusiasm at her accomplishment that she felt bubbling up inside her. She jumped off the stool, snatched up the stick, and bounced into the parlor to find Yara standing at the front door, talking to someone outside.

"It worked!" Kilisha burst out happily.

Yara turned, startled. "Thani?" she asked.

Much of Kilisha's good cheer abruptly evaporated. "No, Mistress," she said. "But I got the restoration spell to work. See?" She held up the stick.

Yara looked at it.

"It's a stick," she said.

"Yes, but it was *broken,* and now it isn't," Kilisha explained.

"And this will fix Thani?"

"It should," Kilisha said. "The mirror thinks it will."

"But you need the jewelweed and the couch, first?"

"I *have* the jewelweed, Mistress. All I need is the couch. And the other furniture, and the spriggan." She gestured at her surroundings, where the chair and bench appeared to be watching her, the coatrack was pacing back and forth on its tether, and the spriggan was perched atop the end table, dancing from foot to foot as the table rocked back and forth.

"You hear that?" Yara said, turning back to the door. "We just need the couch!"

"We're looking," someone replied, and Kilisha recognized Nissitha's voice.

"Well, please keep looking," Yara said. Then she closed the door and turned to Kilisha. "You can do the spell? You're sure?"

"Well, I did it once," Kilisha said. "I think I can do it again."

"Won't it be harder putting together so many parts of a living person than just unbreaking a stick?"

"Um . . ." Kilisha hadn't thought about that. She remembered how she had had to shape the magical smoke cloud to fit the shape of the pieces and force them back together, then tried to imagine wrapping a cloud around the mirror, the dish, the spoon, the rug, and all the rest. . . .

"Probably," she admitted.

"Then I think you should practice some more. Keep practicing until we find the couch! I don't want it going wrong when you try it on my husband."

"Yes, Mistress," Kilisha said. She looked down at the stick in her hand, a simple object that had been broken into two simple pieces, and considered how many complicated pieces Ithanalin was in. Then she looked back at Yara and said, "May I have an egg, please?"

✦

Chapter Twenty-five

Reassembling a smashed egg with Javan's Restorative was different from repairing a stick—largely because of the liquid nature of its contents—but was not, Kilisha was pleasantly surprised to discover, significantly more difficult. A shattered earthenware mug was midway between the two.

She ignored the occasional voices in the parlor and kitchen, and the frequent activities of the spriggan.

Allowing for rest periods and preparation time those few iterations of the spell used up most of the afternoon, and after the last Kilisha decided that further attempts could wait until after supper. She undertook her usual chores, sweeping out the kitchen and picking up after the children, then did a quick inventory of the furniture and the spriggan before returning to the kitchen to assist Yara with dinner preparations.

As she chopped carrots and onions for the soup Kilisha asked whether there was any news of the couch, and Yara responded with a detailed report that lasted well into the meal but, in the end, came down to "no."

Kelder had mobilized the city guard—that portion of it not committed to other, more urgent activities such as guarding the

Fortress in case Empress Tabaea launched an attack, or running errands for the Wizards' Guild in their attempts to analyze and neutralize the self-proclaimed empress, or preparing refuges for the fleeing nobility of Ethshar of the Sands. The guards at all eight gates had denied seeing any ambulatory furniture leave the city, and at least a hundred other guards were patrolling the streets, looking for the couch and spreading the news that it was wanted.

Of course, they would be patrolling the streets in any case, as part of their ordinary duties, but Kelder had assured Yara that they would also be searching for the missing couch.

Opir had all of Kilisha's friends and family from Eastgate and the surrounding neighborhoods making inquiries through the usual network of chatter and gossip. Yara thought it very unlikely that the couch could be in Eastgate, or would even have passed through—it would have been seen, and the news would have been reported by now. The search had now spread to Eastside, Lakeshore, and Farmgate, and should eventually take in the entire city—save perhaps the wealthy areas where neighbors gossiped at fancy balls and dinners, rather than in the streets and shared courtyards.

Istram had brought word to the Wizards' Guild, and the missing couch would be placed on the agenda for discussion as soon as Tabaea had been dealt with. In the meantime, several wizards and apprentices had promised to tell him if they saw such a couch.

And in their own neighborhood, on Wizard Street between Lakeshore and Center City, Adagan and Nissitha and others were making inquiries. Nissitha was very proud of the effort she was putting in, but as yet had no positive results.

Kilisha was impressed by the extent of the net being cast, but even so, after a moment she remarked, "Except for the soldiers, we haven't heard anything from the south half of the city, or from the waterfront."

"Not yet," Yara agreed. "If the couch isn't found soon, we'll have to start looking there."

"What if we *never* find it?" Lirrin asked, worried, and Pirra burst out crying. Yara quickly jumped from her chair and snatched up her youngest to comfort her, hugging her to one shoulder. Pirra's weeping faded to a whimper.

"We'll find it," Kilisha said. "You can't hide something as big as a couch forever!"

"You can if it's invisible," Telleth said.

"Yes, but it's not invisible," Kilisha said.

"How do you know?" the boy asked.

"It wasn't invisible when it left here. Kelder saw it go. And it doesn't have any hands to work spells with, so it couldn't turn itself invisible."

"Well, what if some evil magician, a demonologist or a sorcerer or someone, turned it invisible?"

Kilisha glowered at him. "Why would anyone do that?"

"I don't know—but why else hasn't anyone found it yet?"

"There are plenty of places to hide in this city," Kilisha said. "Someone will find it eventually. You'll see."

And with that she pushed away her half-finished meal and stalked back into the workshop, where she went through Ithanalin's book of spells once more, looking for some magic that might help find the couch.

She found none, and in the end set about practicing Javan's Restorative again, failing her first attempt to reassemble a shattered jar, then getting it right on the second try.

She also repaired and cleaned a torn tunic, and fixed a toy juggler Telleth had broken a twelvenight before; she had decided that if she was going to work the spell, she might as well make it useful, rather than specifically breaking things so that she might restore them.

The jar, the tunic, and the toy all came out as good as new, gleaming and flawless. By the time she finally went to bed she wondered why the spell wasn't used more often.

Of course, the ingredients weren't free, and it took at least an hour, usually more, of a wizard's time—hardly reasonable for repairing broken toys. It really wasn't an especially difficult spell, though. She was confident that she would be able to use it to restore Ithanalin, once she had all the pieces.

All she needed was the couch, and with so many friends out looking for it, it would surely turn up soon. She told herself, as she lay on her narrow bed, that it would probably be found within a day or so.

It wasn't. The nineteenth and twentieth of Harvest passed without any news. Kilisha grew very tired of working the same spell over and over, and eventually, despite Yara's insistence that she practice the Restorative, she began reviewing some of her other spells instead. The possibility of making a few homunculi to join the search for the couch occurred to her, but a careful study of a few likely spells in Ithanalin's book convinced her that she was not yet ready to attempt them on her own, with no master to guide her hand—or to interpret Ithanalin's sometimes cryptic phrasing.

She wished she could go out looking for the couch herself. When the searchers continued to report no success she had begun to wonder whether it might have somehow gotten up on a rooftop, or in a ditch somewhere; she wanted to levitate herself again and see if she could spot it from above. She almost managed to convince herself that she had missed it before because she had only looked at ground level, at streets and courtyards and gardens.

Yara, however, forbade Kilisha to leave the house. "I don't trust the furniture, let alone that spriggan," she explained. "I want someone here who knows magic, and who can catch them if they get away. And I want someone here in case the couch comes back, or someone comes by with news."

Kilisha was tempted to argue, but resisted. "Yes, Mistress," she said.

Yara herself, though, felt free to go out searching, or recruiting more searchers. By the afternoon of the twenty-first it seemed as if half the city was looking for that red velvet fugitive. Yara and the children had gone to Arena and Bath to post more announcements on the message boards and see whether anyone had responded to yesterday's crop, and Kilisha had the house to herself—except for the furniture, milling about the parlor and tangling the ropes, and the smaller pieces thumping in their boxes, and the spriggan swinging by its fingertips from the edge of the workbench.

She was staring at the heap of jewelweed, trying to decide whether to attempt yet another iteration of Javan's Restorative and wondering what she could try it on this time, when someone knocked on the front door.

The distraction was welcome, and the possibility that someone might have found the couch gave her steps speed as she leapt from the stool and hurried to the parlor. She dodged the bench as she ran to the door.

The latch had already unlocked itself; Kilisha had to give it only the slightest tug to open the door and find herself staring at the tall, dark-haired beauty who stood on the stoop.

Kilisha had expected Kelder or Opir or Adagan, or perhaps Istram. It took her a moment to adjust to the reality and recognize this visitor.

"Lady Nuvielle!!" she said. She bowed hastily. "A pleasure to see you, my lady; but alas, my master is indisposed."

"Is he still? I'm sorry to hear that," Nuvielle replied. "But perhaps you can answer my question, apprentice—Kinsha, is it?"

"Kilisha, my lady. And I fear I have not yet studied animations, and can tell you very little about your pet dragon."

"It's not about the dragon."

Kilisha blinked, trying to imagine what else the noblewoman might want. "Did you wish to order another creation, then? Or some other spell?"

"No. I came here to ask a question. I came here three days ago to ask the same question and was turned away, and this time I am resolute—I will have an answer."

Kilisha remembered almost bumping into Nuvielle while chasing the spriggan; it had not occurred to her that the Lady Treasurer might have been headed to Ithanalin's door. Kelder had told her he had turned away a customer, and she had not bothered to ask who the customer might have been, but presumably that had been Nuvielle.

If it wasn't about the dragon, though, then what could she want? Was there a problem with the taxes, perhaps?

Whatever the aristocrat wanted, she was clearly determined, and the simplest thing to do was to cooperate. "Of course, my lady," Kilisha said. "I apologize for the inconvenience." She hesitated, then said, "I would invite you in, but I fear the shop is disordered at the moment."

"Is it?"

"Very much so."

"Is your couch missing, then? The rather good one, dark wood with crimson velvet upholstery?"

Kilisha's jaw dropped—something that until that moment she had thought merely a figure of speech. She quickly snapped it shut again, and said, "How did you know? I mean . . . have you seen it?"

"I believe I have, yes. That was the basis for my question."

"Then by all means, my lady, please tell me more! The couch's absence has been a matter of great concern to us!"

"It's quite an unusual couch, isn't it? I've never seen another quite like it, have you?"

"No, my lady." Kilisha fought down the urge to say more, to demand an immediate explanation; Nuvielle would come to the point eventually, and there was no need to antagonize her.

"Do you know where it's from?"

"No, my lady. My master had it when I first came here, and I never thought to ask."

"I rather admired it when I came here before, and I did not recall ever seeing another quite like it, which seemed entirely fitting for a wizard's parlor couch—and then a few days ago I *did* see another like it, under surprising circumstances, in a room I had visited a hundred times, and it seemed a very curious coincidence—so curious that I wondered whether it *was* merely a coincidence, or whether that same couch had somehow been transported."

"Where is it, my lady?"

"Well, that's what's so strange about it—how is it you don't *know*?"

Kilisha began to suspect that Nuvielle was deliberately teasing her. "It escaped, my lady," she said. "The accident that left my master indisposed animated that couch, and it fled. We are very eager for its return, but we don't know where it went."

"Ah."

She *was* teasing. "My lady, please," Kilisha said. "Where is it?"

"I wonder how it got past the guards? It must be quite clever. For a couch."

"Guards?"

"At the Fortress door," Nuvielle said.

"It's in the *Fortress*?"

There had been sign after sign that some of the furniture had wanted to get into the Fortress—Kilisha couldn't begin to imagine why—but she had thought that was impossible. The doors were locked and guarded, and surely something the size of a *couch* couldn't have slipped in unnoticed!

Nuvielle nodded. "It is, in fact, in the overlord's private apartments. He thought the household staff must have placed it there as a surprise for his birthday. He was very puzzled when they denied it, but he's been too busy with other concerns to pursue the matter. And I was quite startled to see it there."

Kilisha swallowed. The notion that the overlord himself was involved in Ithanalin's little disaster was rather distressing. "Did you tell him where it came from, my lady?"

"No, because I wasn't certain," Nuvielle said. "I did say I'd seen one like it once, and would make some inquiries, and here I am. You say it *escaped*?"

"Yes, my lady. A tax collector interrupted one of my master's spells, then left the door open, allowing the couch to escape."

"A tax collector? One of *my* tax collectors?"

"Yes, my lady."

For a moment the two women stared at one another, then Nuvielle said, "That was very careless of him."

"Yes, my lady."

"And you want the couch back?"

"Very much so, my lady."

"The overlord rather likes it."

"I'm sorry to hear that, my lady, as we really must *insist* upon its return." Kilisha's voice was unsteady as she said this—she was defying the lords of the Hegemony! "My master's indisposition is related," she explained. "We must have the couch to restore him to health."

"Ah. And you say one of my tax collectors is responsible?"

"Only indirectly, my lady. A spriggan was involved, as well, and simple misfortune."

"Still," she mused, "it would seem that I owe it to you to make amends."

"If you could aid us in recovering the couch . . ."

"I can get you into the Fortress and to the overlord's door," Nuvielle said, "but beyond that I'm afraid it's between you and Wulran."

"Wulr—Wulran?"

"My nephew Wulran. The overlord."

"Of—of course, my lady." Kilisha's voice squeaked embarrassingly as she spoke. Between her and Wulran? But "Wulran" was Wulran III, Overlord of Ethshar of the Rocks, Triumvir of the Hegemony of the Three Ethshars, Commander of the Holy Armies and Defender of the Gods. And she was just Kilisha of Eastgate, a mere apprentice.

"Would you care to accompany me back to the Fortress right now, to take care of this?"

Kilisha started to say yes, then stopped.

All her life, and never more than these past few days, she had always rushed into things, never planning ahead but just doing whatever she thought needed doing. She had gone chasing cats without stopping to think, had gone chasing furniture unprepared, and had just generally hurried off thoughtlessly. Ithanalin had spent the past five years trying to teach her to plan out her actions, to make sure everything was ready before she began a spell; she had been lectured repeatedly about the dangers of haste, especially where something as dangerous as wizardry was involved. While she had finally learned to prepare spells properly, she still often dashed headlong into everything else.

This time, though, she wouldn't. This time she would take the time to plan and prepare, to think it through.

For one thing, Yara had ordered her to stay in the house.

For another, she wanted to have suitable magic ready, in case she needed it.

For a third, tackling something as big and smart as the couch alone seemed foolhardy. It clearly *was* clever—whatever portion of Ithanalin's spirit it had gotten had plainly included the wiles necessary to get past the Fortress guards and into the overlord's apartments, and furthermore it had *chosen* to do so, so its motivations were, to say the least, not obvious. Kilisha thought she might want all the help she could get.

"I must make some preparations, my lady," she said. "The couch may not be entirely cooperative, and I want to be ready."

"As you choose. When shall I expect you, then?"

Kilisha hesitated. Surely, the Lady Treasurer of Ethshar of the Rocks was not about to rearrange her schedule to suit the preferences of a wizard's apprentice!

"Would midmorning suit you, perhaps?" Nuvielle suggested.

"Tomorrow?"

"Yes, tomorrow; shall we say, two hours before noon, at the north door of the Fortress?"

Kilisha bowed deeply. "That would be *excellent*, my lady. I am most grateful for your assistance."

"Tomorrow, then," Nuvielle said, acknowledging the bow with a nod. She turned.

Kilisha stood in the door and watched her go, then stepped inside. She closed the door, made certain the latch was behaving itself, and then allowed herself a broad smile.

"Tomorrow!" she said. "Tomorrow, tomorrow, tomorrow!"

Behind her the spriggan giggled, and chirped happily, "To-morrow!"

Chapter Twenty-six

When Yara returned home to prepare supper she encountered Kilisha standing in the kitchen, grinning foolishly. "I found it!" the apprentice said.

Yara started to smile; then her brows lowered and she frowned. She called in the children and sent them upstairs with a few quick pats, then turned back to Kilisha. "You found the couch?"

"Yes!"

"But I told you to stay here!"

"I *did* stay here!" Kilisha protested.

"You used magic?" Yara said, the frown softening.

"No," Kilisha admitted. "Someone told me where it is. I've arranged to meet her tomorrow morning, and we'll go get it."

"What if it runs away again tonight, though?"

"I don't think it will," Kilisha said. "It's in the Fortress."

Yara blinked. "How did it get in *there*? There are guards everywhere!"

"I don't know. Nobody seems to know. That's where it is, though."

"Why are you waiting until morning?"

"Because I promised you I wouldn't leave the house today!

And besides, I want to have some time to prepare, and I want to bring along some help—I was thinking Opir and Kelder and Adagan would be good, if they're willing. The couch is heavy, and it might be hard to catch."

"Do you think so? Will the four of you be enough to carry it all the way down from the Fortress, then, and up here?"

"Oh, once we've caught it and gotten it outside I intend to levitate it," Kilisha said. "I'm a wizard, after all."

"You're an *apprentice*."

"And a *wizard*, Mistress," Kilisha insisted. "I'm a member of the Guild, even if I am just an apprentice."

Yara looked at her silently for a moment, then said, "I suppose that's true. You're sure you can levitate it safely?"

"Absolutely sure, Mistress. I have the spell already prepared and tested." She patted her belt pouch. "It's in a potion."

Yara considered her husband's apprentice a moment longer, then said, "Good. Then help me with supper."

A few minutes later, as Kilisha lifted a heavy pot of water onto the stove and Yara trimmed a leg of lamb, Yara said, "I'm not sure Opir and Adagan and Kelder will all be stopping by this evening."

"That's all right," Kilisha said as she pushed the pot into place on the hottest spot. "I'll send them a message tonight."

Yara put down the knife she had been wielding. "How? I don't want you or Telleth running around the streets—"

"The Spell of Invaded Dreams," Kilisha interrupted. She stepped back from the stove, then glanced at Yara. "At least, I know I can reach Opir that way. I'm assuming Kelder told the guard at the Fortress his true name, and I think I remember it. Adagan I'm not sure about, since so many magicians use false names, but he lives so close that I could stop by easily enough."

"The Spell of Invaded Dreams?"

"Yes, Mistress."

"And you thought of that yourself, instead of rushing out on foot?"

"Yes, Mistress."

"Then you really *are* starting to think like a wizard, finally!"

Kilisha smiled. "Yes, Mistress," she said.

Yara picked up the knife and went back to work. It was several minutes later that Kilisha heard her mutter, "Good!"

That night Kilisha gave the spriggan careful instructions, laced with the most terrifying threats she could think of, then went to bed early.

The spriggan obeyed, awakening her around midnight—though she wished that it had found another method, rather than jumping up and down on her head shrieking, "Wake, wake! You said wake!"

"Shut up!" she hissed, grabbing for the creature in the dark but missing it as it danced aside. "You'll wake the whole house!"

"You said wake," it insisted.

"I said wake *me*," Kilisha said, sitting up. "Just me, nobody else!"

"Sorry, sorry," the spriggan replied.

Kilisha yawned, blinked, and then reluctantly said, "Thank you. You did well."

"Happy happy!"

"Now shut up and go downstairs." She knew she shouldn't tell even the tiniest part of her master to shut up, but the spriggan could be *so* stupid and annoying. . . .

The spriggan bounced away, and she groped for her robe.

A few moments later she was in the workshop, preparing the Lesser Spell of Invaded Dreams, which would let her send a message to one of her chosen assistants as he slept, a message that the recipient would, at least in theory, remember clearly when he woke up, without the fuzziness of ordinary dreams.

Unfortunately, she would have no way of knowing whether the spell had worked properly. If Kelder had been given late-night duty, or Adagan had sat up late working on his witchcraft, then her message might not go through—the recipient had to be asleep. If that happened she wouldn't know it until they failed to show up in the morning, so for those two she intended to use the much more difficult Greater Spell of Invaded Dreams—or at least attempt it. For her brother Opir, who always liked his sleep, she could use the Lesser.

It took half an hour of ritual with her athame, incense, and a pinch of dust, but she was fairly certain it had gone properly and her message had been sent.

That done, she started on the Greater, directed at Kelder, which called for blood and silver as well as the other ingredients. For this one, by the end of over an hour of preparation she had worked herself into a trance, and although she knew she was still sitting cross-legged on the workshop floor she felt herself standing in a strange stone room where half a dozen men lay sleeping on narrow cots. This, she supposed, was a barracks room somewhere in the city, and the men were presumably soldiers.

One of them was Kelder. She called to him.

He sat up, startled, knocking his blanket aside, and she saw he was naked. She blushed, and almost let the spell break, but caught herself at the last instant.

"It's me," she said. "Ithanalin's apprentice, Kilisha. I'm in your dream."

"Well, that's nothing new," he said, pulling up his blanket.

"No, I . . ." Then the meaning of his words sank in, and she blushed again. She gathered herself up mentally, then decided that she needed to assert her power a little more obviously. She waved her hands, and the barracks room disappeared. Kelder's uniform appeared, and the two of them were standing side by side on the city wall, looking out over the farms to the southeast.

Kilisha had never been on the city wall, though she had levitated high enough to see over it; she supposed she had somehow pulled this scene from Kelder's memory.

"This dream is magic," she said. "I'm using the Spell of Invaded Dreams to tell you that I want your help. I've learned that the couch is in the Fortress, and I would be grateful if you could meet me at the north door tomorrow morning, two hours before noon, and help me retrieve it."

"Two hours before noon? I think I have collection duty—"

"Tell your officer that Lady Nuvielle sent for you," Kilisha interrupted. "She's the one who found the couch and will be letting us into the Fortress."

"The treasurer herself found it? The overlord's aunt?"

"That's right," Kilisha said. "Please be there!" She twisted the spell's magic, and the two of them were standing at the north door of the Fortress, with the sun two-thirds of the way up the eastern sky. "Here, at this hour."

"I'll try," Kelder said. "If I remember."

"You'll remember," Kilisha told him. "That's how the spell works. That's how you'll know it was magic, and not just an ordinary dream."

"I think I've heard about that," Kelder said. "I'll be there, if I can."

Kilisha smiled at him. "Good!"

He smiled back. "Now what?" he asked.

"What do you mean?"

"Well, I mean here we are, in a perfectly good dream, and you've delivered your message—what do you want to do next? I see you can change the scenery, and make clothes appear and disappear; how long will the dream last? What else can we do?" He stepped toward her.

"I—I need to get some sleep," Kilisha said, pushing him away. "I'll see you in the morning." She broke the spell.

Then she sat there on the floor as the smoke dissipated and said, "Stupid. That was stupid. I should have . . ."

But she didn't know what she should have done. The thought of spending more time with Kelder was certainly not unpleasant, but really, she had far more urgent things to deal with. And he had been dreadfully forward. . . .

But it was a *dream*, not real, and she couldn't decide whether that made his attentions more or less acceptable.

She sat there a moment longer, trying to forget about Kelder and concentrate on preparing a final iteration to contact Adagan. Finally she said, "Oh, to the Void with it. It's late and I'm tired and I'm not even sure it's his real name. I'll go down there in the morning."

"We go together?" the spriggan asked.

"Ask me in the morning," Kilisha said as she got to her feet and headed for the stairs.

She slept later than she had intended, and rushed through her breakfast. As she ate she tried to plan out the rest of the morning. Should she talk to Adagan first, then come back and get herself ready, or should she make her own preparations and then stop at Adagan's shop on the way?

Adagan, she decided, might have his own preparations to make. She would talk to him first.

She had just decided this when Yara asked her, "Did you reach everyone last night?"

"I talked to Kelder," she said, "and I sent Opir a message. I didn't get to Adagan."

"I'll send Telleth, then," Yara replied—and that, Kilisha saw, was the best solution all around.

When she had finished eating she went to the workshop, and as she began gathering supplies she heard the rear door slam as Telleth left on his errand.

Her athame was in the sheath on her belt, but everything else she needed would have to go in her belt pouch. She took a quick inventory of the little leather container.

There were the three potions she had prepared, with their smudged labels. She frowned, pulled them out, and found a pen, planning to make new labels.

Then she paused. Each vial held seven doses, all she had of each spell. What if one of them were to be spilled? She wanted to plan for every eventuality, for once. Maybe there was such a thing as being too cautious—but then she glanced over her shoulder at Ithanalin, crouching in the corner.

Things could go wrong. Things often *did* go wrong. Best to be ready when they did.

Accordingly, she found three more vials, smaller ones, and wrote new labels for them: STRENGTH, V'S LEV., T'S LEV. Then she poured part of the contents of each of the original vials into the appropriate new container, so that she had, as best she could tell, four doses of each spell in the old vials and three of each in the new. She capped them all securely, wrapped them in a soft cloth, and tucked them back in the pouch.

Her vial of brimstone, useful for Thrindle's Combustion, was almost empty; she refilled it.

The tiny bottle of dragon's blood was still in its place; she debated adding more, but decided against it, as Ithanalin's supply was limited—and really, there was no point in taking the ingredients for any spell that required more than a few heartbeats to prepare, and the only really quick spell she knew that needed dragon's blood was Fendel's Spectacular Illusion. She could imagine how that might possibly be useful once, but not how repeating it could help.

There were a few fast spells that called for nothing more than a pinch of dust, and the bottom of the pouch looked a little too clean, so she quickly wiped a handful of powder and fluff from the tops of a row of jars, then poured it into the pouch.

The bit of chrysolite she kept ready for conjuring the Yellow Cloud was still in its rag wrapping, where it belonged.

That was everything in the pouch; she looked over the shelves above the workbench, trying to decide what to add—and trying to ignore the brown goo in the brass bowl atop the oil lamp. She had been refilling that lamp faithfully ever since Ithanalin's accident, and the stuff in the bowl had cooked down from a liquid to an ugly paste that was now starting to dry out and crack; she hoped that wouldn't do anything terrible to whatever magic it might hold—if it held any, and wasn't just a forbidden sauce or gravy.

She spotted the big earthenware jar where the entire family stored any spiders they were able to catch and crush. There were at least two handy spells that called for powdered spider and took no more than half a minute, so she added an envelope of that, and then took a mummified bat's wing from the drawer and tucked that in, in case she wanted to use the Spell of Stupefaction.

If the couch wasn't feeling cooperative the Spell of Stupefaction might be very helpful. In fact, putting the Spell of Stupefaction in a potion, instead of Tracel's Levitation, might have been clever, but she hadn't thought of it at the time and it was too late now.

And of course, she couldn't really be sure it would *work* on something that was animated, but not truly alive.

The Displaced Whistle might be useful as a distraction, and she started to reach for the required curly seashell, but then she remembered that it also called for a fresh-plucked blade of grass. She could hardly hope to find grass growing inside the Fortress. She left the seashell where it was, and looked around thoughtfully.

Ash might be useful; the Polychrome Smoke used ash. Usually she assumed that she would be able to find that readily wherever she went, but perhaps the overlord's hearth was cleaned regularly—especially since it was still summer, and not yet chilly enough to really need a fire even at night. She made a quick trip to the kitchen and returned with a vial of fine gray powder from the stove.

She hoped that this would be enough; she couldn't think of any other quick spells she knew. If she had time for anything more elaborate, anything requiring extensive preparation or other ingredients, she would just have to come back here, or ask another magician for help.

Of course, she might want things other than magic. She added the linen purse containing all her money—which came to six bits in copper and one in silver, hardly enough to be useful in bribing the Fortress guards, but it might be useful somewhere. Ordinarily she let the little bag hang from her belt, but this was not the time to worry about cutpurses, so into the pouch it went.

If she needed a blade, her athame would work as well as any other knife—or better, really, as it was stronger and sharper than an ordinary knife, and had its ability to keep her free of any bonds.

She looked down at the pouch for a moment, trying to guess what more she might need, and could not think of anything.

Her plan was to go to the overlord's apartments with Lady Nuvielle, bringing Kelder and Opir and Adagan with her, then to simply carry the couch out. Getting it home from the Fortress might involve leading it, or hiring a wagon, or perhaps even levitating it—it would depend on circumstances.

Leading it might call for a rope. That wouldn't fit in the pouch, but she intended to bring plenty of rope. Most of the household's lighter cords were already in use holding the other furniture, but there was the coil of rope she had used to bring back the bench and chair—she had replaced it with shorter, lighter strands when tying them to the line in the chimney.

She straightened up, fastened her belt and pouch and knife securely around her waist, and slung the rope on her shoulder. Then she told Ithanalin, "It won't be much longer, Master," and marched out into the morning sun.

Chapter Twenty-seven

Adagan was waiting at his door, just as Kilisha had hoped he would be, and the two of them strolled down Wizard Street together, then turned north on Cross Avenue.

As they walked Kilisha asked Adagan what magic he had brought, and was answered with a rambling disquisition on how witchcraft differed from wizardry in requiring no specific ingredients or preparatory rituals.

"What about herbs?" Kilisha asked as they rounded the corner from Cross Avenue onto the East Road. "Or those crystals?"

"Oh, well, that's not the same thing," Adagan said. "The crystals are just to aid in focusing the mind, and the herbs—that's really herbalism, not true witchcraft. Most of us learn some of that, but it's not really the same thing."

"So you know *two* kinds of magic? I thought the Brotherhood didn't approve of that—and I *know* the Wizards' Guild doesn't."

"No, no, it's all still witchcraft!"

"You just said it wasn't."

"But it's . . . well, herbalism isn't *really* magic. . . ."

"Don't let Urrel hear you say that."

"But it isn't! Herbalism is just the knowledge of the natural properties of plants, while magic is the *altering* of nature!"

"Oh, I don't accept that," Kilisha said. "How are you defining nature?"

That debate lasted until they reached Market Street, where they crossed to the Old East Road, which wound its way up the hill toward the Fortress.

It wasn't quite as steep as Steep Street, but it was steep enough that the conversation faded away for a time; both were saving their breath for climbing.

As they neared Fortress Street, though, and the gray stone walls towered ahead of them, Kilisha asked, "Why didn't you levitate up here?" She didn't look at Adagan as she spoke; she was trying to gauge the sun's angle from the shadows on the pavement.

"Because it would take just as much energy as walking," he replied. "Witchcraft doesn't create energy, just redirects it."

"And that's different from herbalism?" The shadows looked right; Kilisha judged that it was very close to the appointed time of two hours before noon.

Adagan refused to revive the argument and instead retorted, "Why didn't *you* levitate?"

"I'm saving my spells for later, just in case," Kilisha replied. "Besides, it wouldn't be very polite to leave you behind." The truth was that it hadn't occurred to her.

"I thought you didn't have the ingredients. You wizards always need your strange powders and stones and smoke."

"I have a potion right here," Kilisha said, patting her pouch. "But it would only lift *me*, and I didn't want to leave you behind."

"I'd have levitated if you did," Adagan said. "It doesn't take *more* energy than climbing, it just doesn't take any *less*."

"Ah. I'm sorry I didn't suggest it, then, but there's no point now."

And in fact, there wasn't, as they had reached Fortress Street. Kilisha turned right and led the way to the north door.

Kelder was waiting for them, chatting idly with the guards, and Kilisha, remembering the dream they had shared, almost blushed at the sight of him.

There was no sign of Opir. Kilisha wondered whether the dream had reached him. There was no sign of Lady Nuvielle, either, which was rather more important.

Kelder fell silent and watched their approach, then said, "I haven't seen the treasurer yet."

"She'll be here," Kilisha said, not meeting Kelder's eyes. She hoped her certainty wasn't misplaced. She didn't really know Lady Nuvielle, but she assumed anyone the overlord trusted to manage the city's finances must be fairly reliable. Wulran III wouldn't have given her the job just because she was his aunt; for one thing, he had plenty of aunts to choose from. Wulran's father, Doran IV, had had eleven sisters, ten of whom were still alive, and eight of whom were still in the city. Nuvielle was one of those eight, and had been chosen for her current job, so Kilisha assumed she must be at least reasonably trustworthy.

Opir she wasn't quite so certain of. Her brother was generally sensible enough, but he had been known to miss an appointment or two. She looked worriedly down the street that dropped away steeply behind her, then realized she was looking north down the Old Coast Road, which was not a route Opir would use, any more than she had.

Then a metallic thumping sounded, and the heavy door swung open. Two more guards appeared in the opening, stepping out onto the pavement, blinking in the bright sun.

Behind them came Lady Nuvielle, attired in a gown like nothing Kilisha had ever seen before. This was not the velvet dress she wore when going about the city on business, a dress that had impressed Kilisha as exceptionally beautiful; no, this was what she wore at home, when she had no need to worry about dusty streets or adventurous thieves.

It was made in layers—an outer layer of fine white lace and gold filigree over a dress of blue silk, and here and there the silk was slashed dramatically to reveal a golden lining. Kilisha could not help staring at this elaborate garment.

Kelder, she noticed, was staring, as well—but not at the dress, exactly. She felt a twinge of jealousy.

She silently chastised herself; she was taking that dream too seriously. Kelder had every right to admire a beautiful woman.

Adagan seemed unimpressed with Nuvielle's appearance; he bowed, belatedly reminding Kilisha of her own manners. "My lady," she said as she curtsied.

"Kilisha," Nuvielle said. "I'm pleased to see you; do come in! And introduce me to your companions."

Kilisha rose, and took a last desperate glance down Fortress Street, and saw Opir hurrying toward them.

"This is Kelder, one of your tax collectors," Kilisha said. "He was the one who was at the door when the spell went awry."

Kelder bowed. "Kelder Goran's son of Sixth Company, my lady."

Kilisha was pleased she had remembered that name from when Kelder had given it to the Fortress guard a few days earlier; without the patronymic she could not have invoked the Spell of Invaded Dreams, since there were so many Kelders in the World. She smiled at him at the memory of that dream. But Lady Nuvielle was waiting, so Kilisha turned and said, "And this is Adagan the Witch, one of my neighbors. He and Kelder have been aiding me in the search for the missing couch, and have agreed to help me capture it and carry it home."

"Kilisha!" Opir called, as he came trotting up.

"And my brother, Opir of Eastgate," Kilisha said. "Opir, this is Nuvielle, Lady Treasurer, who has found my master's couch."

Opir bowed hastily.

"And is this everyone, then?" Nuvielle asked.

"Yes, my lady," Kilisha said.

"You know, I would have assigned a few guardsmen to carry the couch for you, had you asked."

"Oh." Kilisha felt her cheeks grow warm. "I hadn't thought of . . . I wouldn't want to trouble you, my lady. The couch is my responsibility."

Nuvielle turned up an empty palm. "In any case, you're all here now," she said. "Come inside, and I will show you the way." She turned and strode into the dim interior.

Kilisha followed, mentally cursing herself. Of *course* Lady Nuvielle would have provided soldiers! She was the Lady Treasurer, the overlord's aunt—she must have a hundred guards and servants ready to tend to her every whim. Just because she had come to a wizard's shop unattended did not mean she could not summon a dozen strong men in an instant in her own home; it wouldn't have cost her a thing.

And here Kilisha had brought three assorted strangers along uninvited, not just into the Fortress, but to the overlord's own apartments. She had wanted to be prepared, and to plan everything out in advance for once, but that was no reason to forgo common courtesy. She needed to use common sense, as well as plan ahead!

She was glad that the light in the stone passageway was dim and cool, so that her flushed cheeks would be less noticeable, and she could attribute their color to stepping in out of the bright sun. She marched on silently, not trusting herself to say anything more.

After a slight hesitation, Kelder and Opir and Adagan followed the two women inside. The two guards who had accompanied the Lady Treasurer then brought up the rear, closing the doors behind them, leaving the outside guards to resume their vigil.

Kilisha's upset at her own foolishness was sufficient that she had gone a dozen yards down the passage before she realized that she was inside the Fortress for the first time in her life, and she really ought to pay attention to her surroundings. She might never have another chance to see the interior of the overlord's stronghold.

Nuvielle was leading the party down a stone corridor, broad enough for Kilisha's three helpers to walk abreast without crowding, but still far taller than it was wide. Kilisha looked up to see an arched stone ceiling perhaps fifteen or twenty feet above her.

The stone was surprisingly plain. Kilisha knew that the Fortress had been built during the Great War as a bastion against the Northern Empire, and of course she had seen the unadorned exterior often enough, but she had still expected the interior of the overlord's home to display at least *some* of the trappings of wealth and power. After all, the overlord and his family had had more than two centuries to make improvements.

This corridor, though, was bare—no carvings, no tapestries or other hangings, no carpets. The stone blocks in the walls were square and unpolished, the corners not even rounded, and the joints in the masonry clearly visible. The few doors they passed were heavy oak planking bound in black iron, dark with age but uncarved and unpainted. The only sign of wealth was the numerous oil lamps that lit the passage; these were large and bright, and wrought of brass and crystal. Kilisha assumed they were not the wartime originals, but a later addition—for one thing, they didn't match the plain black iron brackets on which they hung.

Then Lady Nuvielle turned a corner and led them up a stone staircase, likewise straight and unadorned; sunlight trickled in faintly from an unseen window somewhere ahead and above.

They ascended two stories and emerged into another corridor, narrower than the previous one and with a ceiling no more than twelve feet high. Here, at last, the Fortress began to look less like a dungeon—the floor and walls were still plain gray stone, but a strip of lush red and brown carpet ran along the passage, and a few tapestries hung between doors that had been painted with bright floral designs.

Nuvielle led them down the passage, through a salon that was far more in keeping with Kilisha's expectations, along a side passage, and around a corner into an anteroom.

There she stopped dead, evidently surprised by the presence of four guards. Kilisha almost walked into her. The others had left a little more space, and halted without crowding each other—but by the time Nuvielle's own guards entered, the antechamber was rather full. The room was not especially large.

The four guards, standing two on either side of an elaborately carved pair of doors, had been chatting idly; at the sight of the treasurer they snapped to attention and thumped the butts of their spears on the stone floor. Kilisha blinked at them, noticing that their uniforms were much cleaner and better-made than Kelder's, and that their spears and breastplates were wonderfully polished. Two of the four wore unfamiliar golden insignia on their right arms.

"Wulran is in?" Nuvielle asked.

"Yes, my lady," the guard nearest the right-hand side of the doors replied. He was one of the two with the insignia.

"I thought that at this hour he would be conducting business downstairs."

"The overlord found the discussions wearisome and decided to take a brief rest, my lady."

"Ah."

Kilisha thought that Nuvielle's tone managed to convey an amazing amount of information in that single meaningless word; it was clearly a tone of unsurprised resigned disapproval.

For a moment no one spoke; the eleven people in the room simply stood there, considering the situation. Then Nuvielle said, "I suppose I'll want to speak with him sooner or later in any case; could you tell him I'm here, please, and that I've brought guests?"

The guard bowed, but stayed where he was; it was the other insignia-bearing guard, to the left, who opened the door and stepped silently through.

The door closed, and the party waited.

Kilisha was uneasy, standing here surrounded by soldiers; even Kelder seemed slightly threatening now. She glanced at the others in her group, and saw Adagan studying the overlord's guards with evident interest while Opir looked acutely uncomfortable.

That was hardly surprising. She had told him that they were going to the Fortress to retrieve the couch; she hadn't said anything about meeting the overlord himself!

She hadn't expected it herself; she had assumed, as Nuvielle apparently had, that the overlord would be busy elsewhere, allowing them to slip into his apartments and take the couch without his knowledge.

His presence did complicate matters, but after all, it really was Ithanalin's couch, it wasn't as if she had come to steal something.

Nuvielle and the others would all testify that it was Ithanalin's couch. The overlord would surely have no objection to letting them take it back.

She might need to explain how it had come here, though. It wouldn't do to lie to the overlord, or even to *seem* to lie; she started to plan out what she would say, if he asked.

And she needed to remember to curtsy, as deeply as she could—or would it be better to bow? He was the overlord, ruler of the city and master of one-third of the Hegemony, heir and direct descendant of General Gor, who had turned the Western Command into the peacetime city of Ethshar of the Rocks; she wanted to be as deferential as possible.

She could feel herself starting to tremble at the thought of speaking to him, and she tried to prevent it. She reminded herself that Wulran III was just a man, even if he was the overlord. He was only twenty-six, not so very much older than herself. He deserved respect and deference, but there was nothing to be frightened of. . . .

Well, except that he could order the soldiers to kill or imprison or torture her on his slightest whim.

But he wouldn't. He was said to be a generous and kind young man, and besides, even an overlord didn't dare anger the Wizards' Guild by abusing a wizard's apprentice without cause. The Guild had never yet killed an overlord, but they had reportedly come close more than once—most recently Azrad VI, in Ethshar of the Spices, was said to have been given a very direct threat over his treatment of the early warlocks a quarter century ago.

She took a deep breath and stood up straight. She started to put her hand on the hilt of her athame—she always found the feel of the knife reassuring—but then noticed one of the guards watching her closely and shifting his spear slightly, and she stopped before her fingers touched the leather.

She hoped she would be permitted to carry the weapon into the overlord's rooms; if she needed any magic to restrain the couch, she would need her athame.

Then the door opened and the guardsman reappeared. He bowed to Lady Nuvielle.

"My lady," he said, "the overlord consents to see you, but says he would prefer not to deal with a horde of strangers just now."

Nuvielle glanced at the others, then said, "Of course. I will be accompanied only by Kilisha, and the others will wait here."

The soldier bowed again, then turned, and he and his partner swung open the doors. Nuvielle strode in, Kilisha following with a gait far more timid; the two guards stepped in behind them, then closed the door, leaving Kilisha's three friends, Nuvielle's two guards, and the overlord's other two guards in the antechamber.

The two women found themselves in a large and elegant room; Kilisha could not tell whether the walls or floor here were stone, as they were all covered with draperies and carpets, but the high ceiling was painted wood, depicting clouds and birds and butterflies against a blue background. A few sculptures, mostly statues of young women, stood about; a gilded shrine gleamed in one corner. Assorted couches, tables, and chairs were arranged in three neat groupings. Kilisha took all this in quickly, but then her attention focused on one specific couch in the nearest group.

There it was, at last—the crimson velvet couch that had stood so long in Ithanalin's parlor. It blended surprisingly well with its surroundings.

And a handsome young man who she realized must be the overlord was sprawled on it, looking at her.

Chapter Twenty-eight

Kilisha managed to not burst out, "You're on my couch!" Instead she caught herself, remembered her manners, and curtsied deeply.

Beside her, Nuvielle said, "Hello, Wulran."

"Aunt Nuvielle," Wulran said, folding his hands on his chest. "What brings you here, and who is this young lady?"

Kilisha hastily curtsied again and said, "I am Kilisha the Wizard's Apprentice, my lord." She thought that sounded more suitable for the situation than "of Eastgate." When her head came back up from the ceremonial bob she took a good look at the overlord.

He was a tall, thin man, dark-haired and dark-eyed, his complexion rather pale; his face was narrow and his jaw pointed, the sharp angle exaggerated by a neatly trimmed triangular beard. He wore a loose beige tunic embroidered in three shades of brown, black suede breeches, and very practical-looking brown boots, one of which was hooked under an arm of the couch, as the seat was really rather short for a man of his height to lie on.

Under other circumstances she wouldn't have minded meeting such a man at all, but this man was the city's overlord. His clothes might not be especially fancy, and he wore no crown or medallion or other token of office, but still, he had the power of life and death over tens of thousands of people.

"A pleasure to meet you," he said, nodding politely. "I hope you'll forgive me for not rising, but my bowels are in knots and my head is throbbing. My advisers have been shouting at me all morning about this blasted usurper in the Sands, and I haven't been eating well for the past few days, and I'm afraid it's all catching up to me."

"Have you been sleeping well?" Nuvielle asked.

"No, I haven't been sleeping well," he snapped. "Aunt Kinthera and Uncle Ederd and Ederd's father are out at sea somewhere with this madwoman threatening to kill them all, and there's talk that I may be next after them, and dozens of people are *already* dead and Ederd's palace is full of thieves and beggars sleeping wrapped in the tapestries—how am I supposed to sleep?"

"I hadn't realized how much it troubled you, my lord," Nuvielle said. "When we spoke yesterday you seemed quite calm."

Wulran flung one arm over the back of the couch and pulled himself up partway to shout, "I'm *supposed* to seem calm! It's part of the job." Then he sank back down, letting his arm fall across his eyes, and said, "What did you want, my lady? Is there some new complication? Has Tabaea turned all our gold to seawater?"

"No, my lord, nothing like that. Nothing to do with Tabaea at all. I'm here because this wizard's couch has run away."

For a moment Wulran did not move, or respond in any way, and Kilisha wondered whether he had heard; then he said slowly, without moving, "Her *couch* has run away?"

Kilisha decided that the time had come to speak for herself, even to the overlord. "My master's couch, actually, my lord," she said. "The one you're lying on." She managed to keep her voice steady.

He lifted the arm from his face and turned his head to look at her. "*This* couch?" he said, tapping the velvet-upholstered back with one finger.

"Yes, my lord."

"It ran away?"

"And came to the Fortress to hide, my lord, yes." Each sentence came more easily than the one before; the overlord was too human, too *ordinary*, to stay frightening.

"It came here under its own power, then? It was alive?"

"Well, animated, anyway. I'm not sure *alive* is quite the right word."

"That's how it got in here? The servants didn't bring it?"

"It ran away, my lord, and seems to have come here by its own choice."

"And it just walked in here? How did it get past my guards?"

"I don't know, my lord. I've wondered that myself. It's apparently quite clever."

"I see." He let his raised arm drape over the back again. "And you've come here because you want it back?"

"Yes, my lord. Without it, I can't undo a spell that has transformed my master."

"Interesting." He stroked the velvet upholstery. "You say it was animated—it doesn't appear to be animated *now*. I've never seen it move."

That had puzzled and troubled Kilisha. "I can't explain that, my lord—it *should* still be animated."

"Well, perhaps it's been getting the sleep I haven't. If you can prove it's yours, then I'll be happy to return it—though it's been quite comfortable having it here."

"I saw it in the wizard's parlor," Lady Nuvielle offered, before Kilisha could reply.

"And I have neighbors who will attest to it, as well, my lord," Kilisha said. "One is in the antechamber right now."

"She brought some friends to help carry it," Nuvielle explained.

The overlord sighed. "Then I suppose I had better get off it and let you take it," he said. He started to lower his arm, to push himself into a sitting position—and the couch bolted.

It dashed wildly across the room, narrowly dodging a table; its stubby curved legs were moving so fast Kilisha could see only a blur. The overlord was still half-lying, half-sitting on it, one foot hooked under an arm and his eyes wide with astonishment as it bounded in a zigzag across the carpet.

The couch's arm was not its original gracefully curved shape, Kilisha saw; it had closed down on Wulran's ankle, trapping him.

"Guards!" Nuvielle called, far louder than Kilisha would have thought possible for a woman her size.

The two guards in the room were already moving, arms spread and knees bent, spears held horizontally, trying to corner the couch and force it back against one wall, away from any doors. At Nuvielle's shout, however, the door burst open and the other four guardsmen—no, five, Kilisha saw, as Kelder was with them—came rushing in.

The couch was rocking madly back and forth, bouncing first one end off the floor, then the other; the overlord was clinging to the velvet with both hands. He looked terrified.

The couch knocked over a pedestal, sending a large vase crashing to the floor; flowers, peacock plumes, shards of porcelain, and dirty water sprayed across the carpets as the vase shattered spectacularly. One of the first two guards shied away, raising his spear for a moment, and the couch dashed forward, ducking underneath. The overlord did not duck quite as quickly, and the shaft of the spear caught Wulran on the top of the head with a horrifying *crack*.

Then the couch was past that pair, and the other five had not yet had time to take in the situation; the maddened sofa charged through them, knocking one man to the floor, and leapt through the door to the antechamber.

Where it had previously moved freely in every direction—forward, backward, or side to side—it now seemed to have settled onto treating the end that held the overlord's foot as its front, and the end where the dazed young man's head rested on a pillow as its rear. Rather than bouncing about wildly it was now running full tilt, like a fleeing animal, with the overlord on its back.

"Catch it!" both Kilisha and Nuvielle shouted. Suiting her actions to her words, Kilisha ran after the fleeing furniture; she had been quickest to react, but the soldiers followed close on her heels.

Nuvielle did not join the pursuit, but Opir and Adagan, after watching in motionless surprise as the couch, the apprentice, and half a dozen soldiers ran past, fell in behind, chasing the couch up the passage from the antechamber.

Kilisha had expected the couch to turn left at the salon and head for the stairs by which she and her party had arrived, but instead it scrambled straight across, past a drapery into another passage, then turned right at the next crossing.

That brought it to a staircase, but a staircase going *up*. It bounded upward, almost catlike in its motion.

Kilisha followed, but even as she ran she tried to think of something she could do to stop the berserk thing without hurting either it or its passenger. While it would be bad enough if the couch smashed itself, Kilisha *really* didn't want to be involved in anything that injured the overlord—or worse, killed him. That would be bad enough at any time, but now, when a usurper had already disrupted the government of the Hegemony, and Wulran had not yet sired an heir, it might be disastrous. Kilisha suspected that wizard or no, the Guild notwithstanding, if she got the overlord killed her head would wind up on a pike on the Fortress ramparts.

She reached for the flap on her belt pouch, trying to think what she could do with the spells she had prepared. Would the Spell of Stupefaction work on a couch?

Even if it would, the spell took several seconds to prepare, and she couldn't do it while she was running. Maybe if the couch ever held still for half a minute. . . .

The couch wheeled about on the next landing and bounded up another flight, Kilisha struggling to keep up.

The Spell of Optimum Strength—if she ever did get a hand on the couch she wanted to be able to hold onto it. She couldn't drink the potion while she was running, though, any more than she could cast a stupefaction.

Sooner or later, though, if the couch kept going up, it would be trapped, wouldn't it? It must be panicking, she thought, to be going up instead of down. If it had gotten out in the streets it might have been able to dodge them forever, but it wouldn't be able to come back down these stairs without getting caught.

Of course, there might be other stairs....

"Someone go back down and make sure all the doors are closed!" she called back over her shoulder. "We mustn't let it get out of the Fortress!"

"Right," someone said—a deep male voice she did not recognize. She still heard boots pounding up the stairs behind her, but perhaps not quite as many. She could not risk looking back; she might lose her footing. A stumble here would not merely let the couch increase its lead over her, but might send her tumbling down the stairs on top of the guards.

It rounded a second landing, charged up one final flight, and at the top bounded across half a dozen feet of floor, then slammed into a door.

And bounced off.

Kilisha almost ran into the couch as it rebounded off the oak and iron barrier. It had clearly expected to smash right through, but the door had been stronger than it thought.

It was trapped! Kilisha grabbed for it, and felt the overlord's hair brush her fingers, but then the couch veered to one side, to the left, and Kilisha saw that no, it was *not* trapped, as a long corridor extended from the head of the stairs in that direction.

The couch ran desperately down the corridor, gaining ground on its pursuers, then suddenly stopped, turned, and rammed its way through a large window.

"Gods!" Kilisha said, horrified. They were several stories up— she was not sure just how far. The couch and the overlord would be smashed to pieces! She dashed to the opening and looked out past the shattered glass and twisted leading, expecting to see empty air and the couch plummeting to its doom.

Instead she saw a broad sunlit and stone-paved courtyard— the one atop the Fortress that she had seen from the air three days before. The couch was galloping across it, the overlord still trapped on the seat.

It was already several yards away, and she was not about to

just dive through the jagged remains of the window; she was not going to catch it just by running after it. She stood panting for a second or two, then reached for her pouch.

"It's in the courtyard!"

"It went through the window!"

"Open this door!"

Kilisha ignored the shouting soldiers as she pulled out a vial and looked at the label, then dropped it back and grabbed the next.

On the third try she finally read STRENGTH; she pulled the cork and took a sip.

A flood of warmth rushed through her; her legs straightened and her hands tightened into fists, and she had to catch herself before she crushed the vial of potion. She carefully pressed the cork back into place, not allowing herself to push on it. She had used this spell before, and knew how easy it was to break things while enchanted.

She hoped that it would give her the speed and endurance she needed to catch the couch, and the strength to hold it.

She tucked the vial back in her pouch and jumped through the shattered window just as the soldiers got the door opened and poured through into the courtyard.

Chapter Twenty-nine

The couch was bounding up a staircase on the far side of the courtyard, up onto the ramparts. The overlord was still aboard, his foot still trapped under the arm; he appeared to be conscious, but was not struggling or gesturing or saying anything Kilisha could hear. Kilisha charged forward, across the court, after them.

The soldiers were shouting, and other soldiers, who had been patrolling the battlements, shouted replies. Several of them were already moving along the ramparts, closing in from both sides toward the top of the staircase the couch was climbing.

The couch reached the top of the stairs and turned left, trotting a quick dozen yards, only to find itself confronted by two approaching guardsmen. It wheeled on one leg and headed back in the other direction to find two more soldiers on the walkway and Kilisha already halfway up the stairs, the other pursuers close behind her.

It was apparently cornered—but Kilisha saw that there was another way out. "Some of you get below it, so it doesn't jump!" she called. As she reached the top of the stair she grabbed the railing and glanced back to see that Adagan and one of the guards

had heard her and taken heed; they were moving across the courtyard instead of climbing the stair, positioning themselves so that if
the couch dove from the ramparts to the courtyard it would find
them waiting.

Opir hesitated on the bottom step, then turned and followed
Adagan.

Kilisha turned her attention back to the battlements.

The two patrolling soldiers from the north had come up beside
her, and the three of them formed a barrier closing in one end of
a box. The couch stood a dozen feet to the south, and another
dozen feet beyond were two more guardsmen. To the east was a
sheer drop of about eight or ten feet to the courtyard, and Adagan,
Opir, and a soldier were waiting at the bottom; other soldiers and
curiosity-seekers were emerging from various doors and corners
and gathering there, as well.

To the west was a parapet, perhaps three feet high and a foot
thick, pierced by foot-square crenelations, and beyond that wall
was nothing but sky and sea. Kilisha knew that they were atop the
Fortress, which stood atop the sea cliffs, which stood in turn atop
the wave-washed rocks that gave the city its name; anything that
went over that parapet would fall a hundred feet down a sheer
stone wall and smash on the rocks below, and when the tide came
in the pieces would be washed out to sea.

The couch was trapped, cornered on a strip of stone eight feet
wide and eight yards long.

For a moment everything seemed to freeze; the couch, apparently realizing its situation, had stopped where it was. The guards
on the ramparts had paused, unsure of what was happening. And
Kilisha stood at the top of the steps, taking in the situation and
preventing the men behind her from moving forward.

"Don't hurt it!" she called. "It doesn't know what it's doing—
it doesn't remember who it is!"

"Who in the World *is* it?" someone asked. "And why does it
look like a couch?"

"It *is* a couch," Kilisha shouted back. "But it has a piece of a wizard's soul trapped in it. Only it didn't get the wizard's *memories.*"

"It's holding the overlord," another soldier called. "I don't care *who* it is, it can't do that!"

The couch turned back and forth as they spoke; at the last sentence it backed up against the parapet and squeezed down on the overlord's leg.

"*Ow!*" Wulran bellowed. "It's crushing my leg!" He reached for the couch's arm, and pried at it helplessly. The couch was clearly stronger than he was; it clamped down, and Wulran was unable to loosen its grip.

"Don't go any closer," Kilisha called, as the four soldiers started forward. "It might break his leg!"

"But . . ." The nearest guardsman looked at her helplessly. "We have to do *something!*"

"She's just an apprentice," one of the soldiers on the stairs behind her said.

"She's a *wizard's* apprentice," Kelder retorted. "She knows what's going on here better than we do!"

Kilisha was grateful for the vote of confidence; she wished she deserved it, but in truth, she really knew very little more than anyone else. She could only guess what the couch was thinking, what it wanted. . . .

But maybe she could figure it out. Maybe she could talk it into releasing the overlord and coming home peacefully—and if not, she could try the Spell of Stupefaction. She stepped forward.

"Couch," she called, "do you remember me? Kilisha, your apprentice?"

The couch turned, and seemed to be listening—though Kilisha had no idea why she thought so. It had no ears, no eyes, no features, but it somehow seemed alert and attentive.

"Nobody wants to hurt you," she said, taking another step forward.

The couch backed away, tight against the parapet. It lifted one back leg up into the nearest crenelation, hoisting itself and the overlord up at an awkward angle. The soldiers started forward.

"Calm down!" Kilisha called, raising one hand—but her other hand was fumbling with her pouch. She needed the bat wing and the envelope of powdered spider and about thirty or forty seconds to work the Spell of Stupefaction, and she doubted she would have the forty seconds, but at the very least she could have the bat wing and powdered spider ready.

The soldiers and the couch stopped.

"Couch," Kilisha called, "you're a spell gone wrong. We just want to put it right. Half of you is an ordinary couch, and the other half is a piece of my master, the wizard Ithanalin. Do you remember any of that?"

The couch turned back and forth, clearly signaling a negative—it didn't remember anything of the sort.

"It's true, I promise," Kilisha said. "I swear it by all the gods." The powdered spider was eluding her fingers. She had found the vial of strength potion, though, and closed her hand around it. She had an idea of how she might use that, and it wouldn't require time she didn't have. "We just want to put everything back where it belongs—put the couch back in the parlor, and put Ithanalin's soul back in his body. Won't you let us do that?"

The back-and-forth was far more emphatic this time.

"But don't you understand, it'll be putting everything right?"

The couch did not bother with a mere shake this time; instead it gathered itself and sprang up onto the parapet, only just barely catching itself before it went over the edge. Several people gasped as it balanced there on two legs, one front and one rear, its other front leg hanging over the battlements, its other rear leg over that fearsome hundred-foot drop to the rocks.

The overlord, who had been moving about trying to get more comfortable, froze in terror.

Kilisha knew that any chance of stupefying the couch had just vanished; if she tried it now it might fall the wrong way. She forgot about the bat wing and spider.

"Let me past," a soldier said in Kilisha's ear as he tried to move behind her to get at the parapet.

"Don't go near it!" Kilisha shouted. "Don't you see? It's saying it would rather die than let us catch it—and it's ready to take the overlord with it!"

The soldier stopped. "Oh," he said.

"Everyone stay right where you are," Kilisha said, taking another step toward the couch. "Let me talk to it. I'm sure we can come to some sort of agreement."

"I hope so," the overlord said, so quietly that Kilisha doubted any of the soldiers heard him. He was looking over his shoulder at the ocean far below.

Kilisha hoped so, too—though she had no intention of keeping any agreement that might get made. Once the overlord and the couch were safe and separated, she intended to take the couch home with her, no matter what it might mean. She would gladly break oaths, disobey her master, *anything* that would get this all settled safely and restore Ithanalin to himself!

She was trying to plan out what she could do, and had a few ideas, but it was so hard to think clearly in a situation like this!

She needed to get the couch down off the parapet, and get the overlord off the couch, and it didn't matter which order she did it in, so long as she kept them both from falling. If she got the overlord to safety first, it would be easier to deal with the couch.

"My lord," Kilisha called, "how is your ankle?"

"It hurts," Wulran replied. "So does my head, for that matter."

"Let me give you something for the pain, then." She pulled the vial of strength potion from her pouch and held it up with the label turned away—she had no idea how the couch could see, or whether it knew how to read, and preferred to take as few chances as necessary.

If Wulran drank the potion he would be strong enough to pry the arm off his ankle—or at least, she certainly hoped so! Once he was loose, she could worry about the couch.

Wulran squinted at her. "What is that?"

"Just a potion to relieve pain," she lied.

"You know, apprentice, I'm not at all sure I can trust you. I don't know you; all I have to convince me of your identity and honesty is Nuvielle's word, and you might have enchanted her."

"My lord," Kilisha said desperately, "I am just an apprentice—do you think I would dare put a spell on the Lady Treasurer? You know the Wizards' Guild forbids us to interfere in politics. This potion is harmless, I assure you—you can read the label for yourself."

"Oh, fine—I *would* like this headache to go away, and my ankle is starting to throb splendidly, and I can't feel my toes. Bring it here." He held out a hand.

Kilisha started to step forward.

The couch backed up a fraction of an inch, moving ever so slightly closer to plummeting from the fortress ramparts to the rocks.

Kilisha froze.

"I'll toss it," she said. "Catch, my lord!" She threw the vial underhand, hoping the overlord was reasonably coordinated; she did have one more vial of strength potion, but only one.

Fortunately, Wulran caught it easily. He glanced at the label, then at Kilisha; she nodded toward his pinned ankle.

"Pain reliever," he said. "Thank you." He pulled the cork and lifted the bottle.

"Just half, my lord!" Kilisha called, as he began to drink.

As she spoke she was thinking quickly. The real danger here was falling. If she tried to work any sort of spell—not just the Spell of Stupefaction, but anything—the couch would see it, and probably think it was an attack. She did still have her other potions—would she be able to use those without sending the couch over the edge?

She wondered what weird portion of Ithanalin's mind had wound up in the couch to drive it to this sort of behavior. All his fears and irrational whims, perhaps? Whatever the reason, the couch was clearly insane, perhaps suicidal.

She groped in her pouch for the other potions. Both of them were levitation spells, and since the big threat was a fall there ought to be some way to use those here. . . .

The overlord recorked the vial and tucked it into his belt.

"Thank you," he said. "I feel better already." He started to reach for his ankle.

The couch leaned dangerously seaward. Soldiers started forward, then froze.

"My lord!" Kilisha called. "Wait a moment, please!"

"Urk," Wulran said, as he felt the couch shift. He cast an uneasy glance over his shoulder at the watery western horizon again, and straightened up.

"I have another potion," she called. She pulled out more vials and glanced at the labels.

"If you think it would help," Wulran said.

V'S LEV. and T'S LEV., she read. She hadn't really thought out whether Tracel's or Varen's would be more appropriate, but these were what she had. She quickly tossed one to the overlord.

He caught it, glanced at the label, and looked puzzled. "Tracel's what?" he said.

"Just drink it," Kilisha said desperately. "About a fourth of it." She reached down and uncorked her own vial.

The overlord shrugged, pulled the cork, and lifted the potion to his lips. Kilisha took a step forward.

And at that, the couch teetered one last time, then plunged over the edge.

✦

Chapter Thirty

Kilisha did not hesitate for an instant; she dashed forward and dove through the crenelation after the couch. As she dove she screamed, "Drink it *now!*"

Behind her she heard several shouts and screams, but she ignored them.

She jammed her own vial of potion between her teeth as she pushed off from the parapet, before she really even began falling; then she reached up to brush the hair from her eyes.

She was falling through empty air, the rocks and breaking waves rushing up at her at hideous speed, and there was the couch, and the overlord, falling just ahead of her, and the overlord was drinking the potion. She grabbed for the couch, felt her hand close on it; she tipped her head back and swallowed.

And she was suddenly weightless. She stopped falling so suddenly that her head snapped back, dazing her, and her gorge rose. The couch jerked at her arm, and she felt as if her shoulder was coming apart. For an instant everything vanished in a burst of pain; then she opened her eyes.

She was hanging in midair a few feet out from the wall of the Fortress, several stories below the parapet but a few feet above where the gray stone wall rested on the cliff. The couch was hanging from her right hand, which was closed tight around one of its legs. The overlord was still on the couch, still pinned under one arm—but his upper body was floating at an odd angle.

"You drank the potion, my lord?" she said.

The couch squirmed in her grasp as Wulran nodded. She tightened her grip, pleasantly aware of her own superhuman strength.

"Then get your foot loose," she said. "You won't fall."

Wulran stared down at the rocks. "You're sure of that?"

"I'm sure," Kilisha said. "It's Tracel's Levitation, the same thing that's keeping me from falling. You'll stay at this height until you say the release word."

Wulran glanced up at her, then back down at the sea. "Young woman, I trust you realize that if I die today, you'll be in an absolutely amazing amount of trouble."

Kilisha managed to laugh. "Oh, believe me, my lord, I'm very well aware of that!"

"All right, then." He bent down.

The couch thrashed wildly.

Suddenly nervous, Kilisha called, "Do you have the rest of the potion?"

"Yes," Wulran said warily, holding up the vial. "Why do you ask?"

Kilisha laughed again. "Well, I'm only an apprentice. I *think* you'll levitate right where you are, but if I'm wrong, you'll have a couple of seconds to drink the rest of that before you hit."

"Oh, you are *so* comforting!" Wulran glanced up past her, then bent down again and pried at the wooden arm encircling his ankle.

The couch struggled, and Kilisha had to devote her entire attention to keeping her grip on it. She could hear wood creak as the overlord fought to free his foot.

"Hurry, please," she said. "This strength spell only has a few more minutes left."

"*Now* you tell me!"

Wood cracked suddenly, and the overlord's leg jerked up—but his boot, still caught, pulled off and fell.

Both of them watched silently as the empty boot spiraled down and splashed into the surf—but now the overlord was hanging alone in midair, a few inches of space separating him from the couch. He looked around, taking in his situation, then reached out and pushed himself away from the couch so that it could not grab him again, extending that few inches to almost a yard.

And the couch seemed suddenly heavier in Kilisha's grasp. She realized she really did only have a few minutes before the Spell of Optimum Strength wore off, and when that happened she wouldn't be able to hold the couch. *She* would be safe, and the overlord as well, but the *couch* would fall, and probably be smashed on the rocks or swept out to sea.

After all this, she did not want to let Ithanalin down.

With her left hand she reached across and pawed at her belt pouch, and managed to find another vial. She turned it in her fingers and read the label.

V'S LEV.

She lifted it to her mouth, pulled the cork with her teeth, then spat the cork out. It fell and vanished.

Varen's Levitation took two forms, and she knew which one she wanted—but would the potion *do* that?

When the spell was cast directly it could be placed on either the wizard casting it, which would allow him or her to walk on air, or it could be cast on an object, which could then be placed at any height and would stay there. Could a potion cast a spell on an object? It *ought* to be possible, and she had certainly thought it was when she prepared the potion, but she realized now that she wasn't sure how to determine which form the spell took from a potion. She couldn't place the lantern on the chosen object when she *had* no lantern.

She hoped she could choose simply by willing it. If so, then she could suspend the couch here and come back for it at leisure.

If not, though . . .

She decided not to risk it after all. She would walk up, carrying the couch and hoping that the Spell of Optimum Strength lasted until she got it safely back in the Fortress.

And there was also the question of whether she could use Varen's Levitation at all while Tracel's Levitation was still in effect. She wouldn't try it. Spells could interact in dangerous ways. She would break Tracel's Levitation, *then* use Varen's.

"My lord," she said, "I'm going to say a word, and then I'm going to fall, and then I *hope* I'll catch myself and levitate myself and the couch back up away from here. I'm afraid that will leave you hanging here, drifting—but I'm sure someone will come for you soon."

"Wait a minute," Wulran began, but Kilisha ignored him. She had no time to spare.

She tilted the vial, and as the first drop of potion touched her lips she spoke the single word that negated Tracel's Levitation.

She and the couch dropped instantly, plummeting past the overlord as she quickly gulped the potion.

They were falling down the cliff, the rocks zooming toward them, the pounding of the surf increasing from a quiet whooshing to a roar, and then she took a step and caught herself on air.

As before, the couch's weight jerked hard at her shoulder as she came to a stop, but again she held on.

She blinked and unsteadily took another step upward, then began climbing an invisible staircase of air, as she had a few days before, gaining confidence with every step. This time, instead of an axe with a rope dangling from it, she held a struggling couch.

As she climbed she looked around, and saw that she had stopped no more than ten feet from the first jagged black edge of broken stone. For the first time she let herself realize that she had deliberately dived off a hundred-foot cliff toward the rocks, magically caught herself in midair, and then more or less *done it again.*

Well, magic was dangerous, and she was a wizard. She swallowed, and trudged on, walking upward. She turned her steps, making her ascent a spiral, and looked up.

The overlord was still hanging where she had left him, watching her. Above them, the battlements were lined with faces and waving arms as soldiers and others leaned out to see what had happened. A rope was being lowered—to the overlord, as was only fitting.

She walked on, dragging the squirming, thrashing couch.

"Oh, stop it," she snapped, as it gave a particularly vigorous twist. "I'm taking you home, and you don't have any choice in the matter."

A moment later she reached the overlord's level. He had noticed the rope, but for the moment he was ignoring it and watching her. "Are you all right?" he called.

"I'm fine," she replied, not stopping. "As long as I get back to the top before any of the magic wears off, everything will be just fine."

He glanced up at the distance she still had to go. "Are you sure you'll make it?"

"I'll just have to," she said.

"There are other ropes coming," he said, pointing.

There were, indeed, more ropes being lowered, she saw. "Well, they'll be there if I need them," she said. "But I'd rather do it myself." A thought struck her. "My lord?"

"Yes?"

"Once you're securely tied on, and there's no danger of falling, you'll need to break the spell," she said. "I don't think you can go down *or up* while it's on you."

"Not even with the rope pulling me?"

"I'm not sure," she admitted. "But just in case—don't say this now, but the word to break the spell . . ."

She stopped in midsentence. It was only human nature to repeat a word you wanted to learn, even if you had been told not to.

He had not yet caught the rope, and she was already above him, too far away to catch him if he fell.

"I'll tell you later," she said. "If you need it."

He frowned, then turned his attention to the rope.

She waved farewell with her free hand and kept climbing.

By the time she neared the top her right arm was almost numb, and she could feel herself weakening. As she rose above the parapet she called, "I need some help here!"

The ramparts and courtyard were swarming with soldiers and courtiers, and although most of them were focused on pulling the overlord up to safety, a dozen rushed to her aid.

"Bring ropes," she said. "Tie the couch down! Don't let it escape! It's stronger than it looks."

Strong, eager arms reached out as she kept climbing. She turned her steps eastward and strode up above the parapet, across the ramparts—and finally she stopped, with the couch dangling a few feet above the stones.

Soldiers grabbed it from every side; ropes were thrown hastily around it.

"Have you got it?" she called feebly. The Spell of Optimum Strength was gone; she was just a tired teenaged girl holding a heavy couch by one leg, trying desperately not to drop it. Her arm was trembling, her fingers red and straining.

"We have it," a familiar voice said, and she looked down at Kelder's broad face. She knew it was not a particularly handsome face by most people's standards, but right now she thought it was beautiful.

"Good," she said, releasing her hold.

Then she paused, and instead of setting her right foot above the left on her next step she carefully placed it below, beginning her descent.

Varen's Levitation needed no magic words to dispel it; with or without the lantern, the instant her foot touched anything solid the spell would break. She walked wearily down the air until at last her sandal touched the stone pavement of the courtyard.

And then all her magic was done, at least for the moment, and she collapsed onto the pavement, exhausted.

She sat there for a long moment, eyes closed, trying to catch her breath; then she heard her name.

She opened her eyes to find Kelder and Opir on either side, watching her with concern on their faces; she smiled up at Kelder, so focused on his worried eyes that she hardly noticed her brother.

But it was Adagan who had called her. He was up on the battlements, helping to haul in the overlord. "Kilisha!" he called again. "Can you please break this spell?"

She looked up and saw several large men struggling to support the overlord as Tracel's Levitation tried to drag him back down to the level at which it had been cast.

Kilisha took a deep breath, let it out slowly, then called back, "I'll be right there!" Then she waved away assistance and got to her feet unaided. As soon as she was upright and reasonably confident of staying that way, she walked over to the rampart to teach Wulran III the word that would end Tracel's Levitation.

It took him six tries before he could pronounce it properly— Wulran was obviously no wizard, or even much of a linguist. When at last he managed it the sudden cessation of pressure flung him upward from the courtyard pavement, but his guards caught him before he fell back to the stone.

Kilisha, still a trifle unsteady on her feet, watched it all with a broad smile on her face, and with guards standing respectfully at either side.

❦

Chapter Thirty-one

The couch was kept restrained under heavy guard, while Kilisha rested on a cot in one of the little watch rooms below the parapet. The only intrusion on her recuperation was a message of gratitude from the overlord, assuring her that he was safe and telling her that at some point in the future, when time permitted, he would want to speak to her at length about the day's events.

She blinked foolishly at the messenger, trying to absorb this— the overlord wanted to speak to her again?

Well, of *course* he did; naturally he would want an explanation of the whole affair. She thought she could provide that, once she was recovered a little—and once Ithanalin was restored to himself.

"Is there a reply, my lady?" the messenger asked.

"No, I . . . just my thanks," she said. "I'm glad he's safe."

The messenger bowed and vanished, and Kilisha lay back, staring at the ceiling and breathing deeply as she let her strength return. A guardsman stood by the door, waiting for her to rise.

When she was sufficiently recovered to travel a dozen guardsmen carried the couch downstairs, loaded it onto a wagon, and tied it down securely. Then they escorted her and the couch home.

She rode on the wagon—but not on the couch. Adagan rode beside her, the only other passenger; Kelder had long since returned to his duties, and Opir, once he was sure his sister was intact and on her way back to Ithanalin's shop, headed home on his own.

Kilisha's long-delayed return found Yara and the children waiting anxiously; Telleth had been standing watch at the front window and called out when the wagon and its burden came in sight, whereupon the entire family had come swarming out into the street. Their faces all showed concern; even the spriggan seemed to be worried by her long absence and the presence of the soldiers.

The racket was enough to rouse the neighbors, as well; Nissitha emerged from her own front door before the wagon had come to a halt, and joined the party. They all gathered around the wagon as six of the soldiers unloaded the struggling couch, hefted it onto their shoulders, and brought it into the wizard's parlor.

"What happened?" Yara asked, staring at the couch.

"She saved the overlord's life," one of the guardsmen said.

Kilisha, who had just clambered down from the wagon, blinked in surprise at that. She hadn't thought of it that way at all; she had thought she had *endangered* the overlord's life by triggering the couch's rampage.

But really, how could she have avoided it? Perhaps if she had waited until Wulran wasn't *on* the couch before she said anything. . . .

But how could she have known he would be resting there, with his foot under the arm? And once the couch began running she had done everything she could to stop it without getting anyone killed.

Really, she *had* saved the overlord's life.

This was quite a shocking realization, and for a moment she was too stunned to speak.

"I knew she would find the couch," Nissitha said, standing by one of the wagon's wheels.

Adagan, who was just then climbing down, looked at her and said, "You did not."

Nissitha's mouth fell open in surprise as she stared at him—
and, Kilisha noticed, she had already been looking at Adagan, making the stare easier.

"Of course I did!" Nissitha managed, as a few of the soldiers—
those who were not trying to maneuver the writhing couch
through the doorway—turned to listen. "I'm a seer!"

"No, you did not," Adagan repeated. "And no, you are not."

Nissitha gaped at him again. "How *dare* you say that?" she
demanded.

"I dare because I'm a witch, and can tell truth from falsehood,
and I'm tired of hearing your self-serving lies," Adagan said wearily. "A seer? You don't even see what everyone else does, let alone
anything more. You don't realize everyone on the street knows
you're a fraud. You can't see that I've no more interest in you than
I would in a toad. Today Kilisha has performed the most astonishing feat of bravery I have ever seen, and deserves to have a
moment to glory in it before attempting a complex and difficult
spell on Ithanalin's behalf, yet here you are, thrusting yourself forward and trying to take attention away from her. It's disgusting.
Why don't you go away and let these soldiers do their jobs, and
let Kilisha attend to her master?"

By the end of this speech not just Nissitha, but everyone in
the street had fallen into stunned silence, staring at Adagan and
listening to every word. When he finished Nissitha let out a stran-
gled gasp, turned, and stamped back into her shop, slamming the
door hard behind her.

Another brief silence fell; then Kilisha said, "That was cruel."

Adagan let out a sigh. "I know," he said. "She'll never forgive
me. But I'm tired of having her following me around, trying to
seduce me, and she might have eventually gotten over anything less
vicious."

"I don't think she'll get over *that* any time soon," Kilisha said,
gazing at Nissitha's door.

"I'm not sure I will, either," Adagan said. "If you'll excuse me,
I think I need to go home and throw up."

"Of course," Kilisha said.

She was watching Adagan walk away when one of the soldiers cleared his throat behind her. She turned.

The men had gotten the couch into the house and tied it down amid the rest of the furniture; now they were tossing extra ropes back onto the empty wagon.

"Is there anything else we can do for you, lady?" a soldier asked her.

Kilisha blinked at him for a moment, and then, startled by her own daring, said, "Yes, actually. Would you stand guard here for the next hour or so? I need to perform a spell, and it's very important that no one interrupt me, and that nothing escape during that time."

"Escape?" The soldier looked at one of his companions. "You mean the couch?"

"Or any of the other furniture, or the bowl, or the spoon, or one particular spriggan," Kilisha said. "I need them all here."

The guardsmen exchanged glances; then one turned up a palm. "As you say, lady."

That settled, Kilisha entered the house smiling.

Yara met her in the parlor as the furniture bumped and clattered around her. "Kilisha, what happened?"

"I'll tell you later, Mistress," Kilisha said. "Right now, I want to perform Javan's Restorative before anything escapes again. Could you help me fetch everything I need?"

Yara started to say something—presumably, Kilisha thought, to reprimand this insubordinate Apprentice—but then she stopped, frowned, and said, "What will you need?"

"The spriggan, the door latch, the mirror, the bowl, the spoon, the rug, the bench, the couch, the chair, the coatrack, the table—and Ithanalin," she said. "In the parlor. Oh, and I'll need incense and jewelweed and . . . well, I'll get those."

Fifteen minutes later everything was in place.

Attempting a spell of this difficulty so soon after the exhausting events at the Fortress might have been foolish, but Kilisha felt strangely invigorated, rather than tired; the ride home had given her time to recover, and Adagan had called her astonishingly brave, and the soldiers had said she had saved the overlord's life, and she felt inspired. She could not bear to wait any longer to perform this act of wizardry and put an end to Ithanalin's dispersal.

This particular performance of Javan's Restorative turned out to be far and away the most difficult Kilisha had ever managed; the furniture kept trying to move about, the spriggan squeaked and struggled constantly as Yara held it in place, and simply coordinating so many pieces amid the clouds of magical smoke was a severe strain. Kilisha's initial flush of vigor and enthusiasm faded quickly, and there were times she didn't think she would be able to finish. The work dragged on and on, well past the hour she had asked of the soldiers, past sunset and suppertime, and still she worked.

And finally, when her reserves were completely exhausted and she knew she could do no more, a sudden silence fell across the furniture, and the clouds of magical smoke began to dissipate. Kilisha let out a breath and turned to her master.

Ithanalin straightened up from his crouch, stretched, smiled, then turned to her and said, "I'm impressed, Apprentice. That was excellent."

Kilisha smiled at him, and then fainted.

❧

Chapter Thirty-two

Kilisha awoke in her own familiar little bed, with Telleth sitting beside her and a familiar spriggan standing on her feet. She opened her eyes and turned her head to see the morning sunlight through the window.

"She's awake!" Telleth called, leaping up. "Dad! She's awake!"

"Awake awake awake!" the spriggan squealed, jumping up and down on Kilisha's ankle. She kicked it off, and it danced happily on the bed. By the time she looked up from the spriggan Telleth was on the stairs, heading down.

"Thank you, thank you!" the spriggan said. "Got wizard out of head!"

"I didn't do it for *you*," Kilisha retorted—but secretly, she was pleased that the spriggan hadn't been hurt, and didn't mind being back to itself. She brushed it off the bed, sat up, and reached for her robe.

A few minutes later she ambled down the stairs into the kitchen and found the entire household gathered around the breakfast table, waiting for her. Ithanalin rose from his chair as she entered.

"Kilisha," he said, "I want to thank you. I saw most of what happened—I remember everything that happened to all the pieces, which is the *oddest* sensation. I remember you demanding that you be given the bowl and spoon, I remember you coaxing the coatrack to follow you, I remember you chasing the bench, all of it."

Kilisha swallowed hard. "You *remember* it all?"

Ithanalin nodded.

Kilisha remembered, too. She remembered yelling at various fragments of her master, chasing them recklessly through the streets, tricking them and trapping them and tying them up, lying to them and bribing them and threatening them. She remembered sitting on them. She remembered the love spell on the rug, she remembered the spoon wrapped around her arm and trying to get under her clothes, she remembered holding the coatrack over her head, and grabbing the spriggan by the throat. . . .

"I'm sorry, Master," she said. "I didn't mean to be disrespectful."

"*Sorry?*" Ithanalin chuckled. "Oh, don't be foolish. I remember you doing what had to be done to collect a bunch of idiot fragments; any disrespect involved was entirely justified. I remember some rudeness, yes, but I remember persistence and ingenuity, as well. Most particularly, I remember the very fine performance you gave when I dove off the Fortress with the overlord—it was a remarkable display of courage and foresight. You must have put a great deal of thought and effort into preparing those potions! That was excellent work, worthy of a master wizard, let alone a journeyman. You're clearly ready for more than just the Spell of the Obedient Object."

"Thank you, Master," Kilisha said, somewhat overwhelmed by this praise. Then a thought struck her. "You remember *everything?*"

"Yes, I think so. Why?"

"Could you tell me, then, how the couch got into the Fortress, and why?"

"Ah!" Ithanalin smiled and reached for his chair. "Well, I'm sure you know how sometimes when you're working on a long spell odd, irrelevant thoughts will wander through your mind. That was happening as I stirred the mixture, and I was remembering an incident several years back when I spoke with someone who had once been a rat, who had told me about finding the legendary escape tunnel from the Fortress."

"Escape tunnel?" Telleth asked from his seat at the table, his eyes wide.

"Yes," Ithanalin said, sitting down again. "When the Fortress was built, during the Great War, the possibility of a long siege by Northern forces was considered, and a secret tunnel was built from deep in the Fortress crypts to a nearby cave, so that messengers could slip in and out undetected. After the war knowledge of the tunnel's location was lost, but this rat—well, former rat—had rediscovered it, and she told me where it was, and I was thinking about that when that tax collector started pounding on the door."

"Kelder, you mean," Kilisha said, as she took her own seat at the table. It was hard for her to think of him as just a tax collector again, but of course that was all he was to Ithanalin.

Kilisha knew that Kelder was at least a friend to her now, and well on the way to becoming something more. She felt pleased and warm at the thought, but brushed it aside to listen to her master's explanation.

"Yes, I suppose so," Ithanalin said. "At any rate, when I realized it was a tax collector interrupting my work I was somewhat annoyed, and the thought occurred to me that perhaps I could trade my knowledge of the tunnel's whereabouts to the overlord for a lifetime exemption from our taxes. That was foremost in my mind when I tripped, and that thought became the driving obsession of two of my fragments—the one in the bench, and the one in the couch. Both wanted to meet the overlord to discuss it, but only the couch remembered where the tunnel is. So the couch was able to slip inside unseen, while the bench roamed uselessly about, looking for an entrance, until you apprehended it. And that was why I—that is, why the couch would not release the overlord. I wanted to make my bargain with him, but of course, I had no way to say so. It was quite frustrating, really." He sighed. "Most of my pieces were frustrated. The latch had my social instincts, and wanted to invite everyone in, and you kept demanding it stay locked. The chair wanted to cooperate with everything—that's why it was eager to follow the other pieces, but it was dreadfully confused about *you*, and couldn't decide whether you were trying to harm it or not. I'm afraid it had very little of my intelligence."

That all made a remarkable amount of sense to Kilisha, but it also left several new questions—where was the secret tunnel mouth? Who was this former rat?

But there were always new questions, and there was no hurry about answering them all.

One more did come immediately to mind, though. She glanced at the workshop door and asked, "What was in that brass bowl?"

Ithanalin flushed, and cast an unhappy look at Yara before saying, "Soup. Spiced beef soup. That was to have been my lunch when I completed the spell."

Kilisha had begun to suspect as much when it had done nothing after days of neglect, but it was still a relief to have the mystery explained.

"The only magic on it was the Spell of the Obedient Object, to make it chime when it was ready to eat," Ithanalin said hastily, looking at his wife again. "And I wasn't going to let anyone else eat any of it, so I didn't think it violated my promise—"

"It doesn't matter now," Yara said, waving a hand in dismissal. "We're all safe and sound."

Ithanalin relaxed at that, and turned back to Kilisha. "I think there can be no question that you are ready to complete your apprenticeship," he said. "I will be happy to teach you whatever spells I can between now and your eighteenth birthday, but whenever you feel you're ready after that, I will certify you to the Guild and you will be free to go."

"Ah . . ." Kilisha began, startled. "But there are still so many spells. . . ."

"You're welcome to stay and learn them as a journeyman, if you choose."

"Thank you, Master."

"Thank *you*, Apprentice. You saved my life."

"And the overlord," Telleth said happily.

"Is Kilisha going to go away?" Pirra asked, suddenly woebegone.

"Not for months," Yara said. "And not if she doesn't want to."

"I'll have to go eventually," Kilisha said. "To make way for another apprentice, if nothing else."

"Well, there's no hurry about *that*," Ithanalin said. "It's almost two years yet before Telleth's twelfth birthday, and he needn't start until he's almost thirteen." He gazed proudly at his son.

"Uh . . ." Telleth's smile vanished; he suddenly slumped in his seat and looked helplessly at his mother.

Ithanalin looked at the boy, then at Yara, then back at Telleth. "What is it?" he asked.

"Well, Dad," Telleth said hesitantly. "I . . . uh . . ." He looked at Yara again, then pleadingly at Kilisha.

Kilisha had no idea what Telleth wanted of her, and turned up an empty palm.

"Come on, lad, what is it?" Ithanalin demanded.

Telleth swallowed, then said, "Well, Dad, the truth is that you . . . well, when I was five you turned me into a squid, and a sixnight ago you trapped yourself in a bunch of runaway furniture, and yesterday you almost got the overlord himself killed. Wizardry is *dangerous*." He looked down at his plate and poked at his food. "I was thinking I might try another line of work. . . ."

His voice trailed off.

Ithanalin stared at him for a moment, then said, "Well, it's your choice, of course. And it *is* dangerous."

Kilisha remembered plunging from the Fortress parapet with nothing but a tiny vial of Tracel's Adaptable Potion to keep her from a gruesome death on the rocks below. She remembered the feel of Javan's Restorative coming apart around her when the spriggan interrupted her. She remembered the coatrack threatening her with an uncurled hook, the bench careening along Fortress Street, the couch galloping wildly through the Fortress, and a dozen other bizarre scenes she had recently survived. Dangerous? Undoubtedly. She smiled.

"Of course it's dangerous," she said. "That's what makes it fun!"

❦
Author's Notes

1. Pronunciation

It's come to my attention that some readers, thrown by the central cluster of consonants, have had difficulty pronouncing the name "Ethshar."

It isn't really that hard. It's a compound word. "Eth" rhymes with "Beth" and is Ethsharitic for "good" or "safe," while "shar" rhymes with "car" and is Ethsharitic for "harbor" or "port." ("Ethsharitic" rhymes with "he's a critic.")

Ethsharitic names are generally pronounced more or less as if they were American English. If there's any doubt, I hope the following rules will help:

The accent is on the first syllable unless the vowel is marked (as in "Adréan" or "Kluréa"), or unless there is a double consonant, in which case the syllable ending in the double consonant is accented (such as "Falissa," accented on the second syllable, or "Karanissa," accented on the third). Names of four or more syllables will usually be partially accented on the third syllable, as well as having the primary accent on the first.

There are no silent letters, not even the K in "Ksinallion," except for the silent E following a double consonant at the end of feminine names, as in "Nuvielle," or indicating a long vowel, as in "Haldane." (That really ought to be "Haldeyn," but I couldn't quite bring myself to spell it that way.)

A is always as in "father," never as in "cat."

AI is always as in "hai!," never as in "rain."

C is always as in "cat," never as in "Cynthia."

CH is always as in "church," never as in "Achtung!" or "champagne" or any of the other possibilities.

É is pronounced as in "Renée."

G is always as in "get," never as in "gem."

I is always as in "kit," never as in "kite."

J is always as in "jet," never as in "Bjorn" or "je ne sais quoi" or "José." (It's also fairly rare.)

LL is always as in "frill," never as in "La Jolla."

OO is always as in "pool," never as in "book."

TH is always as in "thin," never as in "the."

U is always as in "rune," never as in "run."

Y (as a vowel) is always as in "any," never as in "try."

And of course, you need not put too much effort into this; no one is going to hassle you for mispronouncing Ethsharitic. If in doubt, just say it however is easiest for you!

2. Locations

This novel takes place in a city named Ethshar of the Rocks. Most of the events in *The Spell of the Black Dagger* take place in Ethshar of the Sands. Several of the other Ethshar stories take place largely in Ethshar of the Spices. Despite their similarities, these are three separate cities—that's why the lands they dominate are called the Hegemony of the *Three* Ethshars. If the street names and descriptions herein don't match those in, say, *Night of Madness,* it's because this is not the same city, any more than Alexandria, Virginia, is the same city as Alexandria, Egypt. I regret any confusion on this point.

LAWRENCE WATT-EVANS